Poster Girl

Jack Adams

Atlas Productions

Poster Girl

First published 2022.
Copyright © Jack Adams and Helen Goltz

Edited by Sally Odgers.
Proofreading by Dr Amanda Apthorpe, Kris Sheather and Brenda Telford.
Cover images by Abel Delgado, Joshua Brits, Moose photos.
Cover design by Atlas Productions.

NATIONAL LIBRARY OF AUSTRALIA

A catalogue record for this book is available from the National Library of Australia

For Blair

My handsome, witty, and charming cousin

Oh what a tangled web we weave,
When first we practise to deceive!

– Sir Walter Scott, Marmion

Chapter 1

NOW...

Coen

The first time I saw Soleil's face I was holding a blunt knife. But it did the job. I wedged it in the kitchen drawer and levered it until it cracked open. Everything you'd expect to open and close in my new abode effectively didn't. I guess that was the price you paid for living by the sea in a timber house; I would have negotiated the rent better if I'd known.

Unlike all the other kitchen drawers, this one wasn't empty – a couple of notepads, pens, and a small pile of faded papers were left behind. I pulled them out – they were posters, advertising leaflets... faded but not so badly that I couldn't read them.

I paused when I realised exactly what they were... these were no ordinary 'missing cat' or ironing service flyers.

'MISSING'. *French backpack Soleil Reyer, 22, last seen at the Rest-up Backpackers' Hostel.*

Even faded, I could make out that Soleil was a good-looking girl. I read the date she went missing and did the math; she'd be 37 now if she were still alive. In her photo she

3

looked beautiful, blonde, full of life, laughing. Yep, she was something.

In the same drawer were a few blank sheets of paper and underneath them, more copies of the faded poster. Odd. Perhaps the former owner was on the search committee or maybe he or she knew Soleil Reyer.

I smelt one removalist before I saw him… hot work that. He broke my concentration as he stomped into the kitchen, announcing he had another large box marked 'Kitchen – Fragile.'

'Your best china, mate?' he asked and laughed. I'd left most of my stuff in storage in Brisbane given I didn't know how long this writing sabbatical would be. I'd only taken a six months lease at this stage. Not that I had a lot of stuff after the split. Five years together and my partner wanted out and wanted to take what was hers and some of mine. We weren't married, that was the problem. She wanted to be, I wanted to just continue as we were. It came to a head and she left and I stopped writing – I guess I missed her more than I thought I would.

But not enough to marry her.

My publisher, Natalie, suggested a green change or sea change so I could find myself or find inspiration. So here I was renting a place that looked out at the ocean in Strand Harbour, population 28,000 plus one now.

'That's a blast from the past,' the removalist said, unceremoniously dumping the fragile box on the table and running his arm over his face to wipe away sweat. He was a big guy, a Kiwi, his arms were bigger than my head. He nodded at the flyer.

'Yeah? You know about this?' I asked, curiously.

'Sure, everyone who lives here knows about it – or did. I

don't think they ever found her. Good sort,' he said, glancing at the poster girl over my shoulder. 'It was all anyone was talking about then… I was about eighteen and remember the drama. Well back to it,' he said and moved out of the room.

Stuffing the papers back in the drawer, I vowed to do an online search on Soleil later. But now… time to unpack; there was no avoiding it. But Soleil Reyer stayed with me.

Chapter 2

THEN... 15 years earlier

Jessica

Some days it seemed so wonderful. My sparkling life was everything I've ever dreamt of: a gorgeous house, a beautiful husband – a doctor no less – a job at a newspaper. Where I'm from, they'd say that I'd made it.

We're renovating, Adam and I; we've left the original timber house standing and we were building around it. It's almost done inside and Adam's looking after the landscaping outside. We were putting in a plunge pool too. Cold, small, and deep.

But I never dreamed of a beach house or expected to live in this coastal village; water scares me. You can't relax around it... it's sneaky. We had mountains and ranges in my home town, no water.

My plans included a big-city career, so after graduation, I left home and went to the big smoke, to Sydney. Such a culture shock, but I slid into that life like it was in my blood. After two years on the job, they made everyone from editorial to advertising to the design team redundant, and the paper went under. There was no returning home, it was too much of a step backward. You know, like those actors who went to Hollywood and scored a few commercials but ended up going home and getting 'real' jobs.

But along came a job on the *Strand Harbour Daily*, only ninety minutes' drive from the city on a good traffic day, and so I moved here and met Adam. I miss Sydney, my friends and the buzz of the city – restless was in my DNA; my father was the same, well so Mum said… he was so restless he cleared out before I was five. Always moving, always needing change. Adam gets frustrated with me. Before he bought this house, I tried to talk him into going back to the city but he didn't want to go anywhere; he had concrete boots on.

My family was expecting me to move back home and become the editor of the local rag. You always come back to your roots, that's what my grandma said, and she said it every time I was home for Easter and Christmas. Allegedly, wanting to return home comes in stages. The first stage – you grew up in a small town and you didn't know any different, it's your world. Then you hit your late teens and that world was not big enough and you wanted out – you have to get out, you can't breathe. You go to the 'big smoke' and become someone. Then, in the third stage, you realised you're not someone because the city was too big and no one knew you or cared who you were – you were just a small fish in a big sea. So, you came back home where you belonged and felt at peace.

Me, I'm not there yet, stage two was my goal but it got interrupted. Every time I returned home to visit, it sure as shit still felt like a small town to me. Adam's not going there, no way. Sure, Strand Harbour was no different to my hometown except for geography, but at least I hadn't returned home for a job or to live off my parents while I found one. A good marriage, wealth and security – that part of my life was sorted while chasing the dream job. Adam's a top surgeon; a wife who works on a small-town rag won't satisfy him forever. Neither will I.

This was the big plan – the dream husband, dream house, to be the editor of a daily and receive awards for my writing. I wanted it so badly that I could taste it and it tasted like success.

But in the interim, who knows, maybe something big might happen in this little seaside town and be the story of my career!

Chapter 3

NOW…

Coen

Job over. The removalists finished up and left with a good tip and a tepid carton of beer for their efforts – they had my fridge in the van for half the day so cold beer was out of the question. But you've got to look after the workers, they'll look after you, and the lads did a good job. Now, the mission was to unpack all the essentials first, despite the pull to get to my laptop, set up my writing room, and put my books in the bookcase. There's something exciting about seeing a row of books with my name on the spine all lined up, even after all these years.

The subject of a book had been spinning in my mind when I came here… well, that's the line Natalie, my agent got. The truth was I was still struggling after the break-up and couldn't get a word down. Coming here to this small seaside village felt like getting back to my roots. My people were water people; my trust in it was marrow-deep, it was healing and I'm counting on that. Why Strand Harbour? I was a guest at the Strand Harbour Writers' Festival last year and met a guy from the University here. He suggested if I ever wanted a sea change, he'd love to have me. Bad luck if he was just mouthing off because 'hello', the idea was timely; he was good to his word and offered me some sessional lecturing in creative writing – two lectures a week and two tutorial groups. It's not about the money, it's about the human contact. Plus, having those hours occupied reduces my writing time and increases the pressure on me to get it done. Who doesn't work better on a deadline?

I wasn't ready to take a walk on the beach or explore the town just yet, best to ease into these things. Flipping the small espresso machine on – a gift from the publisher – I found the pods and a mug, and made myself a good strong coffee to inspire me to finish unpacking the boxes of kitchen wear, linen, towels, and clothes that came along with me on this adventure. My navy couch didn't match the creamy tones of the open plan living area, but whatever… the editor of *Vogue Living* wasn't dropping by anytime soon. My writing desk stood in the right place and my bookshelf beside it, that's all that mattered. They stood empty, waiting patiently for me to unpack my office box of goods and fill them.

Finally done unpacking the essentials, I allowed myself to set up my office, also known as the dining room. It's not like I'd be entertaining, and this room had a great view of the ocean. From here, the TV was in view, and the fridge and coffee pot were exactly twelve paces away. Perfect. At least my white desk seemed to fit the house theme – anaemic.

I found the Wi-Fi connection on my laptop and checked emails. Then as the sun set across the ocean, I topped up my coffee and did what I had been wanting to do all afternoon – search for Soleil Reyer. She had been on the fringes of my subconscious like a treat you could only get after eating your dinner first. I was a disciplined person and the anticipation gave me something to look forward to… I could smell a story.

Typing in the words '*Soleil Reyer missing backpacker*' in the search engine produced… woah… 452,000 results. Seriously!

"Let's start with the basics," I said, talking to my coffee. I should get a dog for company… can a dog stay here? I'd need to check the fine print on the lease. For the amount I'm paying, I should be allowed an elephant if that's my heart's desire. Back to the task at hand and sorting the articles by latest first, scrolling down the list. The last article was about five years old and written on the 10th anniversary of her disappearance; clearly, Soleil Reyer was still missing and there were no fresh leads according to the story. Soleil had just vanished. Now that I knew this, I changed the order and started at the very first story 15 years ago.

I opened it and noted the journalist's name – an occupational hazard – Jessica Steyne. I read a few of the news stories about Soleil's disappearance and the requests to call Crime Stoppers or Detective Nick Clarkson with any information.

Jot that down and the journalist's name as well… it might come in handy later.

In the top drawer of the desk was a pad and pen – it was one of the rare times I could find anything in my desk so might as well take advantage of its recent unpacking and make notes. If the detective's still in town, I could draw him out for a chat with the bribe of a beer. Then I saw a longer editorial piece by the same journalist, Jessica Steyne and sat back to read it:

The Strand Times – *Editorial*

Missing Sunny
By Jessica Steyne, crime reporter

Soleil 'Sunny' Reyer, 22 of Lyon, France, was last seen on Saturday 9 September around 6.30pm leaving the Rest-up Backpackers' Hostel where she had been living for the past month. Sunny had plans to stay there a few weeks longer; I know because Sunny and I rode together.

I'm not in the habit of picking up hitchhikers; not that our much-needed and transient labour force were not good people, but a single girl alone in a car has to be a little cautious. I saw Sunny walking back to the hostel alone several times before plucking up the courage to give her a ride and keep her safe as well. We've all heard stories about other people appearing when you stop for a solo hitchhiker but that never happened. We rode together about a dozen times after that.

I drove her home on the Friday night before she disappeared, but like a bad omen, the thirteenth time I came her way and looked out for her she wasn't there. No big deal, it was a Saturday, I was working she wasn't. But on Sunday afternoon the news broke, she hadn't returned to the hostel Saturday night … or Sunday morning. On Monday, a poster took her place along the road we normally travelled. It was a shock, frightening to see those large red capital letters – MISSING – and my first thought was that she picked the wrong ride. She may have hitched a ride to the shop or to catch up with a friend; someone must have seen something.

When Sunny and I travelled together we talked of little; weary from a day of fruit-picking, she was happy to get a ride. Sunny told me she had plans to head up north in the next few weeks with two friends. She was keen to see Cairns and to visit the Great Barrier Reef.

She was single, her mother had passed away, no siblings, and she didn't know her father, but from her Facebook page, there was no doubt that Sunny in her twenty-two years of life had touched and gathered many friends and acquaintances.

Come back Sunny, Come back and pick up your life where you left it.

Detective Nick Clarkson of the Coffs Harbour Police has appealed for public help. If you saw Soleil Reyer at any time over the weekend, if you offered Sunny a ride over the past few weeks or can identify drivers or vehicles that were in the area, please contact Crime Stoppers or your local police station.

*****

Good piece, Jessica Steyne. There were more articles by Jessica and a couple of photos of her at social events on the arm of a good-looking guy. The caption read Jessica Steyne and Dr Adam Steyne – husband, I suspected. See, I'm good at this sleuthing stuff.

Then the articles stopped – that's to be expected after a while when someone disappears and the search gets watered down, but it wasn't just the articles on Soleil that stopped – Jessica had written her last article not long after Soleil disappeared. I searched wider for her byline, but no, no more Jessica Steyne articles here in Strand Harbour or anywhere in the country for that matter.

Weird.

Where did she go? What happened to her? Why did she stop writing?

Chapter 4

THEN…

Jessica

Today Sunny was there again and shared my ride; she always slipped into my car with such energy, even after her day of hard labour. She brought sunshine to the front seat – she was well named. I wanted to tell her about my sunny life – my beautiful home, my beautiful husband, my failed pregnancy tests. I wanted to say it out loud so that it was real and happened. Adam doesn't care. He doesn't want to know about the 'baby thing' as he called it, until he's required to drive me to the hospital for the labour. I thought Soleil might help me put it in perspective, but I said nothing… the words wouldn't come out. Instead, I told her about the renovations.

'It sounds wonderful,' she said. 'And you are putting in a pool even though you are right opposite the beach?' 'It's kind of the done thing these days,' I said with a shrug. 'Besides, Adam loves a plunge pool – so deep and cold. I think he is used to the Atlantic waters of the Cape Town beaches, so it has to be cold,' I said with a smile, raving about my fascinating husband.

'It'll be great, I bet you will end up swimming in it all the time,' she said.

We travelled along in silence for a while. I bet Sunny wouldn't dance around Adam's moods, she seemed so sure of herself. She'd coax him out of himself or put her foot down and tell him it was not acceptable. Me, most days I avoided him when he was morose. Was that how it started for battered wives – all sunshine and roses and then it crumbled at the edges, and they did things to avoid conflict and to protect themselves? When people asked 'why didn't you leave', did they know the answer? Maybe because you loved them; they weren't always like that; they might go back to being what they were when you first met them. Or because they loved you – they tell you that all the time; maybe you needed each other.

My handsome, emotional grenade of a husband. I watched where I stepped all the time for fear of being hurt or being hit by shrapnel. He's an excellent surgeon, I've been told. He's excellent at being moody, too.

That's why I loved going to work and I looked forward to picking up Sunny; to relax with her, to indulge in casual and easy chats. We slipped into each other's lives and out of them again – no commitment, neither of us suggesting any more than that. I wondered who she was riding with when I didn't see her. I hoped it was a safe ride.

Chapter 5

NOW...

Coen

Ah, lycra, who doesn't look good in it? I'd ventured out into the belly of Strand Harbour on my bike – a MAMIL – a middle-aged man in lycra, but proud of it. It was a pretty town with a smattering of tourist shops featuring the usual crap in them, plus a real estate agent, several clothing stores, more coffee shops than population – that might be a slight exaggeration – and a Thai and Indian takeaway. There were two old pubs on bookend corners, one had been restored, at least externally.

While securing my bike in the rack out the front of one of the coffee shops, a bus arrived and a handful of university-aged students piled out and the next batch shuffled in. I watched where the students headed since they were locals; they broke off towards a couple of the grungier coffee shops and the unrenovated hotel. Noted. Eventually, I'd get to the bottom of where the locals went for non-tourist prices and the best takeaways.

In my line of view was the cop shop a short distance

away; should I find out if Detective Nick Clarkson was still on the scene? Nah, I'd get a bit more reading under my belt first. As for Soleil, there was some serious digging to do and hopefully, some locals would remember the way it played out.

Last night I found and consumed a few more of Jessica's articles but I was none the wiser – I knew Soleil hadn't been found but was she presumed dead? Could she have cleared out of town and taken on a new identity rather than return to France? Was she living somewhere in Australia under a false name married with kids? Did she ever leave Strand Harbour? I'm yet to find Jessica, the journalist, as well. Maybe she divorced and left town, or she's still here but works under her maiden name. I'd have to check marriage and divorce records. So many maybes, so little time.

I picked a coffee shop that wasn't too trendy and after ordering, made myself at home on their deck. I planned to take a ride to the university campus next and inspect it, given I was starting there next week. Just as my coffee arrived, Natalie – my agent – rang, timing was everything.

'Hey, have a coffee with me,' I said.

'Why where are you?' she asked abruptly.

'In Strand Harbour, in a coffee shop and my latte has just arrived.'

She made a snorting sound. 'I thought you were outside my office!'

There was a lot that I liked about Natalie and in more than a professional way but I'd never explored that before because of the girlfriend, now ex. But Natalie was dry and fiery, attractive, confident, slim and bossy – there's nothing more attractive than a woman who doesn't need you.

'How's the writing coming along?' she asked.

'You'd think I was your meal ticket,' I teased her. 'Give me a break, I only arrived and unpacked yesterday. I've barely plugged in the laptop.'

I thanked the pink-haired waitress who came back to drop off a croissant I had ordered. She would have been in primary school when Soleil went missing.

'Who are you thanking and for what?' Natalie asked. She didn't wait for an answer. 'Since you're not home writing, what happened to the two-thousand words a day goal?'

'If you could see me, you'd see I'm rolling my eyes,' I said, with a sigh. 'I'm thanking the lovely waitress who delivered my latte and a croissant. By the way, you're wasted,' I told her. 'The SAS interrogation unit is looking for you.'

She laughed and then sighed. 'I wish I was in a coastal town having a coffee and a croissant, an almond one preferably.'

'Come and visit. I promise I'll still write while you are here, you can go shopping while I get those words down. My new digs have three bedrooms.' Just establishing she didn't have to share my room, not that I'd be against the idea.

She laughed again but didn't bite. 'Mm, tempting. So when are you going to tell me what the new book is about?'

I took a sip of the coffee – hot, strong with a good head, perfect.

'Let's see… how about tomorrow at 9.30am?'

'Really?' she practically squealed.

'Don't be ridiculous,' I told her. 'I'll tell you when you come to visit; a weekend off and away from the corporate world will do you good. Besides, there are a few places I want to go to do research and it will be easier to go there with a female friend, rather than looking like Joe Desperado.'

'Now you're talking. I can tell the boss it's a business trip. How soon?' she asked.

'Sooner rather than later.'

We talked about some writing festival appearances she wanted me to attend and the politics of publishing. She covered how her boss was a dick and she hoped he would retire soon because he was about one hundred and she'd get the job, and then we hung up. I finished my coffee and pastry and waved my thanks to the café team as I departed.

Stopping on the footpath to look around, I spotted a supermarket up the street, so I left my bike locked up, walked there and got enough groceries to last a few days. They could deliver them to my new home later today. I did an abridged ride around the university campus and then headed home to get back to work for the afternoon. If Natalie came to stay, I'd better have something to show her.

*****

Showered, a hot mug of tea in front of me, and laptop opened, my Soleil research continued. So, she was still missing, but where was the journalist, Jessica?

Let's start with her doctor husband in case he was still in town.

Taking a punt that Steyne was her married name and the Dr Adam Steyne from the press clipping wasn't her brother, I combed the local hospital's website to see if he was on their current staff list. Nope, no Steyne is currently on staff, crap. Next to their marketing area and the annual reports. What were the odds that they'd archive them online so I could check back on when he was last here? Not good by the looks of it, only last year's was available for download.

I sat back and thought for a moment, then left the hospital's website and searched online for the Strand Harbour General Hospital annual report with the year date of 15 years ago, and there it was in PDF format. God, I love the internet, what the hell did we do before it? Opening it, page after page, and then bingo – found him! Dr Adam Steyne – a good-looking guy indeed… bet he pulled the girls, but then Jessica was a looker too. Now for the next year's annual report, yep scored that as well, and he wasn't in it. Hmm. So the year after Soleil disappeared, Dr Steyne was gone.

The next search for him by name revealed three Dr Adam Steyne listings. I clicked on each one until I found a photo and found him – 15 years older, but it was him. It just gets better… he's working in a hospital in Perth. Great, the other side of the country. But, on the bright side, at least he was in the country if I wanted to contact him to talk with his wife, Jessica. I guess if they're divorced he still might be up for a chat about any memories he has of the whole Soleil period given his wife reported on it. I dug a little further; he was South African and had been here at the Strand Harbour local hospital for a few years before taking off to Perth.

Funny choice of town to come to when you could choose anywhere in Australia. Funny that the good doctor left around the same time as Soleil disappeared; funny that was also when his wife's articles stopped appearing.

I loved the dig but I won't get too excited yet, there could be a simple explanation – he might have received a better job offer and off they went; Jessica might be with him but a stay-at-home mum now, or something similar. Hope there's more to the story than that… was that a bad thing to wish for?

Chapter 6

NOW…

Coen

Ihad been hard at the research now for close to three hours, Natalie would be pleased, I might even tell her. It was nearing four o'clock, and I was just about to pack it in for the day when I found this news piece:

The Strand Times online

Missing woman's phone records reveal nothing
Jessica Steyne, crime reporter

Police have had little success determining the whereabouts and last movements of missing French backpacker Soleil Reyer from her phone records.

Detective Nick Clarkson of the Strand Harbour Police said Ms Reyer had left clothes and some personal possessions at the Rest-up Backpackers' Hostel but her handbag and phone were not amongst them. Her phone records had shed no light on her disappearance.

'We have identified most of the calls made and received, except for two blocked numbers that police are still attempting to trace,' Det. Clarkson said. 'The phone records indicated that the missing woman's phone was last used in the Rest-up Backpackers' Hostel district around 5pm on the evening she went missing.

'No calls were made or received since then and we have tracked the phone to within a ten-kilometre zone of the hostel,' he said.

'This doesn't mean that Ms Reyer is in the vicinity; her phone may remain in this area, be damaged or switched off in the general vicinity of the city block and phone tower.'

Ms Reyer, 22, was last seen leaving the Rest-up Backpackers' Hostel around 6.30pm early evening on Saturday 10 September. Strand Harbour Police became involved the next evening when she failed to return to the hostel or return phone calls from concerned friends expecting her back for work the next day. Police uncovered a personal diary belonging to Ms Reyer amongst her belongings.

Ms Reyer is 172 cm (five-foot-eight), tanned skin, blue eyes, long blonde-brown hair and approximately sixty-three kilograms (139 pounds).

The police are seeking public help. Please call Crime Stoppers or your local police branch if you have any information.

Share: Facebook | Twitter | Email | In | g+ | Add your comment to this story.

*****

Make my day, Soleil had a diary! I couldn't believe my luck; it was every writer's dream... an insight into the headspace of a subject. If it hadn't been given back to her family, I just had to convince the detective to let me read it.

Given no one has been charged and the case was still open, she obviously didn't write in the diary that she was planning to disappear or that she feared someone was going to bump her off and named them. But the diary would be great to build a picture of her for readers, to flesh her out.

I stopped, realising that I was thinking like someone who was going to write this book. There was a missing woman, a journalist whose byline had disappeared and with her husband, had most likely left town and nothing much else. I had to get out of my head for a while.

Walk time. Finding my runners, it was time to christen the beach, so to speak. After that, I'll sit with my sparkling water on the veranda, look at the sparkling water, and contemplate preparing an evening meal. My day had to have some structure now or else it wouldn't work – a teaching and writing routine had to be established. I was good in my own company and good working at home but only if I had a routine.

With the house locked up, it was only a handful of steps to make before hitting the beach; what a bloody fantastic house to rent. So, where were the owners and why weren't they living here?

It was a bit like central station on the beach… every man and his dog were having a late afternoon walk or jog. Is that sexist? Make that every person and their dog. Got to love small towns though; everyone greeted each other with either a smile, a nod, a full-on 'How are you?' or in my case, 'You're that author, aren't you?' It's good for my ego to be recognised and even though I had seven books published and had been writing for over a decade, it wasn't until one of my books was made into a movie that my name became known. The local newspaper also ran a story that I was coming to town and I think Natalie slipped them the details – she denied it. I'd make it known if I were in her job.

A few people stopped to talk with me, shake my hand, tell me which of my books they liked and didn't – yep, everyone's a critic – and one couple even invited me to lunch one day. Nice. But it was the older woman with the beagle who stopped me in my tracks when she said: 'So you're renting the doctor's house?' She glanced to the end of the beach at the row of houses where I had just come from.

'Uh, I don't know, I just rented from an agent,' I replied. 'So who's the doctor and where's he living? Not homeless now, I hope?'

She laughed at my joke, bless her and said: 'Dr Steyne.'

'I'm in Dr Steyne's house?' Weird coincidence.

'Yes, Adam. His wife was the local journalist, a handsome pair they were. She knew that backpacker who went missing. Now that was an awful affair. Some say it took a toll on the Steynes' marriage,' she shrugged.

'Is that why they left town?' I wanted to know more but Alfy, the beagle, took off and she left my question hanging, wished me well and hurried off to call him back. Thanks for nothing, Alfy!

I was living in Jessica and Adam Steyne's' house. What did that mean? Did it mean anything? Why were there so many flyers still in the drawer? Were they both in the search party or had the newspaper organised printing them? But more importantly, where were all three of them now?

That's it, action stations… first thing in the morning the cop shop was going to get a visit and I'd be making myself a new friend.

What was the detective's name... Nick Clarkson? Yep, Nick, I'm your new best friend.

I headed home with gusto, keen to return to my research and with the weekend ahead of me, there was plenty of time to get stuck in.

THEN...

Jessica

Adam was in the shower when his phone rang. I usually answered it in case it was his work and they called him into the hospital for an emergency. But his time it wasn't; it was a woman and the call was personal.

'Is Adam there please?' she said with a clipped South African accent.

'He can't come to the phone at the moment, but he won't be long. Can I take a message?' I asked.

There was a hesitation before she spoke again. 'It's his wife's sister – deceased wife's sister – he has my number, thanks.' She hung up without leaving her name.

That was like a blow – a body blow that froze me to the spot for what felt like a long time. I felt shocked that I didn't know Adam had a wife, had lost a wife, and shocked by the sister's rudeness. The abruptness of hearing those words out loud – Adam's wife – reverberated through me.

But the look on Adam's face after I had passed on the message suggested he was more shocked than me.

'I'm not married, I assure you,' he rushed to tell me. Adam made me sit down and then told me the details. He delivered them like he'd been rehearsing for this day – the bare facts and no more delivered clinically. It made me wonder how he delivered bad news to his patients and family at the hospital – hopefully with more compassion.

'Chelsey's gone, no longer on the earth,' he told me. 'I met her in my first few months of residency. She was five years older than me, but we didn't care about that. We got married six months after meeting and we were married for four years when she had an accident. Slipped and fell. I had a very public breakdown; now I'm starting anew. No one here is looking at me like I'm a tragic figure; no one here knows my history. Death taints you, Jess; it leaves a stain. People look at you differently.' He took a breath and looked away. 'I've heard it all:

'That's the poor bastard whose wife fell and died.

'In love, happy they were…

'Thank God it's him and not me…

'He needs to get back on the horse and get dating again.

'It's too soon to be dating again, what's he thinking?

'He's hardly mourned her.' He stopped and looked back at me as if testing if his response would suffice.

'No need for you to know anymore, is there? I love you, Jess. You've saved me and I want us to begin from our time together. Can we do that?'

And as far as Adam was concerned, that was it, discussion over. In the days following I tried twice to get him to talk about his deceased wife again, but he would shut the topic down. It was like I was the *Titanic* and I had hit an iceberg named Adam.

'I don't see the point of dredging this up,' he would say, his voice taking on a clipped tone. It was like he divided his life into Anno Jessica – the years before me, and Post Jessica – after meeting me.

26

I wanted us to be just about us too, no baggage. And it consoled me he wasn't mooning around, talking about her all the time, missing her, remembering when she and he did this or that. Nevertheless, I needed to know more – maybe it was the journalist in me or maybe it was human nature. He was clearly a man who fell in love quickly and acted quickly – six months and they married, two weeks and he wanted me to move in with him. I needed the facts; I needed to know that the ground would not shift and I wouldn't be abandoned because he married me too soon.

From then on, when Adam was melancholy, I wondered if he was thinking of her; was it their anniversary or birthday? Or had I said something that reminded him of her? Could I ease the pain or was it best to avoid him… and he was like that a lot – a dark, intense man. I felt like there was always something unsaid, the elephant in the room with us. Was it Chelsey – the beautiful angel smiling down on him from heaven, constantly reminding him of what he's lost, reminding me of my loan?

Chapter 7

NOW…

Coen

Natalie rang me right at eight on Monday morning. She does that on purpose to make sure I'm up preparing to write and not sleeping in… I'm onto her. I wonder if she's this tough on all her authors or am I just special? Fortunately, I'm a morning person and I'm up! I had a jog along the beach, showered and I was eating cereal when she rang.

'I'm coming for a weekend in three weeks; arrive Friday, out Sunday midday. Is that okay, too soon?' she asked, hitting me with a lot of short, sharp statements in a row.

'Brilliant,' I said, 'I'll organise a weekend of activity, writing and free time for you,' I added.

'Don't you want to check your calendar first?' she asked.

What calendar? Since I came here there were no bookings or appearances on my radar, none accepted anyway. I was completely free for the next six months except for my weekly teaching commitments starting next week.

'I'd better,' I said and waited a few moments, ate a spoonful of cereal and then declared, 'all clear and locked in! I'm going to see the local cop this morning, if he's in, he's a source.'

'Source? Ooh, is this for your new book? Great!' she gushed.

'It is, which I'll tell you about when you come to stay.'

We swapped some small talk about our weekends just past and then hung up. Good, I'd look forward to having her here – by that time I'll be desperate for the company of a familiar face.

With breakfast done, dishes stuck in the dishwasher and a promise to turn it on when it was full or when I had used every piece of crockery in the house, whichever came first, I did a bit of grooming – not wanting to be arrested by the fashion police. When presentable, I grabbed my phone, wallet and keys, and headed out the door to the cop shop. I decided to drive today and drop into the university afterwards, since my first class started tomorrow. Probably best to find the room I'm required in and sus out teacher parking arrangements, if there were any.

The cop shop was quiet at 9am; in the big smoke there would have been a stack of leftovers from Sunday night being bailed or released after sleeping off a bad performance of drunk and disorderly. It was a young constable manning the front desk and he looked at me with suspicion – they start young.

I kept it casual. 'Gidday, I was hoping to speak with Detective Nick Clarkson.'

'You're the author!' he said, and his face relaxed.

'Coen Watson,' I said, not sure whether I should shake or salute, after all, one of us was in uniform. I offered my hand anyway and we shook.

'Yeah, I really liked your serial killer series,' he clicked his fingers trying to think of it, then blurted out 'Reiker! Yeah, he was a real nut job. Love to arrest him.'

I laughed. 'Thanks, that's a line I haven't heard before.'

'Couldn't get into the '*Road Kill*' series… not your fault, it's hard to read stories about cops without feeling like you're at work.'

'I understand,' I agreed, pleased that it wasn't my fault. At least he didn't tell me what police procedural errors I made.

'You know your cop couldn't get the DNA results that fast though,' he said. And there it was, took about five minutes for the feedback.

'Yeah, well it is fiction and the reader can't wait around forever,' I said, with a shrug and small smile. I didn't want to get him offside this early.

'Oh, sure. Right, I'll go get Nick,' he said, remembering I hadn't come in to talk books.

I looked at the noticeboard while waiting and scanned the photos of shady folk on the wanted list. I wasn't there; what a relief. I heard footsteps behind and turned to see a tall man in a pale grey suit with equally pale hair, and not much of it, approaching me. He was slim and walked like a man who worked out – straight as a rod back, shoulders back, comfortable in his skin.

'Coen? Detective Nick Clarkson,' he said, and extended his hand. 'You're the author!'

We shook. Was it a good thing that the top cop knew my name? Sometimes it worked against me as authorities immediately thought I was going to write about them.

'Coen Watson,' I agreed prepared to admit that much. 'I was wondering if you could spare me five minutes now or sometime today, or I could shout you a coffee to discuss a story?'

'Yes, to both,' he said. 'A caffeine hit would be good. There's a reasonable place on the corner.'

Well, that was easy, bloody great! He told the constable he could reach him on the mobile phone, and we headed out the door. He was easily a head taller than me.

'Loved your *Road Kill* series. Who's your consultant?' he asked, assuming I had one. I extended the length of my stride to keep up with him.

'A retired cop,' I told him and mentioned my friend's name. 'But sometimes I change the truth just to make the story move along better. Shits him off.'

The detective laughed. 'I imagine it would,' he said.

We entered the coffee shop and he went to a booth near the window. I suspect he's been there a few times before.

'You know, it might start tongues wagging if people see us talking. The author who is new in town and the cop who has been here most of his career,' he said, as he nodded to the waitress that we were ready to order.

'Get out. Don't cops and authors talk all the time?' I asked.

'In the old days, cops and journos shared information. Now it's all done through our media team because the press turned the spotlight on us,' he said with a sigh.

'Blood journos,' I joked, 'wrecked it for all of us.'

He grinned and we both ordered a coffee – Nick had a flat white, I had a cappuccino in a mug.

'Well, welcome to our coastal town,' he said and sat back. 'I'm guessing you haven't sought me out for my conversation skills.'

I liked him; he didn't waste words.

'I've heard you're scintillating,' I said, and he grinned. 'But you're right. I'm looking into one of your cold cases – a prospective book – Soleil Reyer.' Before he could react, I added because I was fishing, 'I just found out that I'm living in Adam and Jessica Steyne's house.'

His eyebrows went up. 'Seriously, you didn't know that when you rented it?'

'Nope, I'd never even heard of Soleil before I arrived. Fate maybe,' I said and nodded my thanks to the young waitress as she served our coffees. I took a sip – good head, hot, the coffee I mean. 'So,' I continued, 'I'm doing a few days' work at the university and the rest of the time I hope to write Soleil's story, this town's story.'

Nick nodded but said nothing. I used that trick too – shut up and they'll keep talking. So I threw it back at him. 'You led the case?'

He took a deep breath. 'Shit case. No idea what happened to her, no closure, no suspects.'

'Really? Not one that you want to share?'

He gave me a look like I was dreaming, and I grinned. 'So, how do you feel about working with me on the book?'

'You mean give you access to all the police resources?' he said, outsmarting me.

I hesitated before answering. My few non-fiction books were mainly historical stories of heroes and villains. This was different and I wanted and needed Detective Nick on board.

'No, I'd be happy to work together. At the end of the day, we both want an outcome. You want an arrest and to find Soleil; I want to solve a mystery, put a case to rest and have a best seller.'

Nick was taking a sip when I said the last point and almost choked on his coffee. He laughed. 'Well, I love that you're upfront about it.'

I shrugged. 'I know I'll get emotionally attached to Soleil and the other victims – family and friends – as I write it, maybe even you,' I warned him with a smirk. 'But sometimes a fresh set of eyes, a new dig, can bring out new leads.'

He nodded. 'I agree with that. There have been some good crime podcasts that have done just that. Sometimes people prefer to talk with someone other than the cops. So, what are you proposing? What do you want from me and how will you represent the police service?' he asked.

'Fair question,' I nodded. I'd prepared for this and knew it could make or break. I took a breath and started. 'I'm negotiable, completely. But how about this…'

THEN…

Jessica

The first time I saw Adam, I watched as women openly flirted with him. Well, that would not be me. I was working – attending one of the hospital's monthly information nights. In a small town, this was news. But my plan to avoid him failed… we reached for a drink at the same time as a waiter went past, and he invited me to go first.

'So, enjoying yourself?' Dr Adam Steyne asked as it then forced us to make some small talk.

'I've had trips to the dentist I've enjoyed more,' I said, with the hint of a smile. May as well be honest – a research launch with a bunch of egg heads wasn't really my favourite assignment, even if the scientific outcomes were occasionally interesting. Still, it was a stupid comment and career-limiting. He could have taken offence, rung my editor, and I could have been packing up and heading out of Strand Harbour before I'd even unpacked my sock drawer.

But he laughed.

'Well, Jessica from *The Strand Times*,' he said, reading my name tag in return, 'how can we make this evening more memorable for you than the dentist?'

'Got any of that gas they use?' I asked, and he laughed again. 'Of course, I am joking,' I assured him. 'I found last month's presentation on the inroads into diabetes studies fascinating,' I mentioned the discussion on using snake venom as an anti-coagulant as well. Rescued from embellishing the truth any further by the screech of the P.A. system, the master of ceremonies called for everyone's attention.

Dr Adam Steyne gave me a smile that said I was lucky this time, and I returned it with a raised eyebrow that hopefully said I wasn't backing away from the challenge. I moved away to put down my glass and turn on my recorder, and an attractive woman filled the space I left. That was it. I got to work, he vanished into the crowd and I never expected to hear from him again. But, as I stepped out of the room to leave, he was there. He asked if he could take me out for a drink, and we were together from that day on.

I hinted to Clare at work how fast my relationship was developing and the 'wet blanket' couldn't help herself; she did some digging on Adam – she's a journalist by name, a journalist by nature. When I got to work on Friday morning, she was ready for me.

'A coffee at lunchtime, you and me? I've got some info for you,' she said, smelling of cigarettes already at seven-thirty in the morning.

'A story?' I naively asked. I'm not waiting for lunch to get that.

'No, personal stuff. I have a friend in the right places who has done a bit of a background check on your man.'

I rolled my eyes.

'You should do it yourself. I check out anyone who I date these days,' she said, waving her pen at me as she wandered off. 'Just looking out for you.'

The cadet who sat opposite me watched Clare depart and then gave me a conspiratorial smile which I didn't return. If she didn't like Clare that was her problem. Sure, Clare was ballsy... butch, but we clicked when I came to *The Strand Times*. So what if she wasn't a fashionista – she had an array of different coloured flannelette shirts – who would have thought they came in red, blue, green and mustard colours? She dressed like she was going to a football game and with her almost crew cut, it wouldn't take much to mistake her for a guy. She was pragmatic and outspoken, and that's what I liked about her.

I've always attracted Clare types, even when I was in primary school. Maybe because I was little, they always wanted to protect me. Throughout high school I had a 'protector' – Julie McConnell, the toughest girl in the school. Pregnant at sixteen and she had breasts before most of us knew they were coming. Now Clare had my back. I knew she meant well about Adam, yet I was head over heels, completely in love, no going back, and I didn't want to hear any bad news.

I tried not to think about it all morning and worked on the story of the day. I was terrified of what Clare was going to tell me. At lunchtime we went to her favourite coffee shop; she didn't eat lunch – well, that's not technically true – Clare's lunch comprised coffee and cigarettes. I don't know what dinner comprised... I'm not asking. I suspect it's something fried with beer.

'He's a widower,' she started.

My eyes widened. 'Crap.'

'I warned you about instant intimacy,' she said.

'I know,' I responded.

'Seven years ago,' she said, stirring sugar into her mug-size latte. 'She died seven years ago.'

'That's good,' I brightened, 'well not good, but you know what I mean,' I tried to cover my insensitive comment, not that Clare cared.

She continued, firing off each sentence in a staccato fashion, oblivious to how the sentences hit my skin and exploded like bullets.

'He worked for a private hospital in Cape Town in South Africa before coming here; I suppose after the death of his wife, he wanted to start a new life. His wife, Chelsey, died from a fall – the coroner deemed it death by accidental injury. Her maiden name was Kotze, that's K-o-t-z-e. She was a social media influencer and ran her own Public Relations consultancy,' Clare said, with a slight sneer; not her scene. She continued: 'She was blonde, five foot eight or 172 centimetres, from wealthy stock, five years older than Adam.' Clare looked at her notes before continuing: 'Married at twenty-six, died at thirty, Adam was twenty-five at the time of her death. He married young, but I guess there's nothing wrong with that. No kids, so it wasn't a shotgun wedding. He's all legit – education, finances – all good and above board.'

I exhaled. 'Well thanks, that's thorough.' I didn't need to hear about his former love, even if Clare meant well. 'How did you get this info again?'

'A friend of mine works in an agency that has access to people's information, he owed me a favour, enough said,' she said, with a double-tap to her nose – the international code for secrecy I believe.

'But now you've wasted that favour on me,' I said.

'Worth it,' she answered. She pushed her findings to me as if she was wiping her hands of them.

I touched her hand. 'Thanks, Clare, I appreciate what you did for me.'

She nodded, embarrassed, and brushed me off. I'm guessing she wasn't used to getting affection or praise. I drank my tea, weirdly grateful for her; I trusted her. But somewhere in my gut, Adam's history and the pace of our relationship concerned me. I couldn't put my finger on it just yet... but I'm fully aware that Chelsey's beauty will never fade in his eyes and mine will; he'll remember the good times with her, but I am yet to make a bank of good memories with him, more than he had with her.

I couldn't get past the fact that not once did he mention a wife, or that he was a widower. Was he broken-hearted, too destroyed to speak of her, or was this a coping mechanism that helped him move on?

What hold did she still have over his heart?

Chapter 8

NOW...

Coen

It was a good thing that I didn't have kids because I offered and agreed to everything except handing over a firstborn to get those files from Nick. He was a tough customer, or he'd been burnt before, or both. Natalie would be pissed off that I was going to work hand-in-hand with him to such an extent, but it was no skin off my nose. It's not like I'm doing an exposé!

Nick agreed to meet me for dinner at the pub which he recommended – my shout of course – to give me a copy of the files and Soleil's diary. After our coffee this morning, he was going back to the office to break it to the young constable that he was on photocopy duty for the next hour or so. Next time I'm nearby, I'll drop in and give the cop kid an autographed set of his favourite of my books, the *Reiker* series. That might win him back a little, or he can sell them online when I die and they might get a few extra dollars. Geez, the things we do to kiss ass.

It was great to have the police files, but I wanted to spend a lot more time talking to Detective Nick. Did he seriously not have one lead? He must have a gut instinct about someone in the town. What was his take on it all? What can he tell me about everyone involved from the journo to the manager at the hostel where Soleil was staying? What wasn't written... the stuff hidden between the lines. At least Nick seems like a decent guy and not a dick. I'll make sure he meets Natalie too; it won't hurt to get the female take on him.

Next, the university and finding a park without the appropriate pass – I swung the car into the teachers' area and nabbed a spot – bad me, I'd have to give myself detention. Come on, this visit will be thirty minutes tops, what's the odds of getting a fine or towed? I bolted into the building, checked out the directory and found the floor for English Studies. Up the staircase, two levels, where a young, good-looking guy with a name badge reading '*Josh Crawford, English Studies Coordinator*' told me that my colleagues from the department were in class. He shook my hand enthusiastically when I introduced myself.

'We're excited you're joining us,' he said. I reciprocated. He was groomed to within an inch of his life; I felt shabby beside him. He showed me where to go tomorrow for the lecture and the room allocated to me where I could work and hold my student appointments. He also gave me a parking pass so I was now legal. Young Josh also recommended the best place to get coffee on campus. Worth his weight in gold and I told him. Done and out of there in twenty minutes.

An afternoon free to write. Soleil, I'm coming for you.

THEN...

Jessica

Adam delivered the news like pulling off a plaster, quickly and abruptly.

'Chelsey's sister wants to visit,' he said, as we had a quick breakfast together before he left for his Saturday rounds at the hospital. He delivered a bit of a bombshell, given he's rarely spoken about his past life. I said nothing for a few moments, I was in shock and I sat there open-mouthed, staring at him in my suspended animation. I didn't even know he'd called her back. Now, his deceased wife's sister was going to be staying with us. Great.

'Only for a couple of weeks from Saturday,' he clarified, rising and heading to the sink.

'A couple of weeks! From this Saturday?' I spun around to look at him. 'How long have you known?'

'I didn't call her back right away, but a few days ago, I guess.'

'What? Did you think the less notice the better and best not to give me an out?' I asked.

Surprisingly, he looked sheepish.

'She messaged me a few months ago, but I didn't take her seriously. She's one of those people who say "let's catch up" to everyone. I thought if I ignored her she would go away,' he said.

'Apparently not,' I replied.

He continued. 'She's coming to visit friends but thought she'd grace me, us, with a visit. We're her first destination.'

'Weeks?' I said again.

His lips tightened and then he explained: 'It's what a lot of friends and relatives do when they come from South Africa… it's a long and expensive trip so you spend quality time with people because you don't do it often.'

My frustration was at boiling point. 'In our entire relationship, you've said two words to me about your first wife, and now you want us to play host to her sister for two weeks?'

He sighed. 'Sorry. She came over last year, but luckily we were away… it was when we went to the Margaret River to sample wines and drank them dry. Can we do this?' he asked, but I knew I wasn't really being asked.

'Well, technically, she's family. Does Chelsey's sister have a name?' He probably told me but she didn't offer it when she called. Best to make sure there were not several of them!

'No. They didn't think to give her one,' he said with a smile to break the tension. He gave me a smirk. 'Skylar, or Sky. She's pleasant enough… four years younger than Chelsey, so she's about thirty-three now.'

'Were they close, the two sisters?' I asked.

He continued to focus on washing the breakfast dishes with great concentration, probably wishing the conversation was over.

'Not really – competitive, more like it. They looked alike. The race was always on to be the better sibling since the day they were born. She even hit on me not long after the funeral,' he said without thinking.

'Did you mean to say that out loud?'

He shook his head. 'Sorry.'

Great, just the sort of house guest every female wanted. This called for another angle. 'I'm owed some annual leave,' I started, 'do you want me to go away for a week and catch up with some of my friends, and leave you to catch up with *Skylar*?' I said her name like it was all too trendy.

He wheeled around to look at me. 'Hell no! I'm not having her anywhere near me unless you're around,' he assured me.

Thank God for that, at least.

He continued: 'We're not going to any trouble. I'll set up the bed in the guest room and she'll have to fit around us and our work schedules. She's a beach girl, she'll be fine.'

Of course she was.

'How is she getting here?' I asked, knowing the drive to the Sydney airport was about ninety minutes away.

Adam had it all worked out. 'She arrives Saturday night on a 10pm flight into Sydney. She'll clear customs about an hour later, so I'll pick her up around eleven. We should be back here just before one in the morning. She'll be wiped out, so you can meet her Sunday morning.'

I nodded. 'That's good of you to do that.'

'It's expected, trust me,' he said with a roll of the eyes. He finished washing, wiped his hands and came over to me, sitting beside me.

'Thank you. Let's just get it over with. It's not like we can keep making excuses every year and once she meets you, maybe she can move on,' he said.

'Maybe,' I agreed with a small smile and feeling a little sorry for Skylar now. 'Will it upset you... you know, the reminder of that life?'

'You're the one who has given me a lot to look forward to,' he said, taking my hand. 'I promise, I won't be regressing into a wallow session.'

I nodded. 'Then let's get it over with.'

He smiled, kissed me and left quickly. Glad that was done, no doubt. Just kill me now. The ex-sister-in-law of the wife, ex-wife, first wife, deceased wife, whatever was coming to visit. I really wouldn't mind going away to the city for a week and catching up with friends, and I'm sure my editor, Oliver, would let me. I trust Adam, I think – though from what he says I shouldn't trust Skylar.

The whole thing was a bit odd. I wondered if Skylar and Adam stayed in regular contact and he wasn't telling me the whole story.

At least I'd be working all next week and the Saturday shift so Adam can play tour guide. God, I hope he doesn't become maudlin during and after her visit. He says he won't wallow; it took all my self-control not to say 'more than usual'. I need him to be moodier like I need a hole in the head.

What's the chances that I'll be ovulating on those days, just my luck. I'm not sure I want to be making love and conceiving our child with his dead wife's sister in the next room. It just gets better and better.

Chapter 9

NOW...

Coen

The hotel dining area and bar were perfect. Not too trendy that it attracted hipsters and cost a bomb for a beer and a meal that consisted of a small mushroom in the middle of the plate surrounded by an unidentifiable sauce. And not too old that it was full of shorts and butt crack. I got there before Nick so I could pick a seat and check out the area. I don't know if it was because I've written crime and thriller books for years, but I have to face the door and have a wall at my back. Maybe it was because fans have approached from behind and scared the shit out of me. One of them trapped me in a bear hug and whispered in my ear that she was my biggest fan. If you've read Stephen King's *Misery*, you'll get why I like to be prepared. If you haven't read it, I highly recommend the book and movie.

What was I saying? Oh yeah, I sat at a table and had a glance at the bar while I waited. I could see the range of drinks from where I was sitting and they had some pretty good beers on tap. They had Holsten in the fridge too, which surprised me – it's my favourite non-alcoholic beer that lets me look like I am being social but I don't have to drink. Don't get me wrong, I'm not a wowser but I do my best writing at night and I need a clear head for that.

A woman approached, wearing the hotel labelled black T-shirt, jeans and a black apron tied around her waist. She'd be hitting late-forties, thin, wiry, her blonde-grey hair tied back and an attractive face that said hard work and good scotch.

'Hello, in for dinner or just a drink?' she asked and smiled. That changed everything, she looked softer.

'Hi, both, just waiting for a friend,' I said.

'You're that writer!' she said, placing a menu down on the table.

I half rose and shook her hand, introducing myself.

'Sandra, but Sandy works,' she said. 'Love your books.'

'Thanks, that's kind,' I nodded. I never tire of hearing it, never. But there was always a *but*. She didn't get a chance to make it before Nick strode in with a large envelope bundled under his arm.

'Gidday, Sandy,' he said, pulling out the chair and dropping next to me.

'Nick! Geez, if I'd known Coen was meeting you, I'd have warned him off,' she said, with a smile and wink.

Nick grinned. 'C'mon this hotel would have gone under years ago if it hadn't been for the amount of alcohol the local constabulary drink.'

Sandy looked at me. 'There's truth in that.' She hesitated and then added, 'I've got to tell you, I was pissed when you killed off Eloise.'

There it was, the *but*...

Nick's eyes widened and I held up my hand to him.

'A character from my book,' I explained. He visibly relaxed.

'I really liked her,' Sandy continued.

'Yeah, me too,' I agreed. 'But she was in love with a serial killer; it would never end well.'

She sighed with sad acceptance and then took our drink orders and left. Nick put the envelope on the chair between us and nodded at it.

'Appreciate it,' I said. 'I feel like I should slip you an envelope back across the table.'

'Would make the picture complete,' he agreed. I felt the paperwork next to me humming; I couldn't wait to get home and start reading. But first I had to ask. 'Nick, where's the journo gone? Jessica Steyne? I can't find one article she's written since she left here.'

'Well you wouldn't,' he agreed. 'She moved back to Sydney and goes by a different name now.' He made sure he had my attention when he said in a warning voice, 'she doesn't want anyone to connect her to her married name, she's forging a new career, a new life.'

'Right, divorced then?' I asked.

'Yep,' he answered, short and sharp.

I studied him. Big deal, lots of people separated or got divorced and started again. I knew several ladies who had reverted to their maiden names. 'At least she's still alive,' I added.

He puffed his cheeks and exhaled.

'God, did you think I had two missing people? Trust me, one missing young woman is enough. Jessica is alive and well.'

'What's her name now?' I asked.

He thought for a minute. 'Escapes me,' he said.

'Sure it does,' I said, narrowing my eyes at him and he laughed. Why was he protecting the journo?

'Is there something you're not telling me?' I asked.

He scoffed. 'I don't know what you want to hear, so yeah, I imagine I'm not telling you a lot.'

Then he leant forward and got intense. 'Coen, I want to solve this case. I can't move on or even leave here with it over my head… the worse kind of unfinished business,' he said, in a hushed voice. 'I want to find Soleil and if she has been murdered, I want to find the bastard who did that too.'

Chapter 10

THEN…

Jessica

It's bizarre how slipping on a pair of high heels can make you feel different; it was fun to dress up, I haven't done it for a while. Tonight was a hen's party for one of the girls in the office, Lara. It would put me out of the house when Skylar arrived, brilliant. I brushed my hair out and wore a fitted red dress with a touch of gold jewellery. I felt good and I felt my age again; I'd forgotten in the course of being a doctor's wife and journalist that I didn't have to be sensible all the time.

Venturing downstairs just before six was enough time to be at Clare's by 6.15pm and get a taxi from there – nothing was too far from anywhere here. Adam whistled and I did a turn for him; he declared me good enough to eat. Maybe it's not a bad thing for him to see his wife looking good and heading out, might make him appreciate me a little more or give me a few days' reprieve from his moodiness.

'Right, got your phone?' he asked, pulling me closer. 'No talking to strange men, leave that wedding ring on and any trouble, call me.'

I loved when he got possessive; it's one thing that I most adored about Adam. He still called me a couple of times a day and asked where I was, just to make sure I'm safe. He made me feel so secure, so protected, as if he had to know where I was all the time. I wonder if losing his wife made him more protective of me, of this relationship.

'What sort of trouble can a hen and her chicks get up to?' I teased him.

'Hmm, maybe I should chaperone,' he said, with one of his rarely seen and gorgeous smiles.

I laughed. 'No way,' I said.

'Are you sure I can't drop you off at Clare's?' he asked.

'No, but thanks. I want to leave my car at her place so I can leave whatever time I like in the morning. Drive safely to Sydney and good luck with Skylar,' I said, and tried to make it sound neutral and not neurotic. I kissed him, grabbed my overnight bag, which I had left nearby on the lounge chair, and moved to the door.

'Miss you already, you hot woman,' he teased.

I laughed and sent him an air kiss and headed out the front door to my car in the garage. It was moments like this that my life felt on track again, despite not being in the city or on a city paper. It didn't happen all the time, but tonight I felt happy to be here. I drove off and gave Adam a wave as he stood silhouetted against the large glass windows of the lounge room watching me leave.

NOW...

Coen

I took Soleil to bed... well, her diary, with good intentions of powering through it but only managed the first two entries before sleep overcame me. I didn't sleep well the first night here; it's a big house and all the night noises were introducing themselves. But in general, once I was horizontal, it was all over.

I opened the diary. She wrote it in small handwriting and all in French. Crap. Then I noticed a stapled wad of paper at the back of the book – bless the police service – they had translated the diary. On closer inspection, it looked like just the relevant bits since her arrival in Australia had been translated. That would save some time and I trust the police service would know what's relevant, hopefully. I'm not sure what was to be gained yet from reading Soleil's entries, if anything, but it fleshes her out for me. It helps me remember Soleil was a person, not just a cold case and not just the subject of a book. She was here for a moment in her life. Where the hell was she now?

Soleil's diary:

Monday 5 June

Once you've been hitchhiking for a while you get your regular lifts. I really like Jessica, she's about my age or maybe a couple of years older and she's picked me up twice now. She's a journalist for the local paper and did different shifts – early for online content, normal shifts for the paper, late shifts to get it to press. The last few weeks she had finished work about the same time as me. She's pale for a girl who lives by the beach; maybe all she did was work. Her job sounded really good; I wish I had done something more than teaching. Her husband sounded good too, a doctor, and she said they were renovating a house. I bet with their joint salaries the house will be right on the beach. Yet, she didn't seem happy.

I glanced at her as she drove. She was biting her bottom lip and staring straight ahead at the road. I thought she might have been quiet because she was shy, but maybe if she talked she might not stop and all the words would pour out of her mouth like an ocean filling up the car with water, drowning us both.

Wednesday 7 June

Good day today, I worked hard and finished early. I loved it here; I planned on staying in this area for three months or so during the fruit picking season. It was hard work, my back ached, much harder than teaching history. But on the positive side, fruit picking took no commitment – no lesson planning, no parent meetings, and no having to control the kids. It was just me and a few of the others from the hostel going out in the morning and working at our own pace through the day, getting intimately acquainted with the stone fruit. We picked in the sun, ate in the sun, laughed in the sun and came home for a night of sharing and drinking and sometimes having casual flings just for fun. Although I had only done that twice since I started my journey! There was this gorgeous German guy I met in London, and I met a real Australian surf lifesaver here and had a brief romance. But why not? I'm single and he was very bronze, just like on the tourist website.

Sometimes, after fruit picking, we all came home together, but most days we left when we had had enough. I was a morning person – I'm an early to start and early to finish person – around three o'clock when my back can't take it anymore. If it rains we don't work because the fruit goes off and rots quickly – see, the things you learn. The guys often worked until sunset. Some days, I tried to slip away without them noticing because I want to walk home by myself and just unwind. Also, it was harder to get a lift when you had a guy with you.

I want to go to the Great Barrier Reef and snorkel. Two guys from the hostel – Julian and Chris – were keen to travel that way with me. Julian has feelings for me, more than just friends.

*****

I closed the book and turned out the light, it was a bit like reading a soap opera. So what's Julian's story? He's next on my list to weed out.

Chapter 11

THEN...

Jessica

I was sober enough to drive home after the Hen's Party, so I caught a taxi back to Clare's place with her, grabbed my car and got home just after 2am. I scared the hell out of Adam; I thought he might still be up talking with Skylar, but he was in bed, alone. His job meant he was often waking me so you win some you lose some in the sleep stakes.

I'm glad he was in bed alone, but did he think Skylar was crawling into bed with him? He pulled me close. Knowing Skylar was somewhere in the house changed things; the atmosphere felt different already.

I woke up with a start; a phone was ringing somewhere in the house – a faint and distant ring. It wasn't my phone and Adam's phone was on the charger beside him. The digital clock read 06:04. Must be Skylar's.

Listening, not breathing... it was coming from upstairs in the new spare bedroom but Skylar was in the guest room, not there.

'Adam,' I nudged him as he slept on beside me.

'What? What's wrong?' he said, stirring.

'Phone. Can you hear it?'

He opened his eyes just as it gave its last ring and then the familiar sound of a message bank buzz.

'Sounds like it's upstairs in the new room,' I said. 'Someone must be up there. Did you move the bed up there for Skylar?'

Adam cleared his throat. 'No. Don't worry; no one is up there. The painter called in yesterday, and we were talking in the second bedroom, discussing colours and timing.' Adam turned to face me and pulled me against him. 'He must have put his phone down and forgotten it. I'll get it later and give him a buzz.'

I breathed a sigh of relief. The sound of a phone ringing early always meant bad news and hearing it somewhere else in the house was just creepy, especially in the unfinished rooms upstairs. A slight overreaction on my part, but apparently Adam didn't find it creepy; he closed his eyes and returned to sleep. I studied him, that beautiful face beside me. A few moments later he opened his eyes.

'I can go check upstairs if you're worried about that phone.'

I smiled. 'No, I'm good,' I whispered, 'go back to sleep.' I must have done that myself because when I next awoke, it was an hour later and I could hear him walking around upstairs in the new bedrooms above our main bedroom – they were like loft rooms. He must have been getting the painter's phone. Who was ringing the painter at 6am? I guess that was tradesmen's hour but on a Sunday? I heard him coming back down the stairs again. He entered the room. I turned to look at him.

'Morning, again,' I said and yawned.

'Hey there party girl,' he said and smiled. 'I've got the

54

phone, but the battery is flat now, so I'll call the painter's landline on the way to work and organise to get it to him.'

'Thanks, babe.' I had forgotten Adam was on a Sunday shift. Crap, I'm in the house with the princess, but at least I can sleep in and hopefully she'll have jetlag and stay in bed until this afternoon.

I felt I should do the 'wifey' thing and while Adam headed for the shower, I got up to put the kettle on and poached some eggs with toast for him. When he came downstairs later, he kissed me on the cheek.

'Thanks, you should have stayed in bed,' he said.

'Knowing you, you won't eat or drink until you get home, so at least you start right,' I said, pushing the plate in front of him. Seriously, could you get a better wife? Ha. 'So, all okay with our guest?'

'Fine. She won't get up until much later and I gave her a spare key so go out if you want to. I should get away mid-afternoon.'

I shrugged. 'I might go for a run, do some reading, talk online with a few friends. I should catch up on some work too,' I said.

'Working on a Sunday,' Adam said, 'trying to make a good impression with the boss?'

'Always,' I said. 'I'll be the editor in a year.'

Adam laughed and looked pleased. He thought I was serious.

He thought I wanted to stay when every day I planned my departure.

Chapter 12

NOW...

Coen

Sunday was a day for reflection and that's just what I did after my morning run on the beach. Finishing with a warm-down walk, I thought about my week of lecturing. It was more enjoyable than I thought it would be. Sure, no one gave me an apple, but no one walked out of the lecture either. Luckily, I've taught a version of this subject before, so it required updating the notes and getting on with it; a lot less work the second time around. The group was about twenty in size. I hoped there was some talent amongst them – usually, there's a couple that shine and the rest were hopeful. Nothing wrong with that though; you never know when you might just tap into the next best thing, even if you have limited talent. I can think of a dozen published books that fall into that category.

I've also tried one of the coffee shops on campus and was planning on sitting down and savouring my brew, but it all seemed a bit trendy and I felt like a dad hanging out with the kids – no thanks. It's funny when you become conscious of no longer being young, but not quite senior.

When I got home from my morning beach exercise and checked my phone messages, there was one from Detective Nick asking me to call back. Excellent. I rang but he wasn't that excited about hearing from me.

'You don't waste any time,' he said when he finally came to the phone after effusive thanks from the constable for his signed book collection that I'd left in his name at the counter this morning.

'How's that?' I asked. I had no idea what Nick was talking about... I barely got through two of Soleil's diary entries last night before giving in to sleep, and I had spent the morning in class. I can't recall doing any damage. He read me a brief paragraph from the '*Around Town*' section of the Strand Harbour newspaper. It was the equivalent of the gossip section assigned to two young and pretty journalists. It read:

'*Best-selling author, Coen Watson, has taken up residence in our town and was spotted at the Pier Café and the Strand Hotel. Our sources can confirm that he is here to write a book about missing backpacker, Soleil Reyer. If you were born yesterday or just moved to town, Soleil Reyer was an attractive French backpacker who might have taken the wrong ride about 15 years ago. It's a cold case, but for how much longer?*'

I sighed. 'Honestly Nick, I did not feed that to the media, that doesn't help me at all.'

'Yeah, I suspected as much,' he said, 'but I think I know who did. My young constable's been known to bed hop with the social reporter on the paper.'

'Do you think she'd reward him for that trivial piece of gossip?' I asked, surprised.

'Hell yeah,' Nick said, 'it's a small town and whether or not you like it, you're news, and Soleil is always just below the surface of the town's fabric for most residents.'

Bizarre.

'Hey while I've got you, Julian from the backpackers—' I began.

He cut me off: '—now if I give you my opinion on every potential suspect it might cloud your judgement, do you want that?'

'Point taken,' I agreed. 'This is my first true crime book, I've got a bit to learn about best techniques,' I confessed to him. 'Although it would save time to know your thoughts.'

'Nuh, he had a good alibi,' Nick decided to tell me. 'He was in love with Soleil, but so were most of the guys at the hostel. But it won't hurt to revisit the Julian papers that I've given you.'

'Thanks,' I said. We talked for a few more minutes and he said if I was at a loss for something to do this weekend, he'd be at Sandy's for dinner tonight. Locked in, it's a date. I'm hoping he gets so relaxed with me that he spilled more than he meant to about the case.

I finished listening to my messages before heading into the kitchen to make brunch. There was a call from one of my two sisters, Carmel, asking me if I'd had enough of small coastal life yet; another call from the university asking if I'd accept two late students – why not, they've only missed one lecture; and the third call was from my publisher, Natalie, passing on the details of a woman trying to track me down. Her name was Lacey Maurier, and she was the receptionist at the hostel when Soleil stayed there. She heard I was writing a book and left her phone number.

It had begun.

THEN…

Jessica

Skylar hadn't surfaced but I was on tenterhooks waiting for her to breeze out all blonde and bright. And then Nick called. It was not like him to call on the weekend, something must be going on. I glanced at the clock, just after 1pm.

'Hey Nick,' I answered, my voice edged with concern.

'Where are you?' he asked.

'I'm at home like normal people on a Sunday afternoon. Not to mention I'm recovering from a Hen's Party,' I said. 'Clearly you don't have the day off.'

'Oh, sorry to bug you then. I just thought you might have been working on the backpacker story,' he said.

'What backpacker story?' I said and my body went on alert; might be a scoop.

'It's probably nothing. A backpacker didn't return to the Y last night, and after midday, her friends rang in to say she was missing,' Nick said. 'But she's not officially missing yet, she might have stayed over at some guy's place. I told them we'll check it out but to call back tomorrow if she isn't back.'

'Who is it? The backpacker?'

I heard Nick shuffle a page. 'Soleil Reyer.'

'Soleil! Sunny!' I said.

'You know her?' he asked.

'I know her well; I've picked her up over a dozen times,' I hesitated. 'That's not illegal, is it?'

'Not in New South Wales, lucky for you or I'd be over to pick you up, frisk you and bring you in,' he warned.

'Phew,' I faked concern.

'If you hear anything from your journo pals that are working today, call me,' he said.

'I will. I hope she's alright,' I said. 'She said she had met someone, so you're probably right, she's having a sleepover and her friends have jumped the gun.' I thought about the first time I slept over with Adam, we didn't get out of bed until late the next day.

'Probably nothing,' he reiterated. 'She's likely to stumble home later today, shoes in one hand, hangover evident. What are you up to then?'

'I'm thinking about doing a load of washing before dropping into the office,' I joked.

'You're a fun girl, Jess,' he teased.

'You have no idea, Detective. I'll let you get back to the all-important job of keeping the town safe.'

'Thanks,' he chuckled. We said our goodbyes and then I worried about Sunny. I wonder if she decided to work on the weekend for extra cash and hitched a lift, a bad lift. I wonder if she was out with that guy she liked… what was his name? Truth be known, Nick called just to chat, I think he's lonely and keeps conveniently forgetting I'm married.

I wandered down to the yard to inspect the renovations and Adam's garden work to date and admire it like a dutiful wife. I glanced up and saw a curtain move slightly in the guest room. Should I go up, knock, and be hospitable, or was Skylar waiting for Adam to come home to make her entrance?

I temporarily filed Soleil to the back of my mind, but my gut told me something was not right.

*****

I pottered around, all the time uncomfortable in my own home knowing Skylar was upstairs, and at a loss to do something to track down Soleil. An hour later unable to relax, I grabbed my keys and bag and headed into work to see if the weekend editor had heard about Soleil, or if not, just give the editorial team the heads-up. The news had reached them but they were treading water on it.

The hour hit 4pm just as I came home and my stomach was churning; I was more anxious about meeting Skylar than I cared to admit to myself. I walked in to find Skylar and Adam sitting on the verandah sharing a wine. Skylar was in my usual chair and I felt a little stab of jealousy because they looked so good together… I felt like I was the guest. Adam rose, kissed me and introduced us.

Skylar, *call me Sky* was all long legs, tan, blonde hair and flashing teeth. Well, that was my first impression. She leapt up and hugged me; she was very sweet – or so I initially thought – as she thanked me for having her stay, and took a genuine interest in my work.

We all relaxed during the night as we shared dinner and drinks – it was actually fun; she didn't flirt with Adam, she sorted of flirted with both of us. Teasing smiles, nudges, drawing us both into her orbit. I liked her and if Chelsey was anything like her, I can imagine she was beautiful, popular, sweet and much missed.

Then, the dynamic changed. I was slow to pick it up but when Adam left the verandah to go top up our wine glasses leaving us momentarily alone, I noticed a subtle change in her. A little later when we had another opportunity to be alone together I realised there was a pattern going on here – without Adam as an audience, she became a little chillier and observed me more critically.

When we were first alone, she said while smiling: 'It's good to meet you Jessica, but I'm really surprised; you're so not Adam's type.' She studied me.

'Really?' I asked, surprised. How many types has he had other than her sister?

'Oh, trust me, I know his taste. He had a brief fling before Chelsey – I only know because she tried to hit on him again after Chelsey passed away.' Sky shook her head in disgust. 'But Adam likes them blonde,' she said, putting a strand of her blonde hair behind her shoulder. 'My sister fitted that bill,' and then Adam rejoined us and she started on a completely different topic. I pulled the knife out of my chest and tried not to think about it too much. I'm sure she meant no harm, it was just a throw-away line – I'm sure she didn't mean to subtly tell me I'm not right for Adam, or that she'd be more his type.

'I'm so disappointed your pool isn't finished,' she pouted at him.

'Tell me about it,' he said. 'The construction is running late. Although they showed up last week to put the plumbing in. If they could just concrete it and get out of here.'

'I bet you can't wait to have that huge, dirt eyesore gone from the garden,' she wrinkled her nose. 'I can remember the pool parties we used to have, so much fun. Are you a swimmer, Jessica?'

I opened my mouth to answer, but Adam jumped in, so to speak.

'Jess is not keen on the pool, let alone a plunge pool – way too cold for her liking,' he said, with a smile as if I was mute and needed someone to speak for me. I smiled at them both and nodded.

'Really?' Sky said, her eyes huge with surprise. 'I love cold water. But we're used to that where we come from,' she said, with a knowing glance at Adam.

On the second occasion when she worked her charm on me, we had moved inside and finished dinner. I rose to clear the table, Adam went to get a bottle of Port from our new cellar, and Sky leant back in the chair not offering to help – but I'm good with that, she's a guest.

'Well,' she said, pushing back from the table and crossing her long legs. 'I imagine this house lends itself to some wonderful parties.' She flicked her hair over her shoulder.

'Actually, we've never had a party here,' I said. 'We've only been here about six months with the renovations going on around us.'

'Really! Six months, oh my God, Chelsey would have had a party every weekend – a launch party, renovation party, beach party, new wallpaper party… any excuse for a party. She loved entertaining, so did Adam. I'm surprised he's not pining for it,' she said, studying me through her long lashes. I think they were fake.

My self-doubt went into overdrive… did Adam like to party? Was I stopping him from doing something he loved or not organising enough get-togethers in our social life to keep him happy? Should I be doing that to help him network and help his career along? I realised Sky was watching me for my reaction.

'Maybe you're right,' I said, feigning a casual shrug. 'We probably work too hard. Once the renovations are done, I'm sure we'll see more people.'

She ignored my comment. 'I think the best party Chelsey ever threw – aside from their engagement party, that was pretty spectacular – was a New Year's Eve party, it broke the mould. I can still see Chelsey and Adam waltzing in the middle of the room at midnight, all their friends around them, the two of them locked in this kiss and the room filled with stars and gold. She had this divine fitted gold dress on, and he was in black-tie. Breathtaking.'

'Sounds beautiful,' I said. Really, could she be any more insensitive? I should have gone away for a week. Who needs this? I felt like crap now. Adam re-entered the room and Sky included him.

'I was just saying to your lovely wife, Jess, how great this place would be for a party,' she gushed.

'Yeah, we're not the party types,' he said.

Sky laughed and rubbed Adam's arm. 'You could have fooled me. I remember you and Chelsey being the life of the party.'

At least Adam had the good grace to look uncomfortable.

'Sky, I'm thirty-two now, not twenty-two,' he said, giving her a smile that would melt any female. The night just gets better and better.

'But you've got a younger wife, you know what they say, you're only as young as—'

Adam cut her off. 'Jess and I are very happy with the pace of our life,' he said. He moved away and went into the living room to get some port glasses out of the china cabinet.

Sky rose, left the table and sat on a swivel chair in front of the counter where I worked.

'Chelsey had so many followers and she was always putting images online, important when you are in PR. I couldn't find your accounts.'

'No, I'm not really into it, except to connect with friends, you know,' I said, knowing she wouldn't know.

'Oh, right,' Sky said, looking at me like I was an alien.

'Well, you've mellowed, Adam. I didn't even hear about the wedding!'

I rinsed the dishes and packed the dishwasher. Moving between the table and the sink, but still, Sky didn't offer to help, leave it to the domestic help!

'We eloped. We wanted an intimate, private day,' I said, with a smug smile. Now I'm trying to match her. I'm pathetic.

'Really? I can't believe Adam wanted to elope, but I guess after his first wedding, which was huge, why compete?'

I didn't know that he'd had a big wedding or a wedding at all, but I bit my tongue. Later I'm sure I would think of a million great comebacks, but right now I just wanted to smack her.

Sky continued. 'Chelsey and Adam's wedding was huge; it was like a celebrity event – the hot doctor and the best-known PR girl in town. Every paper had social photos. I was a bridesmaid along with four of Chelsey's friends.' She finished her wine and swivelled on the stool.

'Wow, I didn't know Adam had five friends to rope in as groomsmen,' I said, leaving myself wide open.

'He has a huge friend network at home. I'm sure they miss him.' It was said like it was my fault he was over here. Again, I had the feeling that every word from her mouth had numerous interpretations; she studied me to see the reaction they were having on my face. I was like a deer in the spotlight.

Sky continued. 'When Chelsey died, Adam was forlorn, just devastated. It was disgraceful how many women just threw themselves at him – a beautiful, rich widower – I completely understood why he had to get away, why he came over here,' she said and narrowed her eyes at me.

I recall Adam saying Sky hit on him at the funeral. Sounds like she had competition.

'You and Chelsey are so different; I can see why he married you.' She smiled at me.

Because I'm not Chelsey? Because I'm not you? Because I'm safe?

I didn't get to be enlightened on that train of thought as Adam re-entered the room.

When I thought over the conversation one hundred times in the weeks after, I was angry at myself for being so placid, but I wasn't used to being on the defensive, especially in my own home. At work and in a business environment I can mix it with the best, but with Sky, I was like some unsophisticated kid who was tripping around in Sky's sister's way-too-big shoes to fill.

Chapter 13

THEN…

Jessica

It was such a shock. I had seen the poster now a few times and each time it affected me. Beautiful Soleil 'Sunny' Reyer, living the dream, staring at me from the power pole. Her face beaming at me, fading from sun exposure. I recognised the photo from her Facebook page – as we say in the media 'in happier days'. I remember her in full colour. It felt like the townsfolk had plastered every street pole and shop window with posters that screamed MISSING. Got to hand it to her friends, they wasted no time getting these posters up.

Despite being on the late shift Monday, my boss, Oliver, called and asked me to come in as soon as possible. This was a huge story; I rushed in, excited and a little sick… every journo worth their salt loves a breaking story.

I walked in and the first thing I saw in our department was the art department scanning Sunny's social media page for useable images. Sunny was officially missing. I saw her on Friday when I gave her a lift back to the hostel. This was freaky.

Where were you?

Clare met me on the way to my desk and gave me the heads-up that Oliver wanted to go all out on this one. We had an all-staff meeting at 9am. Oliver called these once a month but then usually forgot to have them; today, he remembered. Nearly everyone was there when Clare and I entered; Oliver was talking to one of the senior journos about a story in the national paper today. He hated seeing a local story in the national paper unless we covered it first or better – fair enough.

'Okay, order everyone,' he said, sitting down at the head of the table. 'You know management like these meetings so I occasionally have one and besides, we have a hot story on our plate,' he said with a glance to me and then he took in all the team. We weren't a big team, but it was a good team – a mixture of ages and talent. Oliver, as the editor, was in his mid-forties, but he wasn't the most senior; there were a couple of property and sports journos who were older. But with his old-fashioned thin rim glasses, scruffy hair and heavy-set, he easily passed for a decade older. He ran through each of the departments: sport had done a good job of the local footy season and now he wanted the same commitment for the cricket season.

'And Ron,' Oliver began, 'I don't care if you think the ball is the wrong shape, you need to cover the local soccer league. Make yourself known to them.'

Ron frowned and nodded, but not with any great enthusiasm.

Oliver stumbled through his review of the 'Beauty and Lifestyle' department's workings to date – he didn't know a moisturiser from foundation; so that team got the brush over, and then he came to crime reporting. Here we go, he was right at home now.

'A missing backpacker – this is the story of the year. Might be the biggest story for longer than that depending on how it plays out,' Oliver said. 'You're lucky Jess,' he continued singling me out as I usually did the crime reporting, 'many reporters would love to get their teeth into a good missing person case.' At least he said it with a look of apology. 'Don't get me wrong; it's not that we want young women to go missing, but it makes for paper sales.'

I nodded. 'I knew her.'

His jaw dropped open.

'I gave her a lift home over a dozen times.'

'Fan-fucking-tastic,' he said, 'write that up. Write up what she was like, what you spoke about. Do a colour piece and make us cry!'

He was on fire now.

'I'm putting extra resources on this story; Clare, you'll go full-time on it with Jess,' he said. My eyes widened.

'Perfect,' I said, pleased and with a glance at Clare who seemed happy about the news. I was relieved he picked Clare because we worked well together and she knew her stuff, she was a gun at research.

Oliver continued '...and I want to drive more public involvement. Clare, you'll focus on online content, Jess will do the daily paper fill. You can bounce off each other – promote and link to each other's content. Try to drive the reader to the website to take part in helping find Soleil. We're the voice of the town, let's get behind this,' he said.

Clare grimaced; she hated online. I suspected Oliver put her on it because he thought I'd prefer the newspaper, which I do, and he didn't want to take it off me since that's one of the reasons I moved from the city to keep working on a paper. But truth be told, with Soleil's case I could get more stories going if I worked the online audience, especially as Soleil's friends and most people our age probably never picked up a newspaper. Plus, I could break stories any time of the day or night, and I'd be better online than Clare.

'Oliver, it might be better if we swap roles if you and Clare have no objections?' I suggested. 'If we launch a *Find Soleil* campaign like you said to involve the public with the search but link with a sister-site like the Lyons newspaper online in France, it'll have legs. I will invite public comments, approve and publish the ones that will keep the story turning over. Clare can do the grassroots campaign in the paper and maybe Ryan can help us both.'

Clare looked much happier and Oliver loved it. Ryan, the cadet, was keen – he'd been doing lost and found until now.

'Great, perfect, do it, let's ramp this up. Chat to the I.T. boffins – ah sorry guys,' he said, remembering they were present, 'yeah, our I.T. team will help, and also, get our artists to create a dedicated campaign banner for it,' he said with a glance to our two graphic designers. 'Get some of those hashtag things going and let's own this. Plus, tell the cops what we're doing. We want Nick and his lot involved, and we want them to share. Good, good,' he said, nodding his head.

That earned me a few brownie points again; I'm on a roll. He moved onto the motoring guys, and Clare and I exchanged looks. Love a challenge, so let's find you, Soleil! I needed to talk to her friends at the hostel, the hostel owner, the farm owner where she picked fruit, anyone who knew her, had given her a lift, was a friend, went to college or school with her, her stepfather, everyone and anyone who had felt the rays of Sunny. I just had to remember what she told me in our shared car rides.

After the meeting, I put Ryan to work contacting all Sunny's online friends to find out more about her, get comments, get anything we could use including photos.

'Thanks for asking for me,' he gushed.

'We need you,' I assured him but warned: 'Soleil's friends are probably being inundated with messages from the media and weirdos so maybe start by saying we are the only paper on the ground and we're running a local media-driven campaign to find her. Might give us an edge.'

'I'll check the social media pages of her friends too, especially any that are here in Australia, to see what they are saying about her,' he offered.

'Great idea,' I agreed.

I felt like I was walking around in slow motion, I've never personally known anyone who had been a victim of a crime, until now. Sure, I had met crime victims through my work, but this was different. Oliver wanted a story filed within the hour but I had to talk with my detective mate, Nick. We had become a bit chummy; partly because I shared my leads with him if I had any and he didn't like Clare. He thought I wasn't as much of a 'ball breaker' as she was, to quote him. I'm not sure that's a compliment since I'm supposed to be a hard-nose journalist. Still, the relationship had its advantages. He was kind and friendly, not bad looking either, and fit. My editor, Oliver, was pleased I'd established the relationship.

A quick call to Nick after my meeting with Oliver found him free and he met me at our regular coffee shop; he could only stay fifteen minutes, he said. Our coffees arrived, my first for the day, bring it on. Watching the reaction to Nick was priceless; he wore a suit, not a uniform, but most of the locals knew him especially if they'd grown up here. I swear if you sat him in a window at the front of the café, the crowd parted like the Red Sea. Three or four people stopped at the door of the café on spotting Nick, turned around and scuttled away – might have been the hemp pants they were wearing.

Nick leaned closer and lowered his voice. 'Bet she took the wrong ride… happens all the time,' he shrugged. 'Don't know why women hitch.'

He glanced at me before looking down at his cup and stirring a teaspoon of sugar into his coffee. Did he expect me to have the universal answer to that?

'Maybe because we like to think that it would never happen to us and that ultimately all men are good,' I said.

He made a scoffing sound.

'I've got hundreds of files that say otherwise.'

I sighed. 'Such is life. But you're a good guy, case in point.'

'Yeah well, my ex-wife wouldn't agree. She'd say I was a lazy, two-timing bastard,' he said with the hint of a smile. Maybe his occasional jokes about having an affair weren't jokes after all.

'Yeah, women,' I agreed, and rolled my eyes. 'So, anything you can throw my way?' I diverted the conversation back to safe ground.

'I was just going to ask you the same thing,' he said.

I shared with him that Soleil had met someone she was keen on and that she was cagey about it, but her face lit up when she talked about it. I thought he'd be rapt to hear that, but apparently not.

'Yeah, nothing I don't know there,' he said. 'We now have her diary.'

'Oh wow,' I said, 'anything revealing?'

He shrugged. 'It's all in French so we're translating the last few months' entries. We're not finished yet but we've started at the end naturally and are working backward.' Then he gave me a good scrap. 'But she wrote she liked him enough to consider staying if he felt the same.'

I could better that.

'She said he was the first professional guy she'd dated. I didn't push it because I could tell it was new to her and she was keeping it close to her chest. I wish I had asked her more questions now,' I sighed.

'That's good Jess, thanks. She might elaborate in her diary when we get the rest translated.'

He took a sip of coffee and I studied him.

'You know something more,' I said.

'Yeah, but it's off the record for now.'

'Okay, but can I have it first if I give you anything I come across?'

'Don't I always do that?' Nick asked.

'No,' I said, and he laughed. 'What is it? Off the record, I promise.'

'Better be,' he threatened. He glanced around before continuing, 'the hostel receptionist, a dizzy chick took a call for Soleil on Saturday morning. It was from a guy and Soleil was excited,' he said.

'Wow, this is good. Did she get a name or—'

'—none of that yet.' Nick cut me off. 'The young constable was just doing preliminary questions with everyone there so I'm going back there in a few hours with him and we'll get full statements.'

'What's your gut instinct, off the record?' I asked Nick.

'She's in trouble.'

I sighed and did him a trade. 'I'll credit you with the boyfriend lead linked to the diary, even though I heard it from the horse's mouth.'

'Solid of you,' he said with a nod. It took the heat off the police if they looked like they had little break-throughs and besides, it was more credible if it came from the police and then I confirmed it with my memories of girls' talk – Soleil telling me about someone she had met.

'Do me a favour, Jess? A professional guy could be anything, I wouldn't emphasise it for now.'

A groan escaped me.

'I know,' he held up his hand, 'but if there's anyone in town who feels threatened, they are going to bolt as soon as it is out there. Write with a broad stroke, please, and just give me a couple of days.'

I nodded. 'I'll have to check with Oliver, but consider it done.'

He exhaled. 'I'll throw you a bone for doing that for me.'

'Go on,' I leaned forward enthusiastically.

'The last entry of the diary, she wrote that this guy made a mistake.'

Watching Nick, I asked: 'And?'

'That's it. It was her last entry.'

'Fuck,' I said, in a low voice.

'Yeah, my thoughts exactly.'

Then his phone rang and Nick had to go, which was why he always had his coffee as a takeaway.

With a wave of my hand to farewell him, he rose and headed off, still talking on the phone, clutching his coffee. I gulped down my last few mouthfuls and raced back to the office to file a story.

With my hands on the keyboard, words flowed on my character piece about Soleil and her routine before she disappeared. I asked Ryan to select a pic of her looking glowing and full of life. This story had to inspire emotion and action – I was covering the biggest story of my career.

My day was filled with Soleil and Chelsey... Chelsey and Soleil. Ghosts in my life.

*****

The Strand Times

Missing woman was dating local man
By Jessica Steyne, crime reporter

Police have revealed that missing backpacker, Soleil 'Sunny' Reyer, 22 of Lyon, France, may have been dating a local man in the days leading up to her disappearance.

Sunny, as she was known to her friends, was last seen early evening on Saturday 10 September leaving the Rest-up Backpackers' Hostel.

Detective Nick Clarkson of the Strand Harbour Police said it had come to light that Ms Reyer may have been in a short-term relationship before her disappearance.

"According to her diary, which is now in our possession, she met with an unidentified person that evening," Detective Clarkson said.

Friends of Ms Reyer confirmed that on several occasions she did not return to the hostel after a day of fruit picking and that on Saturday, she left the hostel early in the evening to meet with someone.

A spokesperson for the Rest-up Backpackers' Hostel said 'Ms Reyer had joked with her friends about going out to meet the locals and on her return from several outings it was clear she had been drinking, had showered and had changed attire.

'On each occasion, she returned to the hostel late at night and was up early for work the next day. On the night she went missing she left around 6.30pm and did not return that evening or the next morning,' the spokesperson said.

Julian Darby from England who was staying at the hostel with Ms Reyer, said he had known Soleil for several months and her disappearance seemed out of character.

'She was so sensible – she never missed a work shift that she committed to and she didn't drink more than a few drinks at night. She was saving to go to the Great Barrier Reef; she wasn't the wild type,' Mr Darby said.

'We are all really worried about her. She didn't mention anyone specifically to us but I think she was seeing someone casually. Several times, she turned down our group invitations because she had plans to catch up with a person outside our circle,' he said.

Det. Clarkson said the police would like to talk with anyone who may have been socialising with Ms Reyer or saw her in the company of another person.

'Every bit helps. If you have any information, please contact Crime Stoppers or your local police station,' he said.

Share: Facebook | Twitter | Email | In | g+ | Add your comment to this story.

Chapter 14

THEN...

Jessica

Ifiled the colour piece on Soleil as quickly as possible to get out of the office and over to the Rest-up Backpackers' Hostel. My goal was to talk to the receptionist and anyone else available and get out of there before Nick came. Giving Oliver – my editor – the heads-up on my plans, I was off and searching for angles that some of Soleil's fellow residents might shed light on her. Plus it was nearing 3.30pm and they should all be rolling back in from their day fruit picking or sightseeing. I'd give some of them a lift if I passed them, anything for a scoop. Sadly, not one of them was on the road today, neither was Soleil.

I parked in the guests' parking area and headed in. Luck was on my side – at that hour it was a pretty much full house. I'm guessing Nick has asked the residents not to leave town yet.

Like me, everyone liked Soleil; they smiled when they talked about her. They mentioned her sunny nature, her fitting name. No one could believe she would just disappear. Me either... Soleil was in trouble I just knew it, I think we all did. As the hours ticked by, the less hope we held for good news. I caught up with the two guys that were going to travel up north with her – Julian and Chris. We sat opposite each other in the hostel's backyard, which was littered with dark timber picnic tables and chairs, a BBQ that had seen better days and a beautiful, shady mango tree.

'When are you going to take off?'

Julian shrugged. 'I don't feel right leaving now, but I know we'll have to.' He glanced at Chris.

'We're just going to wait a few more weeks,' Chris said. 'We're hoping, you know...'

I nodded.

'There's no way she'd just take off,' Julian cut in. 'We spent a lot of time planning the trip and she was keen, keener than Chris and me.'

'It was her idea,' Chris agreed. 'We were thinking of Perth, but Soleil talked us into going to the Barrier Reef and Cairns.'

An attractive, skinny blonde girl joined us and introduced herself as Astrid. I remember Soleil mentioning her once – her German friend.

'She seemed happier the last week or so,' Astrid told me. 'Don't you think?' she asked the guys. They shrugged. Yep, guys probably wouldn't notice.

'I think she had met someone. A couple of times she came out with us, but when we got back she was here, so maybe she went out, maybe she didn't. But there was one night when she definitely came back here later than us,' Astrid said.

'She came out with us on Friday night, the night before she disappeared,' Julian reminded her. 'But not Saturday night, now that you mention it.'

I sensed a tinge of annoyance emanating from him; I doubt it just occurred to him that Soleil wasn't with them on Saturday night. Was he in love with Soleil and thought he had a chance? Did he find out she was seeing someone else? Did he kill her in a jealous rage? Big call given he seemed so placid but he was big enough to overpower Soleil.

'Did she mention a name to you of anyone she had met?' I prodded them.

They shook their heads.

'Nah,' Chris said. 'The police asked the same thing. We all sort of do our own thing a bit, we don't live in each other's pockets.'

'Matt,' Astrid said. We all turned to look at her. 'I was fruit picking next to her the other day and we were talking guys,' she said with a glance at Chris and Julian. 'She said she'd met a guy she liked and I'm pretty sure she said his name was Matt; he was a lawyer or something like that. You know the big money jobs. They'd gone out a few times; she said she'd think about staying around longer if it went well.'

'That's brilliant, Astrid,' I said. Julian looked less than impressed.

If Detective Nick knew that information he hadn't shared and he certainly hadn't released Matt's name or alleged occupation to us or any other media yet. I'd keep that up my sleeve to offer him later.

I continued: 'Did she say what he looked like, where he worked, what he drove, how she met him, anything like that?'

She shook her head. 'It was hot and we were just throwing a few comments around.' She gave me an apologetic look. Then, with a glance again to the boys, she added, 'she said he was only a bit taller than her and she usually liked them

taller, and he could be rough and she liked that in a guy.'
She blushed as she said it; giving up the girl's talk.

'Mm, interesting,' I agreed. 'I'm not sure what I can do
with that, but it's something. They'd had sex then by the
sound of it, and had it somewhere. His place maybe?

'How tall do you think Soleil was?' I asked.

The receptionist, Lacey, had gotten away from the desk to
have a smoke. I tried to talk with her earlier but the phone
kept ringing. Now she came over to join us and heard the
tail end of my question.

'I've got a photocopy of her passport, we always have to
get photo I.D.,' Lacey said. 'I can tell you in a minute how
tall she is, it'll be on there.'

'Great, thank you,' I said. This trip was turning out to be
worth the visit.

Lacey turned to blow her smoke away from us and then
said to me, 'I'm the one who took the call from that guy
for her on Saturday morning,' she threw the statement in
casually, taking my question right out of my mouth.

My eyes widened. 'Did he say his name? Could you tell it
was a mobile or landline?'

'No name, he just asked for her. It was definitely a mobile,
I think he was driving,' she shrugged.

'What did he sound like? Young, old, accent, any strange
inflections, you know when people say a word kind of
funny,' I dumbed it down.

Lacey exhaled another puff of smoke, it was so pungent
in the fresh outdoor environment and said: 'He sounded
like he was older, in his thirties, maybe and posh. It was
some sort of accent but I'm not sure.'

*I wonder if she told Nick about the 'posh' accent. Lacey
wasn't the sharpest knife in the drawer.*

'Like a British accent maybe?' I prodded.

'I don't know, yes, maybe,' she added. 'Like he was smart.'

I glanced at Julian. Was he jealous of this guy?

'Can I quote you, Lacey and Astrid... you know, about Soleil receiving the phone call and how she talked about the potential boyfriend?' I asked, looking from one to the other. 'It'll go online too. It can just be a quote or I can include your photo if you like?'

They looked at each other and smiled.

'Sure,' Lacey said.

'I won't mention the rough part,' I assured Astrid. Astrid agreed.

Well done, girls. The good thing about my generation compared to older folk was that we loved our fifteen minutes of fame. I snapped a photo of them, confirmed their names and their quote. Witness material was always good and a photo of two attractive girls never hurt.

I was out of there before Nick arrived, although I would tell him about my visit eventually when I traded info. On the way back to the office I realised I had been living vicariously through Soleil. Seeing her, hearing about her plans and her life was releasing my memories of the times when I was excited by travel and adventure and all it promised. But that had to stop. I've been her – now I'm at the next phase of my life. Now her life could be over.

Next, back to the office to file the story. I gave Nick a call and he had just pulled up at the backpacker's hostel. I filled him in.

'Yeah, I knew about the Matt name from her diary, but I can't tell you everything,' he said.

'Well, now I know. But here's something for you—' I told him about the lawyer comment and posh accent. 'Any luck with the hostel phone records?' I asked.

'Yes and no. The call to the hostel is registered on their records, but it came from a burner,' he said.

'So that's a pre-paid phone?' I asked.

'Yeah, pre-paid, often temporary, often not registered. But we're still working on it.'

He asked me to hold off on writing too much about the boyfriend at this stage. I negotiated a compromise – I was rolling with a version of the story: a phone call, the date, the posh accent, the photo of the girls but I promised I wouldn't mention the name – Matt or the possible legal occupation. He wasn't happy – such was the tension between journos and cops but he could live with it. I didn't want to jeopardise finding the guy or Soleil, even though I wanted to break the story. I made Nick promise all scoops were mine in exchange for withholding. The things we do.

Oliver was pleased to see me back and I quickly told him, Clare and Ryan about what I had negotiated for now, just in case they got wind of the story from a source and ran it. I pumped out a story for online and put it up, along with the photo of Astrid and Lacey posing at their glamorous best. I then did a version for tomorrow's paper, which Clare would add her bit to and we'd share a byline.

Next, intern Ryan and I would start tracking down every Matt and lawyer in town or visiting the town with a posh accent! How hard can it be?

The Strand Times online

Boyfriend sought in missing woman's case
By Jessica Steyne, crime reporter

Missing woman, Soleil 'Sunny' Reyer, 22 of Lyon, France,

received a call from a man on Saturday morning, the last day she was seen alive.

The receptionist of the Rest-up Backpackers' Hostel, Lacey Maurier, 19, said she took a call from a man asking for Ms Reyer and she overhead Ms Reyer set up a date for that night.

'He specifically asked for Soleil,' Ms Maurier said. 'We don't take many calls for guests because it's frowned upon – management like to keep the lines free for incoming bookings and most people have their own phones these days. So I remembered him calling.'

Ms Maurier said the man sounded mature and Ms Reyer appeared pleased to hear from him.

'She lit up when she talked to him, and she organised to meet him that night. He was picking her up from the Y.'

Ms Maurier said the caller did not give his name and Ms Reyer did not return to the Y that night or since.

Astrid Meinz, a guest at the hostel who had been fruit picking with Soleil Reyer that week said a boyfriend had been mentioned.

'Soleil said she had met someone that she liked and they had gone out a few times. She said she would stay around longer if it kept going well,' Ms Meinz said. 'She described him as just a bit taller than she was.'

Soleil is 172 centimetres or five foot eight inches.

Detective Nick Clarkson of the Strand Harbour Police has appealed for public help. 'If anyone has offered Soleil a ride at any point in time, or can identify a vehicle or driver that stopped for Soleil, please contact Crime Stoppers or your local police station.'

Share: Facebook | Twitter | Email | In | g+ | Add your comment to this story.

Chapter 15

NOW…

Coen

It was a lecturing morning and the students had returned for another lesson, who would have thought? I had heard bad things about students regularly missing lectures so that was encouraging. I got back from university and made a late lunch – a sandwich that would have won me a place on *Masterchef*. While eating it, I did some quick research on the woman who had left a message, Lacey Maurier. I meant to call her back yesterday but time got away from me. I found a photo of her in a story that the journalist, Jessica, had written. Lacey was pictured with another girl from the hostel, Astrid. Attractive young girls. I read the article. So, Lacey took a call for Soleil from some guy on that very day that Soleil went missing. Excellent.

The 'now' Lacey, fifteen years on, had found me and she was in her mid-to-late thirties, by the look of it. According to her social media accounts, she worked part-time as a checkout chick at one of the local supermarkets. There were a few photos of her with kids and a big guy who looked like a truckie. She was a small, bleached blonde woman. I rang her back. I soon found out that she was an over-sharer, which wasn't a bad thing when you're wanting information.

Lacey mustn't get out much – she wanted to meet for a drink and tell me everything she knew about Soleil. Hopefully, no one would notice this time… I didn't want to appear in the social pages again for wining and dining every potential lead. People would come to expect it and I'd have to get a second job to support it. It was hard to be transparent now that the social pages have outed me. We agreed to meet at a small wine bar that Lacey frequented with her girlfriends near her home. My clock was still on city time – I was there fifteen minutes early due to no traffic; no need to allow for it here. It was nearing six and the winery had the usual after-work crowd in. It was a little upmarket; perhaps Lacey aspired to that, nothing wrong with ambition.

Spotting a small table for two at the back of the room, I nabbed it. I spotted Lacey straight away, she had changed little from her photo, maybe just a little more jaded. My goal was to be home by 7.30pm so I told her my limit was one drink as I was driving and had to be home for some phone calls. It's best to put perimeters on these things. It worked for Lacey – as soon as her glass of wine arrived, she told me she knew who did it and said the police never even considered him.

Lacey spilled, and I mean spilled. I didn't get a word in, but I taped it all which she was pleased about. She began and right at the beginning, sadly.

'I was seeing a guy at the time who was studying law at the university,' she explained. 'Andy and I met at a nightclub. I was studying beauty therapy at college and working part-time at the hostel.' She stopped to sip her wine, and I was going to ask a question but apparently, that wasn't necessary as she began again.

'He thought he was a real hot shot and at the time I guess I liked that. He used to say that he won't be second best and he won't take second best, that he was a big fish in a small pond, and that he was going places. I was pretty then,' she said and paused to sip her wine.

Mm, dangerous ground. Don't want to appear flirtatious or have her say I came onto her.

'I'm sure he still thinks you are very attractive,' I said. Nice one... deflecting the compliment and fishing about their relationship.

'Oh God no, he's long gone,' she said. 'But back then, I had won the local beauty pageant and he enjoyed having me on his arm, he used to say that.'

Can we just get to the Soleil part, please! I try to steer her. 'So Soleil was there around that time?' I asked.

'She sure was, and here's the thing. My guy, Andy, had a thing for her. He came to pick me up from work one day at the hostel and she was talking with me at reception. I introduced them and then I had to go check someone in for the night, and they talked for ages. Then he started wanting to pick me up more and always around the same time. He even told me a few times that he had seen her hitching so he picked her up on the way to get me.'

'Did you think something was going on? Did she seem keen on him?' I asked.

Lacey finished her drink and ordered another. I grabbed a sparkling mineral water.

'I don't know, I couldn't tell with her, but I was pretty sure he was cheating on me, there were signs.'

'Like what?' I asked moving her along.

'He started asking lots of questions about my work, other guests, and then he'd eventually get to her. He must have thought I was stupid and didn't notice,' she scoffed. 'He used to say that he knew her type, that the Soleils of the world – his words not mine – needed to be managed and that she was the type of woman who would walk all over a man if you weren't strong enough for her. He said he knew how to play Soleil's game to perfection.'

'What does that mean?' I asked, and thanked the waiter as he delivered our second round of drinks. I saw a few heads turning our way, I hoped the gossip column didn't have me dating Lacey tomorrow morning. If that truckie guy was her partner, I needed him hunting me down like I needed a reader sending me grammatical tips – it happened.

Lacey started on her second drink before answering. 'I think he thought he could get Soleil, and he probably could, he was a catch,' she assured me.

'But did Soleil know you were going out? Would she make a move on a guy who was spoken for?' I asked.

'I made sure she knew,' Lacey said. 'But Andy loved to see me jealous. Anytime we were out he'd be flirting. He'd say it was good for me to be a little green but if I spoke to any other guy he'd come over to reclaim me right away, like pissing on his property. He just loved to perform,' she said, shaking her head at the memory. 'He'd hold your gaze as he talked to you, he always threw in some flattery and even if he spent less than five minutes talking to you, next time he met you he'd greet you like a long-lost friend that he was so pleased to see again. It made you feel special, he was going to be a brilliant lawyer.'

'What happened to him?' I asked.

'We broke up after about a year, and then he transferred out of here to Sydney University. I never saw him again after that. But four things made me think the police were wrong not treating him as a suspect and I told the cops that.' She held up her four fingers to make sure I got it.

I interrupted her. 'Did they talk with him at all?'

'Yeah, but they said they had nothing on him.'

Her four-finger salute changed to the stop sign – a flat palm – even though I wasn't going to add anything more. 'Before you hear it from the cops, yes, I took a call the Saturday that Soleil disappeared and it was a guy asking for her.'

'Hold up,' I interrupted her now, it was the best thing she had said and the part I most wanted to hear straight from the horse's mouth. 'I saw that in the police files. So Soleil got a call that Saturday morning and—'

'—and she was really excited and agreed to meet this guy, don't know his name, she didn't say, neither did he. I answered the call and yeah, it didn't sound like Andy, but Andy could change his voice. This guy sounded posh.'

'Right,' I said, trying not to sound unconvinced, which I was. Lacey was an important witness for taking the call but the Andy hypothesis was probably off the boil.

'Posh like British posh or—'

'—yeah,' she cut me off, 'like the way the royals talk. But the four things,' she continued, desperate to tell me. 'Soleil told Astrid – Astrid was this girl from Germany who was staying at the hostel too – that this new guy she'd met liked it rough. That's number one – Andy liked it rough.'

'Very interesting,' I agreed. 'And the second thing?'

She finished her wine before answering. 'Soleil said her new guy was just a bit taller than her, and Andy was that.'

I nodded. Fair enough. 'The third thing?'

'His middle name was Matt! You know the police were looking for a guy called Matt, he could have used his middle name,' she said, watching for my reaction.

'Yeah, well that's worth looking into. The fourth and final thing?' I asked, looking to wrap this up.

'He lied about his alibi.'

She had my attention now.

'He said he was home studying but I know he wasn't because he was at my place for a while. And maybe he went somewhere before and after that.' She clapped her hand down on the table. 'That might just solve it for you,' she said.

Lucky me. Andy was worth a look, and I told Lacey just that.

Chapter 16

Then...

Jessica

Ryan and I locked ourselves in the newspaper's boardroom with our laptops and began our Matt search. I assigned Ryan to look for Sydney lawyers in the right age group named Matt, and I started on Strand Harbour and surrounding districts. Sure, Nick and his team would do the same, but it doesn't hurt to have many sets of eyes on the case. I started with the basics and typed into the search engine: *'Matt, lawyer, Strand Harbour'*. Okay, that yielded me four Matts. Jotting down their names, it was back to the search to check out their company websites and networking sites. One Matt turned out to be a Mattina, so I wrote her off. Although it wouldn't surprise me if Soleil had been gay, she was very sensual and flirty.

Three Matts remained. The first Matt would have been about sixty – not to say that Soleil wouldn't fall for an older man, but he's on the back-burner for now. The second Matt looked like a promising candidate except for the photos on his social media pages of him with his partner, a guy. That left me one more Matt. I didn't realise

I was holding my breath until my third Matt's photo came up on the screen and he looked the part – probably in his late thirties, handsome enough to catch Soleil's eye and by the look of the photos on his site, he was a family man. Soleil might have fallen in love with a man who wanted a mistress. Did she find out he was married? Maybe he got rid of her to save his marriage. I jotted down his firm's address so I could stake him out.

In a city the size of Sydney, Ryan only found two that would fit the bill. I gave Detective Nick a call and it went to the message bank. I left a brief message about our 'Matts'. He rang me back five minutes later.

'I'm sorry to say the Matt lead has run cold,' he said straight up.

'Really? What's the story? Oh, I've got Ryan with me, our cadet, so okay if I put you on speaker phone?'

'Fine, hi Ryan, this is not for publication?' he checked.

'Not for publication,' I agreed.

'Well, we checked out all Matts – both local and visiting – and we found a few, but all had solid alibis or were not relevant suspects. We also checked out the Matt that turned out to be a Mattina – girls commit crimes too, you know?'

'We probably do it better,' I said, and he laughed.

Nick continued: 'She's a mother of three and was home all night. Several witnesses confirmed her story. The senior Matt in his sixties was at a conference in Melbourne for a week and that's checked out; gay Matt is definitely gay and his alibi for the night holds up. We discovered a younger Matt, in his early twenties, an article clerk, but he has a watertight alibi – he was in the hospital having surgery, your husband might have performed it!'

'Except he was heading to Sydney airport that night.'

'Right,' Nick agreed and continued: 'Finally, the Matt that appeared to be the most likely contender – the one in his late thirties – is in the clear too.'

I groaned with frustration. 'What's his story?' The suspense was killing me and I knew Nick was dragging it out.

'It appears he was seconded interstate to work on a large case. He's been there for months and was definitely at a dinner event that night in a different State.'

'Crap,' I mumbled.

'Yeah, I said something similar,' he joked.

'But now we're no further ahead than before,' I reminded him. 'So you've ruled out everyone at the hostel?'

'I wouldn't say that. Everyone is a person of interest until they're not. It's just a bummer because the new boyfriend was our best lead. Now we have to work on the basis that his name might not have been Matt and he may not have been a lawyer and of course, he might be transient too. Anyway,' he sighed, 'I have got something.'

'Yeah?' I froze. Ryan leaned forward slightly in anticipation; his eyes lit with excitement.

'Yeah, I'm giving you the scoop okay, as promised.'

'Great, thanks, what is it?' I pushed him impatiently.

'A few witnesses saw Soleil get into a dark blue car that Saturday night. The car could have been black – I think there's a colour called midnight blue – and it was possibly a convertible or a sports car.'

'This is big, Nick, thanks. Any chance you want to call in every blue car in town and check them?' I teased.

'No. I think we'd have a hard time getting that by the civil libertarians but if people want to volunteer to register their cars and have them checked and movements logged, that'd be welcome. Stick that in your story, I'll send you the name of the car witnesses to follow up.'

'Brilliant, thanks. My husband has a black convertible, thank God he's got an alibi. It's about the only good thing his ex-sister-in-law's visit has going for it,' I joked and Nick chuckled.

'Stay in touch, yeah?' he said.

'Yeah thanks, Nick, I appreciate the call,' I said and hung up.

'Fantastic,' Ryan said with a grin. 'It's sad but kind of exciting to be breaking it.'

'You said it,' I agreed. 'I'm going to hunt down the witnesses. Can you move onto businesses that have CCTV footage in the area? I know Nick covered that, but we need quotes from the business owners for a story.'

We'll find you, Soleil, I promise.

Chapter 17

THEN...

Adam

Sky was doing her best to pretend as if nothing had ever happened – like her sister hadn't died and that Jessica wasn't my wife, and that she was still in with a chance. Even with her sister buried, she was still competing. Jessica's bristling the whole time we're with Sky – she's like a cat with her back arched and her fur on end.

I think Sky was having a hard time with it. She was always in Chelsey's shadow and now with her big sister gone, she's in Saint Chelsey's shadow. Instead of being the focus of her parents' life as the only living daughter, she said they were living in a shrine to Chelsey and it was as if Sky didn't exist. Business as usual then.

If I'm being upfront, then I had to admit that Sky's visit brought back memories I didn't care to relive. I remember the day Chelsey died like it was yesterday; I've played it over in my mind, again and again. Sometimes I hear her scream in my sleep and I reach for her but she passes me, falling down the mountainside, her eyes holding my gaze until she falls completely out of sight. She's still falling… I never find her, never hear her hit the bottom.

But that's not how it happened. She was below me, not quite close enough for me to reach – in true "Chelsey form" she always had to be ahead; always had to lead and to be the life of the party. She was showing off, smiling, waving for a photo. It was a beautiful day; you could see forever. We weren't the only abseilers on the rock; there was a tour group going down not far from us. It was Chelsey who wanted to abseil. She was experienced, I was more of a novice but her friends were experienced too. All of them strapped, confident, happy to be the privileged in-group. I fitted in so well – educated, 'pretty' like them, but most of all, married to Chelsey. Anyone Chelsey deigned to be suitable was 'in' and I was the chosen one.

That day I was so busy concentrating on where my hands and feet were going so that I didn't bloody topple, that I didn't have time to give Chelsey the usual adoration she demanded. Normally I'd be expected to notice how hot she looked in her abseiling outfit. I'd be watching the guys watching her, checking out her butt, hardening under the gaze of her teasing smiles. I'd be planning where and how I'd fuck her when we got home if I waited until then.

That day, her death day, I gripped onto the rocks, just above her. She called some encouragement to me and I flashed her a smile before hurriedly returning to refocusing on the rocks under hand and foot. She even took a selfie with her phone, meanwhile, I'm gripping on for life. Then she called out to one of our party below and that's when I heard it; the scream. I gripped tighter; there was never a chance to reach for her or save her; I wasn't that skilled in abseiling, I didn't know how to react or what to do. She was falling like it was in slow motion; the anguished scream, her blonde ponytail flashing in the sun, her hands clawing and scraping as she grabbed the surface on the way down. People were screaming. Maybe it was me, it was so fast and I had so much white noise – panic, words going through my head.

Someone was trying to pull me back up to the top, further away from her. I was yelling for them to lower me. I tore down the rock's surface in enormous leaps, my fear on the back shelf as I stared down at the ground where she had fallen. The pain didn't even register from the number of times I hit against the rocks or missed my footing and scraped skin. If I fell I can't remember, I just tore down. Below more screams, wails, nearer to the ground, someone was on the phone calling for help. My gaze followed the path of the wall where she fell, and then I saw her.

When I touched the ground, her friends at the base tried to stop me from running over, but that wasn't happening and with a shove, I ran to her, falling beside her. One of them told me later that my eyes were huge as if I was looking around for some sort of explanation. More of her friends were coming down in the cable car; others were racing down the gorge route. People on the ground were looking at me, shocked, waiting for me to do something, to react. I could hear the wail of an ambulance. I've never been so blind to what was going on around me; all I could do was hold her as she lay bleeding, smashed.

Everyone moved around me and when the ambulance arrived, her friends pulled me up and away. Propped up between a couple of them, just staring… I don't know for how long or if it was quick or slow, and then it rushed at me, full charge – all the feelings, everything that was going on around me, the strain of everyone's attention focused on my reaction. My legs just went from underneath me, but I didn't fall to the ground; whoever was holding my arms lowered me down, putting my head between my knees.

I can't remember who was beside me or what they were saying; all I could think of was that Chelsey had fallen; Chelsey was dead; and she was gone, gone forever. No one could survive that fall; she was gone from me – that bright light had been extinguished.

It was the happiest fucking day of my life.

Chapter 18

NOW...

Coen

As I sat on the couch with my stir-fry that evening, I had to concede that there was certainly enough weight in Lacey's hypothesis about her ex-boyfriend, Andy, to give it some attention. I'd started going through Nick's police procedural files but had found nothing outrageously interesting yet and I don't recall seeing anything about this guy, Andy. I'd get back to them later.

The footy was on, I flicked through the television channels until it appeared on the screen. As I ate, my mind wandered to my students and my tutorial earlier this morning. They were a good bunch and they sidetracked me once we finished with the formal lesson plan. They wanted to know why I had chosen Soleil's story. Most of them remembered Soleil's disappearance like it was a Grimm's Fairy Tale – they were three or four years of age when she went missing and their parents took the opportunity to reinforce stranger danger warnings – witches in gingerbread houses, missing children, big bad wolves and strangers. Several of them had spoken to their parents about it since they read or heard about the gossip column piece on me and their folks shared their memories. My students had a morbid fascination with true crime, who doesn't?

With the television on in the background, Soleil's diary beckoned and I read on from where I last left it, skim reading through the passages that outlined her vision for the world – we all had those ideals when we were younger. She was an interesting young woman, more mature than her years. I stopped – at last, a piece about the guy she allegedly liked, the one she might stay in town longer to be with:

I decided I would share with Jessica and maybe Astrid because we were becoming close, that I had met someone, but I am not sharing this with anyone else… I want to keep it close to my chest. We met a few weeks ago when he offered me a lift. His name – Matt, he was a lawyer and very wealthy, I think. He drove an expensive car and he told me he was house-sitting for friends – a property on the beach that he said he'd like to show me. He said he will have to move out when his friend, Jeff and Jeff's wife, come back from their six-month working holiday-honeymoon, but then he would buy a house of his own and added with a smile that he would like to buy it with someone special. My heart raced with excitement because we have a connection, early days but sometimes you just know.

Since the first time, he has given me three more lifts, each time on his way home from seeing a client. I love that client! I get a lot more rides than the boys get – it annoys them, but they cannot be angry at something they would do themselves if they were the driver. Few women pick me up, though. I guess I could wait for the bus, but sometimes the wait was as long as fifty minutes. If you cannot get away on the hour,

I could walk 'home' by then. With a ride, I am back at the Y in about fifteen minutes. But the worst days were when you do not even see a car, let alone get a lift. After picking fruit all day, you walk all the way back to the hostel and arrive feeling like you may never move again.

Sure, there's danger in hitchhiking. Maybe my potential new love was a dangerous man; you heard about it all the time. Every country had them. A German girl, Claudia, told of a hitchhiker killer from her country who was not caught until two decades after his crime. He raped and murdered five women and girls and was found after he gave a voluntary DNA test when he was caught stealing scrap metal. Did that conversation stop us from hitching? No, the luck of the draw I guess, and it was still the quickest and cheapest way to get around, but it made us jumpy for a while. When your number was up, your number was up, as the saying goes, but Strand Harbour seemed like a safe little town. Everyone was hitching and had been doing it here for a long time.

The few times Matt offered me a lift, I was dirty and sweaty after a day at work. I really want to show him I can look sophisticated, especially for a potential partner for a lawyer. I need to arrive for a date in a beautiful dress with my hair up. I let myself get carried away; the mindless act of fruit picking lends itself to thinking. Hopefully next time he picks me up he officially asks me on a date. My potential new romance was still a secret... if it kept going as well, I will put off going up north.

*****

Closing the pages of Soleil's diary, I took it all in. She had fallen for this guy, enough to derail her travel plans, but when you were backpacking, that's probably not a big deal.

I couldn't help myself, I flicked through to her very last entry – my heart rate quickened, I sat up, alert. Soleil had written:

Matt, he had so much potential. I thought I could love him but he made a mistake.

Chapter 19

THEN...

Adam

We lost two patients today; one older man from a heart attack, and a young woman in a car crash. Telling her husband she was gone –all the grief and shock on his face seemed so familiar – the worst part of my job... made me relive so many memories. I knew what he was in for now. In the months after Chelsey's death, the things I missed most weren't the milestones or even her for that matter, but the little things you miss after relationships end – having that someone to come home to and have a drink with and talk about nothing or everything; waking up in a shared bed; the messaging randomly during the day. Knowing you had someone who gave a damn.

Speaking of opening wounds, I wish Sky would bloody leave. Won't I ever be free of Chelsey? Suddenly Jessica was obsessed with Chelsey just because Sky was visiting. Enough with the questions! Does she think Chelsey's coming back from the dead? Why were women always insecure, where has this come from? Jessica wasn't an overly confident person, that was part of her charm, but surely me having a dead ex would make her realise she's the only one now! It's not like I talk about Chelsey or Sky… ever. There were no photos of us around, and we don't even know anyone here who knew me in that life. It's filed away, the good and the bad, now if only Jessica would file it too.

Add to that, posters reading MISSING spoiled my drive home from work. Yep, *poster girl* spoiled the mood. Around the first bend, it was there… creepy. *Soleil 'Sunny' Reyer, 22, last seen September 10*. Her face grinned at me. How do they even know she's missing? I mean, what were a few days in the life of a backpacker? Sure, she left a few measly possessions at the hostel, but she could be lying low with a guy she met, or partied a bit too hard and was still recovering at someone's place. Were they considering that maybe she got a ride and took off? Maybe she got the wrong ride, it happened. Maybe a dinner date didn't go that well.

It's all over the media now and Jessica's focused on it too. What will be the next big story that knocks missing Soleil off the front page? Wish it would hurry up, the sooner the better.

NOW…

Coen

Reading the police files and Soleil's diary at night was not good for my dreams; they'd become full of murder and misadventure. Still, something may shake its way to the front of my consciousness during the sleeping hours. So far, that hadn't happened.

It was a lecture day, so I rose early, went for a jog, presented nice and early for my class and wrapped that up by midday. My group were good kids; what they lacked in talent they made up for in enthusiasm, which can be just as useful in the age of influencers. After class, I went to Sandy's pub for lunch; since cooking wasn't on my pastime list, it's best to have my main meal of the day at Sandy's, and you never know who might join me and spill all they know. You'd be surprised how much it happens.

Sandy greeted me like a long-lost friend, which for a new kid in town made me feel very connected... it's the little things. A glance at the lunchtime menu and thank you very much – a latte and a shepherd's pie. I haven't had one since I was a kid – the mince was best rich and dark, and the potato crispy like Nan used to make.

Sure enough, I was only there ten minutes sipping on my latte when a middle-aged man approached. He introduced himself as Luke Bridgeman, a nurse who worked at the hospital during the time Soleil disappeared and apologised for interrupting me.

'Please interrupt me,' I insisted. He was tall and thin, wavy brown receding hair and brown eyes that a writer would describe as kind – must be from years of nursing.

'You're the author, aren't you? I heard you were writing the missing backpacker story,' he said, as I indicated a seat and invited him to take a seat. He sank into it.

Sandy came over. 'Do you want your burger served here, Luke?'

He glanced at me and started to retreat. I said: 'I hate to eat alone.'

He smiled and thanked Sandy. We made some small talk about what brought me to town – a spiel I rattled off that didn't include breaking up with an ex and having writer's block – and I asked him what he was doing these days. Then straight to work for me – I asked him if he had met Soleil or the journalist Jessica or her husband, Dr Steyne. He said yes to all three. Bingo!

'It was freaky at first,' he said. 'You know nothing like that happened here. We had crime, but it was the usual stuff – drugs, muggings, accidents, theft… I couldn't believe it. I gave her a lift once but never saw her again. I picked up a few of the young guys who were fruit picking and dropped them back at the Y too. You know after you see them a few times then they're not transient, you know that they're here for the season and work.'

I nodded. 'What was she like?'

'Charming, beautiful, well-mannered,' he said and thanked Sandy when a large glass of coke arrived.

'Your meals are on the way, gents,' she said and moved on.

Luke drank a mouthful of coke and continued. 'I didn't know until I was driving home and saw the MISSING poster. I'd been on the night shift the days prior, so I would finish up in the morning and go home to bed. It had been a few days since I'd seen the news.'

Our lunch arrived and the Shepherd's Pie looked spectacular. Sandy laughed when she saw my pleased expression.

'If you're not married, Sandy, I might have to take you away from this place,' I told her. She laughed again.

'I bet you say that to all the ladies who cook for you,' she winked and walked off.

'That looks bloody great too,' I said to Luke, admiring his burger.

'Best food in town,' he agreed, 'authentic food, good prices.'

We ate for a bit and talked in between bites.

'Anyone come to town looking for her? Family, friends, an ex-boyfriend?' I asked Luke.

He shook his head. 'I don't think she had anyone. Her friends ran a campaign on social media.'

'So the journalist on the case was Jessica Steyne, and you worked with her husband?' I kept him on track slowly getting to the key questions I wanted to ask. 'Did you know him?'

He leant forward slightly to talk with me as noise increased in the hotel, and I suspect he heard plenty of secrets on his rounds.

'I liked him. Can't say everyone did, but we were both golfers so we had something to talk about,' he thought for a moment before continuing. 'He could be very charming when he wanted to be especially with patients, but he had an aloofness about him.' Luke shrugged, 'Most of the doctors did… I guess it was a time when we held doctors, politicians, church leaders in high esteem, given their positions of power. That's changed over the last fifteen years.'

'Sure has,' I agreed. 'Did you ever hear any rumours about him having an affair or anything of that nature?' Worth a prod, I thought.

'No, can't say I did, but it wouldn't have surprised me. He could have easily if he wanted to… there was plenty of bed-hopping going on when we were all younger and the ladies liked him – he was a really good-looking guy, you know, a face like you'd see in an aftershave commercial.'

I smiled. 'Yeah, got it in one,' I said, knowing what Adam Steyne looked like, and that nailed it.

'We were all surprised when his wife left him... the journalist.'

'Jessica left him?' I asked, surprised as well.

'Yes, that was the rumour that she was the one who called it off. Cleared out and then within a month, he'd transferred and got out of here.'

That was new to me. 'No idea why?'

He shook his head. 'I only saw them together a few times at the work functions where you had to put in an appearance. He was always attentive to her, almost possessive.'

I stored the information away and then he moved into the usual territory.

'Got to say, when Eloise started dating the serial killer, I knew her days were numbered,' he said, and looked rueful.

Yep, everyone's got an opinion on my 'Reiker' series... good on them!

'You and me and every other male, Luke,' I agreed, 'but the ladies, they thought she'd save him.'

We both had a chuckle.

'Love the ladies – they always see the best in us,' he said with a sigh.

Then it occurred to me, was that Soleil's downfall?

Chapter 20

THEN...

Jessica

There's no need to be neurotic, but it's been a losing battle since Skylar's visit. Since being told I'm not Adam's type, I am obsessed with finding out more about Chelsey, but Adam was a closed book on the subject. The last person I intended to ask was Skylar, because I'll get the full gloss version with bonus steak knives thrown in designed to go through my heart.

I found myself looking at him differently. How could we be married and he not think to mention a deceased wife? What else has he not mentioned? But removing myself from the emotion of it all, I figured that maybe that's why he didn't bring it up. People reacted to grief in different ways and maybe his solution was to never talk about it, to bury it away. I'm familiar with it from my work when interviewing victims or their families, you get some strange reactions. Some get angry, others were really helpful and enthusiastic, which was weird too, while I've known some who get addicted to the attention and never stop grieving.

Some completely shut down the topic – it's private, for their memories only.

I had stored the research pages that Clare gave me in my bottom drawer at work, I didn't want to risk Adam finding them at home. But now I had some spare time – I was on the paper late shift and we'd gone to press. Time to do some research of my own before I knocked off.

A mug of tea made and back at my desk, there was a whole sixty minutes up my sleeve before knock-off time. I searched for them – Adam and Chelsey Steyne – it pained me to type that. I was hoping to find more than Clare found – maybe a photo, an old image on a Facebook page or a social photo of the two of them, something, anything. But there was nothing. That was weird. Re-think that... maybe it wasn't weird. I've tried to look up ex-boyfriends before and found nothing on them. No, it was weird. Given how she died there would have been some media coverage.

Equally strange was how little there was on Adam except for recent posts about his appointment to the Strand Harbour hospital and his name in a few research articles. This was definitely weird; there was seriously nothing about him online. Was I expecting too much? Surely not. If Chelsey was killed in a fall, then there should have been heaps of accessible stories, including friends' posts and tributes. Especially when she was in public relations as Clare discovered – she must have been well known around town. But when I searched, I found nothing. Zilch. Just as odd, Adam's name didn't come up in any searches even when I changed the search engine to Google.co.za for South Africa.

Then it occurred to me, maybe when Adam was starting again over here, he used a reputation management firm –

one of those companies that you pay to bury your history online. I did a story once at my last newspaper about a company that did online reputation management. Same thing. They can't erase it, but they can bury it deep enough to be out of the reach of search engines. Maybe he wanted a new start – he didn't want his new employer to know about his history. He didn't want the tragedy of his life to be public fodder. It's not cheap to do – bury your life, but hey, if you're a surgeon on a large salary and probably just scored your deceased wife's life insurance payout, what's five thousand dollars or so?

Or slow down... perhaps she didn't take his name when they married. Sigh, talk about missing the obvious – but that didn't explain why there was so little about Adam online. Clare told me her maiden name and I grabbed the notes searching for it... Kotze. I felt tense typing her name in, like a car accident that I didn't want to look at but couldn't look away from. Several stories came up under that name and I sorted them by illustrated, which showed those articles with photos. For the next fifteen minutes, I clicked and opened articles, but nothing on the Public Relations' Chelsey Kotze, nothing that was the right age and look. There were plenty of other Kotzes. What the hell?

Hmm. Stand, stretch and a short wander around will help and it did – a brainwave! There was a way around this; the online newspaper archives. Trove did a brilliant job of keeping records in Australia, so there must be a similar vehicle overseas. If Adam paid to bury his information online, he couldn't bury newspaper archives. I only wanted to go back about ten years and settling in, sure enough, the records were there – the library was called *Access*. Damn, it required a sign-in, so I used one of the research aliases assigned to me for work and requested a free trial. It didn't take long for the email confirmation to come through, and I was off and running.

First the Cape Town newspapers – I keyed in 'Chelsey Kotze fall to death'. Oh my God! My gasp was loud enough, lucky I wasn't at the library – a list of articles came up. I opened the first one, and there she was. Oh wow. I drew a deep breath, it was a wedding day photo of them in their local newspaper – Adam looking young and beautiful in a tuxedo, Chelsey looked stunning, there was no other word to describe it. So alive, so beautiful – they were the perfect pair. Is that why he picked me? He fell so quickly for me. Was it because I was so unlike her I would never remind him of her?

I couldn't take my eyes off her; the way her arms were wrapped around Adam's neck, and his around her perfect hourglass figure. A Hollywood smile, impossibly long lashes and dead four years after this wedding day photo was taken. I moved to the story.

The Guardian

Woman dies after a tragic fall
Reporter: Suzanne Petersen

A woman has fallen to her death while abseiling with friends at Table Mountain. Chelsey Kotze, 31, was pronounced dead at the scene after suffering fatal injuries; she had abseiled at the location on several previous occasions.

Police officers, who were called shortly before 11.30am yesterday, described her death as a 'tragic accident'.

'Ms Kotze was abseiling with her group and not with a

tour operator. She was a regular participant in the sport,' a police spokesperson said. 'It appears she was halfway down her descent in the popular climbing area when the accident occurred.'

Police said Ms Kotze ran into difficulties when her mainline became tangled. She called for help but fell before help could reach her.

A member of the party who wishes to remain anonymous said Ms Kotze's husband and several of the group had to be treated for shock.

She said: 'It was horrible. We had all been laughing and talking only thirty minutes before. Chelsey and Adam have only been married four years and were living in their dream home which they had designed.'

An ambulance attendant at the scene said they could not save her.

*****

Now I had this, I couldn't stop looking for stories about her in the newspaper catalogue. These shots would have been online and on social media… they had to have been removed if now the only trace of them that remains was in the newspaper archives where they were impossible to erase. I kept searching through hundreds of references: tributes from colleagues, beautiful shots of Chesley through all the major stages of her life and the inevitable funeral shots with Adam, head bowed, at the front of her casket. He looked so beautiful, drawn and alone. My hand was rubbing my heart without me realising it. It was a horrendous way to die; she must have been terrified in her last moments of life. And Adam left behind – I couldn't bear to lose him even after our brief life together.

I was like a junkie; with a deep breath I kept searching, needing to get my fill, so I could put her to rest. Then, maybe I would have a better picture of what was going on in Adam's head when he was quiet and moody. More press clippings, this time one with a full-length photo of the two of them taken at a social event; such a beautiful couple and they looked so suited, so happy. I don't know what he saw in me after Chelsey. I read the story.

The Guardian

Husband pays tribute to tragic cliff victim
By Rod Karnell

South African doctor Adam Steyne spoke to the media after the funeral of his wife of four years, Chelsey Kotze, paying tribute to her spirit and beauty.

Kotze, 31, a Public Relations practitioner, fell to her death last Sunday while abseiling with a party of friends at Table Mountain. Her husband witnessed her fall.

Kotze was well known in public relations and charity circles for her work in promoting good causes and local brands. The pair was regularly seen at social outings and Kotze's Public Relations company, *The Word*, hosted many launches and events for clients.

Mr Steyne said he would carry the loss of his wife until his dying days.

'We had four years together and the rest of our lives planned,' he said. 'I am consumed with pain and sorrow and even though I work with dying patients every day, nothing can prepare you for a loss like this.

'Everyone who knew Chelsey knew she was a beautiful

soul, so full of life. I wish to thank our families, friends, her colleagues and mine for their support at this time of unspeakable sorrow.'

*****

I swallowed a lump in my throat and looked at the photo of the two of them together. Then, I vowed to make Adam the most loved man in the world and the happiest he could be. I scrolled down through the other newspaper references and things began to change. The clippings were taking a decidedly different turn – nasty even. I opened one.

The Guardian

Climber's death may be suspicious
By Mark Ryden

Police are investigating the equipment and the scene of the accident where a young woman's body was found after an abseiling fall on 15 June.

The body of Chelsey Kotze, a 31-year-old Cape Town Public Relations executive, was found at the bottom of Table Mountain after falling during a group abseiling outing.

Authorities initially stated her death appeared consistent with an accidental fall from the cliffs. Police have declined to say what specific evidence resulted in Kotze's death now being considered suspicious.

Her husband, Doctor Adam Steyne, has refused to comment but has released a statement through his lawyers.

'Any suggestion of foul play or suicide is unfounded. Chelsey was a dynamic, confident woman and loved by all.

The distress this speculation is causing to myself, her family and friends is unnecessary and we request understanding to grieve for Chelsey privately.'

A private memorial service was held 22 June at Saint Patrick's Church on Statton Drive.

*****

And on they went: *Was Chelsey's equipment faulty? Who had a grudge against Chelsey? Husband takes time off to deal with rumours; Beauty and some beast; When equipment kills*; and more. I scrolled to more recent dates and found fewer and fewer articles. Time had moved on; they had buried Chelsey. The last article read: *Death of climber ruled accidental.*

No wonder Adam had moved to the other side of the world. I cleared the history searches from my computer.

Chelsey, Chelsey, Chelsey, he's mine now, please don't keep a hold on him.

Chapter 21

THEN…

Jessica

Where the hell were you, Sunny?

I don't know about this guy… this new boyfriend theory; I still think she got the wrong ride. She's beautiful and putting herself in that dangerous situation walking along the road daily as she finished her fruit picking shift. Mark my words, she's already underground, like those poor backpackers who accepted a lift from the Co-ed Killer in the United States or Ivan Milat here in Australia who was convicted of murdering backpackers and burying them in the Belanglo State Forest or… there have been others that Sunny told me about. I bet beautiful, glowing Sunny was under the earth. My arms broke out in goosebumps and I instinctively rubbed them.My mind kept going over and over every encounter with Soleil. Trawling over our talks, trying to find some grain that might help find her. After I picked her up the first time, it was easier to stop each time – it's hardly picking up a hitchhiker when you know them. On most days, Sunny wore long shorts – probably not ideal for fruit picking, but she might have run out of clothes or wanted some sun on her long and already tanned legs. She always looked relieved it was me and I remember one Monday when I pulled over and her smile lit up her face to see me. She was exhausted.

'How is the stone fruit today?' I asked as she slid into the front seat of my Peugeot – my husband liked European cars.

'They are well and send their regards,' she said, with a grin.

I laughed and was going to make small talk but we were both Monday tired, so we sat like family, in comfortable silence. She was intuitive like that. Soleil closed her eyes and rested. I glanced at her and thought about my year overseas doing the backpacker thing, staying in hostels, flat broke and free. Those were the days. It reminded me of the time I was sitting on a beachside bench in Brighton, England, eating baked beans from a tin and an elderly couple that walked past felt sorry for me.

'Poor little thing,' the woman said, thinking I was homeless. Happiest days of my life.

After that, seeing Sunny became a bit of a habit. On my early starts, our finish times would coincide and each time we'd learn a little more about each other.

'So,' she mused on another day that I picked her up, 'a journalist married to an Accident and Emergency doctor, must be some interesting discussions in your house.'

'Yes. Adam says inevitably we both deal in suffering. I'm less inclined to agree with that, it's a little melodramatic. We both have plenty of good news stories too.'

'I hope so,' she said. 'And you are both here, in Strand Harbour? You don't want to work in the city?'

I shrugged; she had hit a sore spot.

'I was working in the city but the paper I was writing for went under – I got a job here,' I told her. 'Adam grew up near the ocean; he likes this lifestyle. I have two different shifts, and he's on-call so we get a bit of variety in our day. Here, he's not always putting people back together or cutting things out, sometimes nothing much happens on his entire shift and I think he likes that.'

'I cut out carbs once, but I really missed them,' she teased, and I laughed again.

Soleil was fun and interesting and the type of person I'd want to spend time with if we were both sticking around.

I had a terrible feeling that Soleil was staying here longer than me.

NOW...

Coen

Time for more of Soleil's diary. Once home in the early afternoon, I went back to finish the extracts that I had skipped to get to the punchline, and a dramatic one it was at that. If I could get a few chapters under my belt and absorb it all, then the reward would be a beach walk – then, maybe something more would come to me while breathing in that fresh salt air. I opened the translated pages of her diary on the page I'd marked.

Friday. I really needed a lift home today; I heard the car, put my thumb out and turned to see if I knew the driver – Jessica, thank goodness. She was smiling at me before she had even pulled to a complete stop. She said it was good to see me, I felt the same and I slipped into her front seat. She was 'Miss

Corporate' again, dressed smartly in a beautifully tailored red dress with high heel shoes and her hair in a high ponytail, she looked great.

She pulled the car back out onto the road and I enjoyed the sensation of the road moving quickly beneath me… more quickly than I could have walked it. Jessica smiled at me and told me she never knew when it might be the last time we rode together.

*****

I stopped to take that in. How very true, but surely Jessica just meant because she was expecting Soleil would head off soon. Still, worth noting – women, the 'fairer sex' as we once called them, have murdered too. There had been some mighty fine ones in history. A quick stop to write the reference and page number before reading on:

It is late now but it has been an emotional day so I wanted to write in the hope that putting down my words will help me sleep. My proposed leaving date has come and gone. Today I gave Jessica a quick update on my love life and even though Julian and Chris are ready to go, I don't want to throw away my chance at love just yet. Is it too early to talk about staying? Jessica agreed it is best I didn't decide under pressure, but it would be awful to leave prematurely and always be wondering. She got it.

I asked her when she knew Adam was the one and she said immediately, the moment he looked at her, and then she looked embarrassed and shrugged. We laughed and I called her a romantic. The hostel came into sight, and Jessica told me she had a hen's party on Saturday night. As for me, no plans. No invitation from my love yet and now that Jessica has picked me up on the way home Friday afternoon, I am not likely to get one. I wished her a good weekend, alighted, and closed the car door. She drove off and even though I was grateful for the lift, I wish it was Matt picking me up. What is he doing tonight and every Friday night for the rest of his life? He hasn't even asked for my phone number.

When I entered the hostel, half a dozen of the fruit pickers were back and some new guests had arrived. I showered, and by the time I got out, we decided to walk into town to the hotel for happy hour, and to welcome the new guests and hear their stories. Good to be busy when you are anxious of heart. At the hotel, I ordered a white wine. From my snooping, I'd found two law firms listed in town; if I had a car, I could go for a drive and maybe drop in and surprise him if I found the right firm. What if he wasn't happy to see me? My ear is only half in the surrounding conversations; I hate feeling like this.

After another couple of wines, I was harder on myself. My mind told me I was kidding myself; it was just sex. Easy sex for him; he picked me up and I 'delivered' in the back seat of his car, that's why he never asked for my number. I am my mother's daughter. It will be a weekend now without seeing him, a whole weekend. Who will he be romancing this weekend since he has no way of contacting me or asking me out? Friday night... Saturday night... Sunday night... without seeing him.

I bet a single man wouldn't do that.

*****

Hmm, a lot of nuances here. Reading Soleil's diary sucked you in. She obviously wrote this after a few drinks, it was more emotional than most of her entries. The angst was coming off the page; I could also remember those early days of dating when you tried to work out when to call, how soon to call, how they felt about you… ah, young love. Did she leave the group and venture into town to the law firms before heading back to the hostel? Is that what happened to her that Friday night? No, she didn't go missing until the next night, so if she met up with Matt, he didn't bump her off that night.

While Soleil's diary had its moments, the police files would put you into a coma, or maybe I shouldn't look at them after a big meal. I shuffled through the pages and found the report on Dr Adam Steyne and his wife Jessica. Reading her alibi, the report said that she had been at a hen's party on the night Soleil went missing but returned home to find her husband tucked up asleep in bed. She had plenty of witnesses and friends that were with her at the hen's party – she didn't have time to run off, pick up Soleil and knock her off, if Soleil had been knocked off. Although, Jessica might have seen Soleil on the way home from the party… it's not like we've got an exact time of disappearance. I'd bloody kill for some CCTV footage. I flipped the page to her husband's alibi – a trip to the airport that night – who was he picking up? Jessica also vouched for him later that night.

As for this Matt guy, Soleil's new love, I kept drawing a blank. Was he a local, a person passing through or did he exist at all? Was her diary for real or if she thought someone might read it, was she creating a false boyfriend for safety reasons? Just a wild thought but was Julian reading her diary? I know Detective Nick had written him off, but I was keeping all my options open. However, that theory might be impossible to prove.

Chapter 22

THEN...

Jessica

Deathly quiet. That's the first thing I noticed as I walked along the road that the fruit pickers staying at the Y walked along every afternoon when their fruit-picking shift finished. But then the sound of the bush started up... it must have paused for me before deciding that I was no threat. Birds and cicadas in a random chorus. Way ahead in the distance were two guys walking; I didn't want them to wait for me so every time one of them turned back to see if a vehicle was coming, I would move closer to the tree line and stop moving.

Right now, I was Soleil – feeling her journey, getting under her skin. What she must have felt like when she was walking back each day from work and waiting for that ride, including, maybe, the ride that would change her life... the ride with Matt, the guy she liked enough to stay in Strand Harbour for while it played out. I parked my car off-road back near some roadwork signs and orange cones. If anyone saw it, they were not likely to check it out... it looked deliberately left. I couldn't see it now, which was disconcerting.

Imagine hitching now... God, Adam would kill me, but I was tempted to have a go. It was eerie walking this road alone. The trees and bush were thick and dense beside me, they could swallow me into them and no one would notice. The traffic was minimal... too late for the school traffic, too early for the few after-workers who came this way – I had knocked off just after four. The cicadas were now in full flight – a constant soundtrack. I heard a snapping sound and wheeled around.

Nothing.

Nothing I could see anyway.

How did Soleil do this? She was on this road about this time, five days a week.

After walking about half a kilometre, it was enough. I'd got the vibe; so important for writing and understanding the victim. I turned to return to my car. The guys were completely out of sight now, and no one was behind me. A car was coming and fast, so I moved behind a tree, pushing my way into the dense scrub. A red Ute went past, spraying up stones and dust from the side of the road at me; I ducked back further behind the tree and waited until it was well out of sight. I didn't want a driver pulling up. There was no noise now, just the sound of the car fading away, and then the cicadas worked their way back to full pitch.

Creepy, I couldn't do this every day. I'd want to walk back to the Y in the safety of a group. I quickened my pace and glanced to the left and right of me. Nothing to see but scrub, but I felt like I was being watched – stupid, I know. My car came into sight, silly how the relief swept through me. Then I heard it again. A loud snap and the cicadas stopped completely. I looked around, an animal surely. I ran in my work gear, my heels, the heat biting me and unlocked my car with my remote as I neared it. Evil chased me but I didn't turn back to see its face. I just kept running, pulled open the car door, jumped in and locked the door.

I sat breathing fast and looking around. I glanced into the back seat. Clear. Of course it was, I'm an idiot... there's nothing out there. Including me now.

NOW...

Coen

It's begun... my writing of Soleil's story. I'm a long way from finishing the research phase, haven't even scratched the surface yet, but I had to write to find out what's missing, what I needed to know. I knew enough about Soleil to paint a picture of her, and I knew enough about the disappearance to write that up. So it begins – the first few chapters drafted that set the scene for the town, the culture, the hostel tourists and Soleil herself.

What I didn't have was pretty much everything that happened after that night – the night Soleil went missing. Well, technically, that's not quite true. I have the police reports and press clippings, but let's face it, if they knew anything then I wouldn't be writing this story. I'd be trying to come up with something else to please Natalie and keep her off my case.

There was also the chance, of course, that Soleil just left town. She wanted to move on, was jacked off with being 'dumped' for the weekend by her new love, and didn't want to tell the other two guys because she'd changed her mind about going to Cairns. There was an online news clipping that supported that theory. It had been printed with the comments below it. I fished around for it, found it and read it again:

The Strand Times online

Possible sighting of missing backpacker in Yamba
By Jessica Steyne, crime reporter

Police are investigating CCTV footage after a witness claimed to have seen missing French backpacker, Soleil Reyer, on Wednesday at the coastal town of Yamba, 140 kilometres north of her last known destination, Strand Harbour.

Police received a tip claiming a woman resembling Ms Reyer was working her way up the coast to her next destination, Cairns, and may be oblivious to the ongoing search.

Detective Nick Clarkson of the Strand Harbour Police said footage is being retrieved from several sites in the area and will be analysed.

'We have spoken with the Yamba hostel who has no guest matching Ms Reyer's description. Yamba police have also circulated Ms Reyer's image in case she is travelling with a friend,' he said.

The Strand Times has contacted local bus and rail providers, but no identification of Ms Reyer has been made.

Ms Reyer was a regular hitchhiker from the Dawson Estate where she had been employed as a casual fruit picker. She was last seen leaving the Rest-up Backpackers' Hostel on Saturday 10 September around 6.30pm to meet a friend. Her handbag and phone were not among the personal effects left at the hostel.

Ms Reyer's friends have been active on social media keeping the search alive, but many suspect foul play; she was a regular hitchhiker to and from the farm where she worked. To date, no footage retrieved from public areas in Strand Harbour at the time of Ms Reyer's disappearance has revealed any useful information. The investigation continues and anyone with information is asked to call Crime Stoppers or their local police station.

Share: Facebook | Twitter | Email | In | g+ |

*****

Under the article, there was a smattering of comments that readers had made:

Soleil kept us updated at least once a week on her Facebook page. The last entry was just before she disappeared. If it was Soleil in Yamba, surely she would have seen this on Facebook and known that we were looking for her, even if she hadn't heard any media reports. This sighting is a hoax. Anja

These sightings are great if they are genuine and not time-wasters from people looking to increase their online followers! Andrew

If Soleil has been spotted, then she might be held against her wishes. Otherwise, why wouldn't she have answered her phone or checked her emails and messages? Was she spotted alone? Ali

I live in Yamba and me and my friends have printed Soleil's poster and put it up around the town. If Soleil is here, she couldn't miss it. So good luck, I hope you hear from her. Jaimee

*****

Back to Soleil's last diary entry, again, so I could read her last sentence:

My potential new love, the lawyer who I have fallen for, made a mistake.

She wrote that before she disappeared, so what had she found out about her new love, and had she seen him that night? Was it enough to make her want to pack up and leave town, telling no one? Did she leave with him, this Matt guy? Or maybe he was violent and tried to hit her and she escaped him? Maybe she discovered he had a few lovers and she was one of the harem. Or did he go psycho on her and freak her out – were there any other missing person cases for females or males in the area around that time? I added to my list of things to pursue.

Or did she confront her lover about his mistake and was it big enough that he had to silence her? She's got her handbag with her, well it's missing so it could be with her, but she hasn't used any of her cards. And why would she want to disappear completely? According to her diary, she was happy to pick up her life at home in France again when this trip was over. Nope, I'm not buying it. For my money, I think she met with her new lover and I think she met her death on that date.

Chapter 23

THEN...

Jessica

My work hours were full of Sunny, while my night was full of Sky and Chelsey. Blondes, blondes everywhere 'nor any drop to drink' and I could use a drink – with apologies to *The Rime of the Ancient Mariner*. I finished writing another 'Sunny is missing' piece and sat back. I knew it was not about me, even so, her disappearance unnerved me as if I was somehow in danger now because she had sat in my car and therefore, I would be next. Every time I got in the car she was in my thoughts; the ghost of her in my front seat. That afternoon driving home from work, the tears came, pouring down my face. I extended my hand to the passenger seat and touched it, but I couldn't feel her. It's crazy crying for someone you hardly know but I miss seeing her on the ride home. I feel heartbroken that she may never be all the things she could have been.

For the second time today, I passed the place where I last picked her up and I pulled over. I don't know why I just did. I sat there for a while, thinking about her, and then the hairs on my arms began to rise. Shivering, I moved the car back onto the road and sped away. Something spooked me and I had to get out of there.

Adam wasn't home, damn him, but neither was Sky thank goodness – even though the lights were on. I gave him a quick call and when he answered, the sounds of the bar and a small crowd drifted through the phone.

'Hey Jess, we're just on our way home now, we slipped out for a drink.' I heard him saying something to Sky and I waited.

'Actually, Sky suggested we go out to dinner. I'll come by and get you.'

'No, stay there and have a drink. I'll meet you out. Where are you thinking for dinner?' I waited while they conferred, glad I had called him before changing out of my work gear. 'Sky's partial to a bit of Asian so let's go to Lemongrass Thai. Alright?'

'Fine. I'll see you there in say thirty minutes unless you two just want to catch up and I'll see you later tonight?' I asked. 'It might be good for you to have some bonding time alone, talk about old times...' *Read into that – leave me out of it. I've been carrying Sunny in my head all day; now I had to front Sky.*

'No, come,' he said, and it sounded like an order. 'Oh, and Jess, bring a few bottles of red wine from the cellar, it's BYO. See you soon.' He hung up.

Yes, sir, will do, I snapped. Nothing would give me less pleasure than to meet the glammy 'couple' for dinner. I sighed and told myself to get over it; Sky's need to be bitchy was her insecurity talking not mine. She'd be off and out of the country soon so it didn't matter. Besides, he's been in a good mood while she was visiting, I guess that's something.

I thought about whether to change from my workwear to something more casual and put on a pair of jeans, with a white T-shirt and navy jacket. I touched up my make-up and hair and grabbed a few bottles of red before heading out, lecturing myself on the way there: *Jessica, let the little things slide – it's not important. She is about a minute in your whole life.*

Funny really, funny odd that was. I was twenty-six, an employed journalist with a handsome husband, a beach house, and yet Sky made me feel like my life was a hoax, and I'm a guest in it, playing an understudy role. I thought about how much of it might be my imagination. I'm younger and I've got the man she wanted – I'm in the driver's seat. I'm also married to her deceased sister's husband and that's probably sad for her and hard to accept, especially if she wanted him. I just had to cut her some slack.

When I arrived they weren't there yet, so I requested a table for three – a window seat – and sat waiting. Adam's car pulled up and as they walked in, she looped her arms through his. Okay, I can handle this, time to bring out the clever, sassy, witty Jessica that Adam knows. Lord help me. There was no room for Chelsey or Skylar in my life – this was my town, my house and the only connection to them was the man they once knew. Bring on the show.

'Hey you two,' I rose to kiss Adam and kiss Sky on the cheek.

'Good thing you were here, or we would have kept partying into the night,' Sky said.

'Good thing I saved you then!' *First little comment laced with meaning.*

'How was your day?' Adam asked as he took the menus from a waiter, thanked him and took over the pouring of the wine.

'Any scoops?' Sky teased. 'What's the biggest story that breaks here?'

Adam grinned at Skylar and it took all my self-control not to throw my wine at them. *Don't push me Adam; it would take very little at the moment to send me back to the city!*

'Today's headline?' I said, joining in, 'The population increased by one tourist.' *Fuck her.* Adam laughed, and Sky didn't like it. How about we've spent the day looking for a missing woman? But why make her feel bad? Why bother? And she was technically my guest too.

'But how was your day, Sky? What did you get up to?' I asked, generously putting the spotlight back on her where she wanted it to be.

'I had a lovely morning on the beach and then we met for lunch,' she said, with a smile to Adam. 'After that, I went for a lovely, long massage to this place that Adam recommended, and then I found a nearby bookstore, I could have spent hours there.'

There was so much wrong with this that my tongue swelled in my mouth and I had this pleasant smile glued to my face. I've never met Adam for lunch; he didn't have time. He recommend a massage place? I didn't even know he liked a massage!

'Jess loves to read too. I'm always dragging her away from bookshops, she can spend hours in there,' Adam said, looking at me fondly. The look Sky gave me was anything but fond, it was cold and her eyes narrowed and to be honest, I felt a little wary. She didn't like Adam speaking about me with any genuine affection, but what did she expect? I'm his wife.

I felt the need suddenly to be a little cautious around her.

*****

Later that night, I needed Adam to come to bed. I was ovulating and today was my peak day and night. I was on a drug that my doctor issued to help induce ovulation. I had been taking it for five days, and my stomach felt like I was carrying a basketball. Adam knew we were trying of course, but he didn't know I was going to this length to get pregnant, and he didn't want to know, but I was getting worried that we had had no success.

Every second day in the past week, my doctor had taken my blood and did a test so I could confirm exactly when I was ovulating. I got the results at lunchtime when I called his office – I'm ripe for it, and Adam needed to do his bit – a small part given my daily blood and time donation to the cause.

But when we got home, Sky wanted to open another bottle and drink on, and Adam was in the mood to party. I told them I was turning in and asked to see him for a moment.

'I'm ovulating tonight,' I said and bit my lip.

He rolled his eyes.

'Tonight is the best night; the doctor's confirmed it,' I continued. I started undressing in front of him hoping that might encourage him or he'd at least give me a quickie.

Instead, his eyes narrowed. 'For fuck's sake, Jess, I'm not in the mood. Besides, I'm sick of sex on a set date, talk about killing the romance.' His voice rose and he got angrier as he thought about it. He hadn't complained about sex before. 'In fact, I don't give a toss if we have kids or not. I'm going to have a drink, go to bed.' With that, he stormed out, slamming the door behind him.

Standing there looking at the door, my stomach was swollen, my body ready, I was alone. Meanwhile, my husband was returning to drink with his ex-wife's beautiful sister on the verandah. I felt ugly, alone, devastated.

Unless he had sex with me in the morning, I'd wasted this month.

I finished undressing, washed my make-up off and climbed into bed on my own. I hugged my knees to my chest and cried. I wish I had listened to Clare right from the start – beware of instant intimacy, but it was too late by then, for me anyway.

For just a moment I wanted Soleil's life again, to be free, until I remembered she was gone.

NOW...

Coen

According to the police notes, there were a few sketchy witness recollections of Soleil being collected that night at the hostel. I know from the reports and straight from the horse's mouth – Lacey – that Soleil had a call that morning and she was happy, a date most likely. So did he pick her up?

Also in the file was a list of registered phone calls where a blue car was mentioned, seen at the hostel that night. Another sheet ticked off those callers after they were interviewed and listed comments which amounted to nothing more than seeing Soleil physically getting into the car. There was no description of the driver – it was night, and nobody got the plate. What about CCTV?

I spent another ten minutes searching for information on any vision captured, but apparently, fifteen years ago there wasn't CCTV at the hostel or in that street. Bummer. Hold up, one of Jessica's newspaper stories covered this subject – the car itself. Shuffling through my online links, I found it.

She was reaching with these stories, trying to keep Soleil in the news when there was little new information to report. It read:

The Strand Times

Blue car sought in connection with missing backpacker
By Jessica Steyne, crime reporter

Two witnesses recall seeing a woman who resembled French backpacker, Soleil Reyer, getting into a dark blue car in the vicinity of the Rest-up Backpackers' Hostel on the night she disappeared.

An eye witness has described watching as a dark blue car of sports appearance pulled up at the hostel around 6.30pm and a blonde woman got into the vehicle.

Jaye Timper was heading out for dinner with a friend when she spotted the car. 'I remember because the girl looked nice and she was happy and smiling as she got into the car. She had a really nice dress on.'

The navy-blue car was also seen by a second witness who wished to remain anonymous. The witnesses could not recall the registration number of the car or its make.

The receptionist at the hostel, Lacey Maurier, has told police that the missing woman was looking forward to seeing a man on the last day she was seen alive.

'She didn't say it was a date,' Ms Maurier said, 'but she went shopping that day for a new dress and was excited.'

Ms Reyer regularly hitchhiked westbound on the Pacific Highway heading back to the Rest-up Backpackers' Hostel after a day of fruit picking at a farm on Bucca Road.

Detective Nick Clarkson of the Strand Harbour Police asked drivers with a car matching the description to voluntarily contact the Strand Harbour Police to be eliminated. Detective Clarkson is also seeking information on the person believed to have begun a relationship with Ms Reyer before her disappearance.

*****

The story went on giving her description and the Crime Stoppers' phone number. So, a blue sports car, no idea who was driving. You're elusive Soleil's new love, I'll give you that much. So, at 6.30pm, looking beautiful, you got into the car for your dream date, Soleil, and were never seen again. Sad and frustrating and I could feel my anger welling; I could only imagine what it must have been like for Nick and his team working the case, and Jessica having known Soleil and trying to do all she can with the power of the press.

I stood; a long walk was called for – up and down the beach to clear my head and let my thoughts flow. Besides, you never know who you'll run into because right now, unless someone wants to share some information, remembers something or I get a lucky break, I've got nothing but what's all been said before. And I couldn't give this up now… I felt like I had an obligation to Nick.

I wanted to find Soleil so badly it was pumping through me like a course of adrenalin every day. It was a bit like falling in love without the passion – a slow realisation that you liked them, maybe loved them; when your eyes were opened, a feeling, a need. Everyone might tell you that they were not right for you, or they were not interested, or you were wasting your time, but it's too late. This story was under my skin and as Julius Caesar said, 'Alea iacta est' – the die was cast.

Chapter 24

THEN...

Jessica

The next morning, I lobbed in at work early so I could get started on my Soleil rounds; Adam was on the morning shift too so it was easy getting up when he was already out of bed. Fortunately, Sky liked a sleep-in so I didn't have to make small talk with her in the morning. Today I planned to do a street walk and talk with people about their thoughts, sightings, and anything they might have heard. Ryan can come along with me to record or make notes while I ask the hard questions.

While logging in, I read our newspaper coverage again – Clare had done a good job – and I checked out the letters to the editor in case anything came in on the deadline that Oliver included. It's always interesting to see what online comments might have collected overnight; I sat down and began scrolling through stories and feeds. The day went so quickly that it was midday before I even surfaced with a few different stories under my belt and having replied to people that had commented and checked they were legitimate so we could publish their comments. I checked in with Ryan and suggested he had a lunch break before we headed off to do our street vox pops.

Because I spent every moment of my working day reporting Soleil's status and trying to find angles to keep her story alive, death was on my mind, which led me to think of Chelsey more often. I wish both of them would get out of my head; if only Soleil could be found safe and well and I could bury Chelsey from my thoughts.

Having Skylar staying wasn't helping, she brought Chelsey with her. Adam was constantly reminded of his beautiful, socialite wife. Everything I am not. Chelsey needs to come off that pedestal and be stored somewhere in my head with limited access.

Last night I lay awake wondering if she got more sex than me? Was he moody with Chelsey too or did that start after she died along with all their plans for their life together? I saw his vacant looks sometimes and worried, does he want out of our marriage? Does he regret his spontaneity and wished he had gone along with my initial suggestions to wait a while and take the relationship slowly? And let's not kid ourselves, our relationship wasn't normal, there were too many unspoken thoughts; maybe it's a cultural thing – our backgrounds and upbringings were so different.

You know the saying that what we love about someone in the beginning will be what we eventually hate – in my case, it was so true. That dark, moody, introverted side of Adam was so sexy, initially. His interest in me was flattering; he wasn't flashy, he had a side to him that everyone else didn't. I loved I got his smiles, his embraces, his protection. Now the dark side was dragging me down like I'm scared to be too happy, scared to be too excited or too positive around him. I'm moderating my behaviour all the time, treading on eggshells. Listen to me, I hardly know myself. When did I become one of those women who plans their lives around their men? Who was Jessica Steyne – wife of Adam Steyne? I think she ate the previous me, Jessica Cartwright, whole.

Chelsey had left me the shell of a man who was going deeper and deeper into a dark depression and now I have Skylar to help that along.

I jumped, sat back with a start as Clare stood in front of me.

'You were a million miles away? This case freaking you out?' she asked.

'Something like that.'

'C'mon, let's get a coffee.'

I rose to follow Clare and suggested to Ryan we leave in thirty minutes. He looked happy; nothing like bad news to fire up a newsroom.

*****

Driving home late afternoon, it still felt weird not seeing Soleil today, but on the upside, Adam's car was there when I got home. Great, I didn't have to entertain Sky.

Please let him be in a good mood.

Please, Chelsey, let me have him all to myself tonight.

I found Adam doing the tour of the house – we did that most days, just to see what the builders had done today and how close we were to finishing. Adam was threatening to throw himself into the garden and do some work, but Skylar's visit kept stopping him, she always had somewhere she wanted to go, and with him. We greeted each other, and I joined him for the final inspection.

'Where's Sky?' I asked.

'Down on the beach.'

Good, ten minutes alone together. He said nothing about my ovulating or 'standing me up' and I didn't bring it up. Whatever. He gave me his verdict.

'They've done well today,' he said, glancing back at the house. 'I'd say they'll be done by the end of the month.'

We finished our inspection at the hole for the plunge pool. It sat like a cavity in the backyard.

'I'm going to have a shower to wash the day off; I'll be quick, then we can have a drink and watch the sunset,' I told him. I saw Sky coming up the front stairs wearing her bikini, her towel over her shoulder. I gave her a wave and smile, she reciprocated in all her sexiness.

I ventured upstairs and blinked back the tears. Why the hell am I teary? Just tired and overwhelmed with it all, I guess. I stripped and moved into the shower; it was a beautiful large shower and rain head. Moments later, Adam entered the shower and wrapped his arms around me. He took me from behind. We came quickly; deprivation had its benefits, but it's probably too late for my cycle.

I am probably imagining things, but I could have sworn I saw a shadow pass our half-open bedroom door. Was Sky out there watching?

*****

Twenty minutes later we were back on the verandah; Sky joined us and we clinked our glasses in a toast.

'Good day at the office?' I asked Adam.

'I did a thousand consultations today and every patient had already done their analysis with Doctor Google. Such a big help, we'll be obsolete soon,' he joked. 'And you?'

'I spent the day on the missing case,' I told him. 'Seeing the MISSING posters freaks me out.'

'Aagh, we're talking about the hitchhiker?' Sky asked, then conceded my point. 'It is eerie seeing the poster,' she agreed and put her hand on Adam's arm. 'We saw it when driving yesterday, remember?'

He nodded. How cosy.

'She's your type,' Sky said and laughed. I snapped to look at her. She can't be serious. Soleil was missing, this was not a subject for our amusement. Adam looked unimpressed.

'You mean she's your type,' he said to her and raised an eyebrow. They smiled at each other and then Adam turned away to look at the beach.

What the hell did all that mean? Was Sky gay?

Or... no, that thought was way too out there. Sky's beautiful blonde sister died in a fall, Sky wouldn't harm her sister, surely she's not running around killing blondes. I almost laughed out loud at the picture in my head.

But still, did Adam mean Soleil was in danger from Sky? Sky didn't arrive in town until the night of Soleil's disappearance.

My mind was racing through the scenarios, ignoring the two of them as they bantered. I'm being crazy, they both didn't get back here until 1am or so, because of the airport trip and it's not like Sky was just going to arrive in town, pick up a hitchhiker and kill her. Why would she? Besides, Adam was with her, he'd never do that. Ha, crazy, Nick would say as a detective I make a good journo.

Still, I wasn't finished here. I turned to Adam and asked: 'Did you ever see her?'

'Who?' he asked, confused.

'Sunny... Soleil,' I said, with impatience. *Who did he think we were talking about?*

'We left that subject ten minutes ago,' he said haughtily. 'And no, I can't say I remember seeing her. I've seen fruit pickers hiking along that road, but I can't recall Soleil in particular.'

'It's weird,' I said. 'I can't believe she sat in my car, on the front seat next to me only last week; now she's gone.' Goosebumps covered my skin, and Adam rubbed my arm.

'I want you to stop picking them up, the hitchers male or female,' he said. 'Promise me?'

I nodded.

'I mean it,' he said.

'I won't, not now.'

'Someone's out there who has seen something and done something, and I don't want you inviting them into your car, so don't court danger,' he said.

Sky smiled sweetly, but the glare she was shooting me was anything but sweet; her lips thinned and her smile was more of a grimace. But that was what I loved about Adam, his possessiveness of me, and that he worried for my safety. I sipped my wine and looked out at the ocean. I can't believe I'm here. The little girl from suburbia was here in a million-dollar beach house with a doctor for a husband. I've made it.

Sometimes, I have to pinch myself to believe it.

Sometimes I have to coach myself to remember just how lucky I am.

Sometimes I have to stop myself from screaming when I'm a hair's breadth away from opening my mouth and just letting it out.

Chapter 25

NOW...

Coen

Tapping away, mind absorbed, I got a bit carried away with my writing, which was a good thing. I had to get up a few times to close the doors and windows as night crept in, and I stopped for long enough to make a toasted cheese sandwich and grab a mug of tea, before returning to the desk and laptop. It was a lovely quiet house once you got used to the sound of the waves. For the first few nights they were so loud they kept me awake, now I don't hear them at all. I woke the other night because I could have sworn there was a break in the waves rolling in. I had a friend who lived near a railway station and he said the same thing... he never heard the trains.

When the moon was out, the view of the ocean at night was amazing – the white seahorses lit by moonlight. It would be quite romantic if I were here with my girlfriend, ex-girlfriend. Nah, she'd hate this place. She nearly drowned as a child and she hadn't gone back in the water since. She used to say it was what lay beneath that frightened her. What would Natalie think of it when she came to stay next weekend?

Back to the writing... which involved transcribing everything I knew so far with no order or chapters, just writing and cross-checking my notes. It took so much longer writing this sort of story because you had to reference all your sources. My fiction books just flowed and while I keep a spreadsheet and noted my fictional character's names, characteristics and relationships, no formal references were required for imagination.

What do I need now besides finding Soleil?

I need to know who Nick thought was ripe for it, but I'm tempted not to ask as well – otherwise, it may end up leading *my* investigation. I'm still not convinced that Julian from the hostel was out of the picture. When can I speak with Jessica and what were her theories, her first-hand perspective of the case and what Soleil was really like? It's good to go in as a virgin, untouched by bias and history. It was time to form my theories.

THEN...

Jessica

Adam was cutting his workday short to take Sky to the airport later this afternoon. Thank God for that, she was going. If I saw her coming out of the bathroom one more time with just a towel wrapped around her, or lying on the beach out the front of the house in her skimpy bikini with her golden tan, I think I would have imploded. I've done my duty, never again and I mean never.

Speaking of swimming, Adam and Sky's fascination with that pool was unbelievable. I suspected her fascination was pure disappointment that she can't sunbake in front of Adam, but he watched it, strode around it, measured it, looked at it. For the love of God, just get it concreted, filled with water and swim in it. Let's hope there was no change of plan and the pool guys came on Monday. There's a bloody big ocean at the front door, swim there!

The office was virtually empty when I arrived first thing this morning, which was often the case – I was used to city hours, but Strand Harbour folk wandered in closer to 9am. There was nothing new on Soleil, and it was a struggle to keep coming up with something that kept her top of mind. There were a lot of online comments I didn't approve of going live; people were nuts. They got stuck into each other, made up sightings, suggested reasons she might have disappeared, many of which were nasty and uncalled for, especially given they probably didn't know Soleil. Seriously, get a life, people. But one got my attention.

She's dead. Serves her right.
Forget it and move on.
She won't be answering her phone or posting on her Facebook
page. A.J.

So A.J., got some insider information? I gave Detective Nick a call, and he answered on the first ring.

'Waiting for my call?' I teased him.

'Every day. Ready for that affair?' he asked.

'So tempting… but no. Hey probably nothing, but I've got a comment online that might be worth checking out.' I read it to him.

144

'Yeah, I'll get my I.T. team to talk with yours. Can you send me the contact?' he asked.

'Sure, I'll email it to you now. Can you let me know the outcome?' I asked.

'Of course, one good favour, etc.,' he said.

We talked for a few more minutes checking that neither of us had anything the other didn't have and I hung up. I suspect he had a lot more than I had. Later that afternoon he called back.

'Nick, you've got news?' I don't know why I was so hopeful; I just wanted some good news.

'Hey, Jess. No, nothing promising. The person who wrote the online comment about Soleil being dead – signed A.J. – knew nothing. But at least our I.T. guys are talking so if you get any more suspicious comments, just let your guys know to flick them over.'

'Sure. So what was A.J.'s story?' I asked. 'Was he just being a smart ass when he said Soleil was not coming back?'

'He's a pimple-faced, room-dwelling teen, addicted to cheap thrills who thought it would be funny to look like he knew something. Nearly shit himself when he saw our cop car pull up out the front of his mother's house.'

'I bet,' I sighed. 'I can't believe Soleil can just vanish. Someone knows something, it's so frustrating.'

'Tell me about frustrating… we wasted a shitload of time on that false photo on her Facebook page and the Yamba lead. Coffee?'

'Make it a double and I'm in,' I agreed.

I slipped out and met Nick in our usual café and on my return drummed up a quick story from the comments received and a few other chased-up quotes. Desperation was sinking in now. Nick had no new leads and all my angles for stories were exhausted. I uploaded:

The Strand Times

Friends concerned for missing backpacker
By Jessica Steyne, crime reporter

International and local friends of missing backpacker, Soleil 'Sunny' Reyer, of Lyon, France, have taken to social media to express their concern for the lack of leads in her disappearance and to plead with anyone who might have any information to come forward.

Ms Reyer's cousin, Adrian Vipond, said Soleil would not put her friends through unnecessary pain and he feared for her safety.

'Soleil was always sensible and mature beyond her years, and she was aware of safety messages, she even taught that to her students,' he said. 'I know her well enough to know that she wouldn't just disappear and cause distress, there's no reason for her to do so.'

'We are concerned that there seems to be so little to go on. For a small town, surely someone saw something,' he said.

Other comments included:

'She would never have knowingly put herself in danger. I'm fearful for her.' *Aimée*

'Please just come back home safely, Sunny.' *Benoit*

'Who would do this to such a bright light? Sunny is living the dream; please return her safely to us.' *Hélène*

'Please tell the police if you know anything, even if it seems unimportant, it may help.' *Quentin*

Ms Reyer completed her teaching qualification and worked for a year before taking a gap year from her career to travel. She spent time in Germany, the United States and England before travelling to Australia.

*****

I finished up with the date and time she was last seen and Detective Nick's message asking people to call with information… the usual drill. Yep, it was a nothing story and I had nothing. It was only a matter of time until we'd have to let Soleil go and move on to the next big thing.

THEN…

Adam

When I got home at dusk after the airport run, Jessica decided to inspect my gardening and talk about how our renovation was going. It was amusing how she says we're *renovating* our beach shack to be a beach home. We're doing nothing – I'm forking out dollars, she's directing tradespeople. It's been the longest renovation project in history. During the time we've been married, we spent about six months thinking about it, another six months drawing up plans and changing them, then we had to get all the required approvals. We met builders, but with her schedule and mine, that took forever. The end was in sight, but neither of us has lifted a paintbrush, a sander, or done a day's work on the 'shack' paid for largely by my dead wife's life insurance payout. Chelsey, always the planner, even now from the grave she's got a hand in my future abode.

We were going to have a house on the beach too, Chelsey and me, she was from money – old money – and I was coming into new money. We spent our weekends driving around picking out blocks of land we could build on. She would drag me onto the block, get a hundred selfies and post it online for everyone's feedback with the view in the background. *Can you see us here? #ChelseyAdam #ournewhome.* God, she excited me.

But she had no idea that we could afford something some of our friends only dreamed of and we were setting ourselves apart. Old money doesn't always realise that. She'd laugh because her 'mommy' and 'daddy' were going to set us up as soon as we picked a house. Chelsey had it all under control, she had everything under control, but me, and that drove her nuts.

If we weren't looking at property, we were partying. The life of the party with her bright white smile and golden hair, Chesley was always partying. Every weekend we were doing something – entertaining friends, socialising – I'd pray to be on the night shift to have a reprieve from her party life, but even then she'd want me to be part of it when the shift was done. Didn't matter that I had just done nine hours on the ward.

Oh, but she tried it on to get a reaction – she'd drop the names of guys that flirted with her to get me stirred up. I don't know where that insecurity came from, but at a guess, I would say years of competing with her sister for her parent's affection had made her crave to be the centre of someone's world. That someone was me. I'd live up to my part. I'd roughly pull her close. 'Do I have any grounds to be jealous, Chelsey?' I'd growl, and she would soften and touch my face.

'I am yours and yours only,' she'd say. Then I would fuck her hard to remind her she was mine. She needed that confirmation more than I did. If I told her about all the women and men that came on to me in the course of my week, she'd be apoplectic.

Chelsey was all about Chelsey. With Jessica, it's different, almost the reverse. She was happy to be the support act and not take the lead role. I've had my fill of blondes, enough to last me a lifetime.

Chapter 26

NOW...

Coen

For reasons that now seem unfathomable to me, I agreed to take part in the Strand Harbour team triathlon. While Nick took the bike leg, and another mate of his, Gavin, did the swim leg – an ocean swim which was even harder than a pool leg – I put my hand up to do the run. So at 6am, there I was on the starting line with about one hundred other dills waiting for the starter gun. I think it was in exchange for a post-triathlon breakfast and information swap. Nick gave me a thumbs-up from the sideline. I gave him a less than enthusiastic morning face which just made him and Gavin laugh.

'Great way to get into the community,' he had said, and a few other clichés. I'm a morning person and like to run, but solo running was my go. It's hard to be pleasant and social at 6am in a pack. The gun went off and scared the shit out of me while I was daydreaming, so like a startled gazelle I raced ahead. I'm not expecting to win or even come close, but we want to finish with a dignified result... maybe just finish.

In all honesty, the 10 kilometres didn't seem that far when you were running in a pack; it's the distraction of the mob and the kick-ass incentive of making sure some kid doesn't pass you. The cyclists came into my line of vision, lined up ready to go as each of their team members came in and Nick was waiting keenly. I gave myself a rev up and reached the finish line and off he went. Thank God that's over, he'd better cough up some decent intel this morning. I grabbed a drink, commiserated with a few other runners and we strolled to the beach to wait for the cyclists to return and to cheer on the swimmers. Gavin looked the part and returning the favour, I gave him an enthusiastic thumbs-up; he smirked. Soon after, the first of the cyclists appeared and eventually Nick came into sight – he'd done alright. Gavin threw his towel aside and prepared to wade into the water and take off. Yeah, we're on fire.

Nick sped in and Gavin was off. When Nick recovered sufficiently to form a sentence we moved to a better vantage point to cheer Gavin home. The first, second, and third place getters all came in – that's the prizes cleaned up, and then another couple of dozen hot shots emerged from the ocean victorious, but they've done this before. By the time we conquer this event a few more times that's bound to be us – who am I kidding. Then Gavin came into sight and our cheering brought him in just that bit faster. We patted each other on the back like we'd won the Olympics. We placed 68 out of 110 competitors… impressive for sure.

After a beach shower and changing in the local beach facilities, we headed to breakfast at the Surf Life Saving Club. Gavin bowed out as he was meeting his girlfriend, who was on another team; fine by me, I was intending to pump Nick for information.

I loved a well-earned breakfast and after we'd ordered a good feed, coffee, and finished congratulating ourselves, I got down to business. I was in writing mode now and I was myopic once I started a project – getting back home to write was all I could think about.

'Got any conclusions yet?' he asked when I broached the subject.

'Sadly, no,' I said. 'But it's only a matter of time.'

He chuckled. 'Right. Want me to tell you who I think did it?'

'Nope.'

He looked surprised.

I explained. 'You're right, what you said earlier, if you tell me that, it's all I'm going to see. I want to approach it like a blank slate. But tell me why you discounted the receptionist from the hostel's boyfriend?'

'Ah,' he said, knowingly, 'you've already heard from Lacey then? She's been pushing that theory for years.'

'Yeah, Andy... his middle name was Matt,' I said.

'So is mine,' Nick said.

'Is that so?' I asked and narrowed my eyes suspiciously. He laughed.

'Nuh, it's James. But the boyfriend was just a peacock and I don't think he'd have the balls to do it, putting it bluntly.' Nick sat back and thought for a moment so I didn't interrupt him.

'Andy had a dark-coloured sports car,' he started again. 'A few witnesses recalled seeing a dark-coloured car – possibly black or navy – in the vicinity of the Rest-up Backpackers' Hostel on that Saturday evening. So, Andy's car was tested for blood and DNA; he offered it up when we asked people in town to come forward, especially drivers with cars fitting the description. Might have looked more suspicious if he didn't.'

'What did you find?' I asked.

'Soleil's DNA was in the car but only in the front seat and he had admitted to having given her a lift a few times. We had nothing on him,' Nick said.

'Right,' I said, trying not to sound disappointed. 'I'm glad you checked out Jessica too.'

'Of course,' Nick added like I was an idiot. 'She gave Soleil a lift numerous times.'

'What about the two blokes from the Y? I know you ruled out Julian but he seemed pretty keen on Soleil.'

We stopped talking as our coffees arrived and meals were promised to arrive shortly.

Nick took a sip before responding. 'The two Poms, Julian and Chris. Yeah, I went down that path, interviewed them a few times. It didn't fit though… they were all staying at the Y, and on the night Soleil got a lift with this so-called Matt, the two Poms were at the pub with other travellers from the Y – they were seen there by a lot of people.' He sighed. 'Drives me nuts.'

'Lacey said the accent of the caller was posh… a pom would pass for that,' I suggested.

'Be my guest and review Julian or any other posh folk you find, you never know what might turn up.' Nick said. 'But at the time it felt like I interviewed *everyone* in town, especially anyone with a blue or black car… I was desperate.'

Our breakfast arrived; they were good size meals for triathletes like us. I dug in and made an appreciative sound on trying my scrambled eggs before asking: 'Did you ever think a female might have had reason to harm Soleil? You know, a jealous friend or psycho?' I wanted to see if Jessica came to mind for that role.

Nick finished a mouthful of his burger before responding. 'I kept an open mind but we believed the last person Soleil was with, was a male.'

I put him on the spot. 'Nick, will you tell me the name Jessica's writing under these days or how to reach her? I want to tell her I'm writing this book. She can speak with me or not, but she should know.'

His eyes narrowed and he studied me.

'I know she's not writing under her maiden name because I checked her marriage certificate and got the name – Cartwright – there are no bylines at the moment under Jessica Cartwright.'

'Clever clog,' he said. 'Let me contact her and tell her. I'll pass your number on. That do?'

'Okay, thanks,' I said. Better than a poke with a stick. 'Tell her I'll do it justice and be fair, and that you're involved, yeah?'

He nodded. 'Alright.'

'Love to solve it,' I said.

'Yeah, get in line, Poirot,' he said, and I chuckled.

Chapter 27

NOW...

Coen

A few days of my week were lost to lecturing and the rest of the week was spent writing what I knew about Soleil and Strand Harbour, and chasing my tail as I followed up my leads and hunches on the 'Soleil case' – my name for it. The waiting game was frustrating – seriously, don't people check their messages every day? How long does it take to respond to a query? Yeah, I've been guilty of ignoring messages myself, but this was different because I'm the one doing the waiting. I'll get over myself.

On a bright note, Natalie arrives late today and I can't wait. The place was spotless, you could eat off my floors. I've allocated her a large room with a bathroom ensuite, a balcony and ocean views, but if she wants to share my room then that's just fine. I'm not expecting that, I'm just hoping for it. While I appreciated the lecturing work and the new friends and contacts I'd made, having a good friend come to stay whom I can relax with was just what I need. I am also hoping Natalie might open a few doors for me... you know how girls like to talk; if she can cut through some of the small-town talk about Soleil, that would be brilliant.

Speaking of which, I had no intention of confessing this to Detective Nick but a while back I made some casual queries with my rental agent – pretending I was interested in possibly owning this house or one like it – to see if I could track down Jessica. You never know she might still own it or Adam Steyne might. That was probably a mistake as the agent, Maree, got excited and offered to show me available homes for sale. I had to calm her down and tell her it was just a seed of a thought and I wouldn't do anything until after the six months lease was up.

But I found out that the house was still owned by the good doctor; the lady I met on the beach with the dog, Alfie, had called it the doctor's house but I didn't make the connection then. God bless Maree, she loved a chat. Supposedly, Jessica wanted out so they put the house on the market but it didn't sell initially – Maree said they had just finished renovating it so it was a little overpriced. Then supposedly Adam decided he wanted to keep it so they came to a settlement, allegedly. Maree said Adam was hoping they'd reconcile and one day move back here. Poor bastard. Well we know that didn't happen, well not in the last fifteen years because that's how long it has been up for rental. Maree said Adam comes over once a year for a few weeks in summer to enjoy the house and check on maintenance. She said it kept them on their toes… he was quite critical, apparently. I didn't ask for his contact details yet, I wanted to talk with Jessica first if that was possible and I wasn't sure what he could tell me in the grand scheme of things. Maree offered to send me before-and-after photos from their files. Why not, let's see what the luxury love shack was like before the touch-up. She had them to me about ten minutes after our chat – must be a quiet day at the real estate agency.

After a grilled cheese for lunch – it was my specialty dish – I printed out the renovation photos and wandered around the house comparing the before and after. I wasn't expecting to find anything but I did find the MISSING posters on my first day here, so maybe other stuff hadn't been cleared, like a notebook of Jessica's for example. Yeah, nice to fantasize.

THEN...

Jessica

I was working from home today on the Soleil online campaign; the boss was in Sydney for management meetings so didn't mind. I saw Adam off at the garage door; such a striking-looking man. It must be something to go through your life knowing that your face can stop traffic, having the advantage of being beautiful over others.

It was nice for a change to work at home on a Monday and not get dressed up and do the hair and make-up. It was pleasant sitting in the home office taking in the panoramic ocean views, the sun coming in. But to work... I had some research to do. My thoughts drifted to Soleil. Where were you, Sunny?

Clare called me just before lunch; she missed me when I wasn't around, she didn't have a lot of coffee buddies, and now that we were covering the same story, we were often rostered on different shifts. Our editor, Oliver, had cut her back to part-time on the Soleil stories. I gave her an update on my discussions with Detective Nick, which amounted to next to nothing.

'It's freaky, you know,' Clare said. 'Someone knows this guy Soleil went on a date with – someone is living with him, working with him, maybe even sleeping with him.'

'He might not even be from here – he could have been someone passing through for a few days and made the whole story up. He could be on the other side of the world by now,' I agreed.

'Did Nick ever check you out?' Clare asked.

'Me?' I almost squealed.

'Yeah, you. You're a suspect; you spent a lot of time with Soleil.'

I snorted in what my grandmother would have said was a most unladylike manner. 'Well he hasn't asked me anything, but I guess he might have checked my hen's party alibi.'

She scoffed. 'He didn't check your alibi with me,' she said.

'Probably because he knows we are friends and you might cover for me,' I said.

She laughed and disregarded my comment. I must remember not to count on Clare for an alibi if I murder someone!

She continued. 'The police constable told me this morning that they have tested just about every blue sports car and sedan in town and that line of enquiry is dead in the water. Did your husband volunteer his car?'

'Adam?'

'Yeah, that's his name,' she teased. 'He drives a navy convertible, doesn't he?'

'Black,' I said. 'But he was in Sydney at the airport.'

'Well you two are both in the clear,' she laughed. 'Got to go, talk later.' She hung up.

My brain started tapping messages to me, whispers in the wiring. A small alarm bell began sounding in my brain again.

I dismissed the thought of Adam or Sky being involved in Sunny's disappearance because it was ridiculous, but I'm living with a guy that drove a dark convertible.

Adam claimed to have never seen Soleil hitchhiking and he didn't recognise her from the poster, but he made a casual remark at dinner… what was it, yes, that Sky looked like Sunny with her tan. Did he see that much detail from the poster after she went missing?

Sky said she was Adam's type, he said she was Sky's and they smiled conspiratorially. Why? Had they seen her?

I stopped the thoughts and then my brain started again, tapping away… his wife died, Sky's sister died. Adam had nothing to do with that; he was broken-hearted. He's never met Soleil. Soleil was missing, last seen with a guy in a dark blue car. Adam's car is black, not blue… close enough, but not blue. Besides, there were lots of blue cars in town.

He was driving to Sydney the night she disappeared. Was he really? Did Sky arrive the night she said she did? Did she come in earlier or later? They were both in bed asleep in the early hours of the morning when I got home from the Hen's Party, they wouldn't do that surely if they just committed a terrible murder. I scoffed, but an implosion of fear was rising within me.

The painters' arrival drew me out of my internal panic. They had a key since our shifts were fairly unpredictable, so I stuck my head out of the office to say hi and let them know I was in the house. They thumped up the stairs with ladders to finish the guest room, greeting me as they passed. Not long after, the builders' cleaners came to remove the leftover timber and roofing sheets from the yard. The place was buzzing with people. I rose to make a coffee and did the rounds to see if anyone would like one. I got a few orders and delivered them with a selection of biscuits which I bought, not baked… I'm not the baking type, although I make a mean jam drop biscuit. I entered the third bedroom with a mug of tea for Ed the painter, who descended the ladder on seeing me.

'Looking good,' I said, and he grinned as he accepted the tea and chose a biscuit. He was an older man with a thick European accent, and by the looks of his painting gear, he'd painted a house or two.

'I like your choice of white,' he said, dunking his biscuit in the tea. 'Timeless. I always say "add your splashes of colour but go with a good base colour". I can't tell you how many times I've been asked to paint some trendy colour which you know next year, they're going to want you to paint over.' He shrugged, 'then again, keeps me in business.'

'Yeah, I'm a big fan of white, too. Makes everything seem bigger and brighter,' I agreed. 'Did you miss many calls when you left your phone here?'

'What's that Luv?' he asked.

'When you left your phone here last week, last weekend, did you feel like you had lost an appendage? I'm so addicted to mine, my whole life is in it.'

'Wasn't me Luv. Me and the boys had another job last week. We haven't been here since a fortnight ago now. Must have been one of the other tradies,' he said.

'Oh, my mistake.' I kept my face neutral, but my heart was pounding. What was going on here? Did Adam have the wrong tradie? Was he just being flippant and didn't tell me it wasn't the painter's phone I heard ringing that morning Sky arrived?

'Well, thanks darlin', Ed said, 'I'll take another biscuit then get back to it.'

I grinned and extended the packet toward him; he took a couple and I departed with a wave. The conversation with Adam from the weekend ran through my head.

'The painter must have left it there; he called in yesterday and we were talking in the second bedroom.'

And later, over wine I had asked him, *'Did Ed get his phone?'*

'Yeah, said he didn't even miss it.'

'I'd be in panic mode,' I remembered saying.

'Might be nice to lose it for a while,' Adam answered.

It's just a mix-up, I told myself. It wasn't Ed's phone, maybe it belonged to one of the other tradies and Adam didn't think it was a story worth correcting. But the voice in my head said it wasn't a mix-up – Ed hadn't dropped in to discuss painting last Saturday, Ed didn't leave the phone, Ed didn't collect it Sunday when I went to work.

That phone was ringing in the early hours of the morning; the caller was looking for someone... looking for someone who should have been home, maybe. That was the weekend that Soleil went missing, a strange coincidence. The weekend that Sky arrived. Or was it a second phone? Did Adam have another phone, maybe that he used for work? But I've never seen it... why wouldn't I know about it? Why would he keep that hidden, unless it was a second phone for an affair?

That doesn't mean he murdered anyone for God's sake; everything was just a strange coincidence or a mix-up. My phone rang, and I jumped. I took a deep breath and smiled. *Crazy.* I pulled it out of my pocket – it was Adam.

'Hi babe, how's things?' his voice sounded like he was just behind me.

'Good, all good, where are you?' I asked, looking behind me even though I knew he wasn't there.

'Just on a break, I thought I'd check up on how the renos were coming along and how you were fairing with the tradies.'

'It's a full house. Painters upstairs and the guys are clearing timber from the yard. All looking good,' I said. I kept my voice light, even if it sounded a bit hysterical to me.

'Great.'

I kept going. 'I've got some stuff done today without the usual interruptions at work,' I added, a slightly hysterical laugh again.

'Bonus,' he said. 'I've got to get back. I should be home by five. See you then.'

Hanging up, I held the phone to my chest. Then it dawned on me… if any of my suspicions were to have a foundation, I had to find that ringing phone. But it had to be done when no one was in the house. I couldn't risk Adam hearing that I was looking for something. All the tradies and Adam had to be gone and then I could begin my search.

Could I turn him in? Did Adam and Sky pick up Sunny on the way home from wherever she had been? Or was Soleil seeing my husband? Was she laughing at me the whole time I was picking her up, knowing she was sharing his bed?

Matt! She called him Matt.

Adam. Matt.

Adam Matthew Steyne.

Chapter 28

THEN…

Jessica

An idea had come to me; slightly weird, but what the heck. I might not want to be seen looking around for a phone, but I sure as hell could subtly make my bed and clean the spa. I ran to our bedroom, to my drawers, and opened one. Finding what I was looking for – long, elbow-length, black satin gloves that I bought to go with a strapless black dress – I slipped them on. Time to play the amateur sleuth – I returned to the bedspread, and I ran my hand over it. Nothing. Now for the other end of the bed. I couldn't believe it. There on my glove was a long strand of blonde hair.

It could be anyone's hair, of course, not just Soleil's – it could be Sky's – but it wasn't mine. I sat on the bed and closed my eyes. The significance of my find hit me, full force. Adam had sex in our bed with another woman. Our vows were broken, my marriage was a farce. All the other worst-case scenarios were knocking at the door now, because he is capable of lying and cheating.

I went to the kitchen, got a sealable plastic lunch bag and

placed the hair in there. I don't know how long hair survives if it has to be tested – I wasn't paying attention during *CSI*. Returning to the bedroom, I pulled back the quilt and did the same, but found nothing on the sheets. But a blonde with long hair had been on my bed. Deep breath. It wasn't me. I can't believe I wanted it to be Sky. My stomach was churning; I always felt my stress there.

If I just stopped looking now, things could go on as usual, I could carry on with my life. That had appeal, a lot of appeal – just whip out a few more stories about Soleil missing, and call it a day on that one. Adam and I would have a very happy life here in our newly renovated beach house. I'll never know if he had Soleil or Sky in our bedroom and what you don't know won't hurt you, right? It would be his secret to live with and my doubts to hide. He'd never know I suspected anything and we'd be happy, as if nothing interrupted our lives. I'd pretend he wasn't capable of killing or cheating and la-de-da, all would be well. Sure.

But being a journalist by trade and by nature, there's the dig. Dig, dig, dig, until I bury myself. I had to know. I'm back to the bathroom like a killer returning to the scene of the crime – they say that happens in real life – I ran my hand around the back of the spa bath, on the ledge. Adam was reluctant to have a spa with me recently, was it because it reminded him of someone else? The ledge yielded one long blonde strand. I looked in the drain, put my satin gloved fingers in and pulled out another couple. Yuk. We hadn't been in the spa bath for weeks, but they could have been Sky's strands. But they could be Soleil's. I put them in the plastic bag too.

Next, upstairs… to our small bedrooms come attic space. Luckily, the painter was in the third bedroom and I returned to the second room where I had heard the phone ringing early last Sunday morning. A glance around satisfied me it was all clear, and I looked in the empty cupboards; there was nothing in them. I stood on tip-toe to see to the back of the top shelf of the built-in-robes, but there was nothing there. If the phone or Soleil's things were ever there, they weren't now. I would do a more thorough look next time I'm completely home alone.

For now, I had to find somewhere to put the plastic bag with the hair in it. Where was somewhere a man would never look? I went back to the main bedroom and pulled out one of my handbags – a silver bag that was bought to match a bridesmaid's dress. I folded up the plastic bag and put it in and pushed the bag back amongst the others. He'd never look there. I peeled the glove off, brushed it down, and returned to our bedroom; I put it back in my lingerie drawer. I moved to the window and looked down at the pool.

Adam went to the airport that night, that's a fact, and he left after 9pm. That'd be a bloody fast date if he had Sunny round beforehand, knocked her off and did what exactly with her body? It just didn't add up. And with Sky here he was never alone to get rid of a body unless they were in it together, but why? Sky just arrived; she didn't even know Soleil.

My gut instinct told me something was wrong, very wrong. I bet Soleil was dating Matt-Adam, a man with a convertible. I bet Soleil was seeing him the night that I was partying with the hens. If I had come home before 9pm, would she be here bedding Adam, her Matt?

I bet I knew where you were, Sunny.

Now it all made sense… why Adam was always staring

at the pool, staring at the corner nearest the shed. His obsession with it and gardening around it; he was nursing her grave until they concreted it over.

Could Soleil be with us forever?

I went to the kitchen and made myself the cup of coffee that I was going to make before, then I moved to the verandah and from afar, I looked at the soon-to-be concreted pool again and breathed in deeply. What would I do if I wasn't emotionally involved? How would I handle this situation?

Think…God, what do I do? This was surreal. You hear about stories like this, I'm not one of them. Should I call the police now? Tell Nick that Soleil could be buried under my new pool? He'd think I was crazy. Besides, what wife calls the cops because she thinks her husband has committed murder?

Just one murder?

The thought paralysed me for a moment; Chelsey fell to her death. Beautiful, full of life, Chesley. Soleil and Chelsey, both Adam's *type*.

What if they dig up the pool and nothing's there? There's no going back from that.

What if Soleil was there? Covered in dirt or blood, beautiful Sunny, her mouth full of concrete. My husband that I loved goes to jail. He wouldn't survive that; he's too pretty. Then I'd become the wife of that killer… people would always wonder about me.

How could she not know?

Was she protecting him? Did she help him do it?

Bet she found out they were having an affair and had a part in the killing. Maybe she did it and he hid the body to protect her. She used to pick that French girl up and give her a lift home, you know.

What would happen to me then? Do I have to change my name or go undercover? If Adam knew that I knew, or suspected as much, would he kill me too? Maybe a pillow over my face, or maybe he would bury me in the new rose garden. Maybe I'd have an accident too. He's a doctor, he'd know how to do that.

I kept running the evidence through my head – blonde hair, a ringing phone in a deserted room, a lie about the painter, a spade in my husband's hand – I tried to dismiss it as coincidental, it could all be explained as an affair.

Stop thinking and just go with it all, see what happens. Remember, I have the best life in the world. Who wouldn't want my life?

THEN…

Adam

Jessica jumped with fright when I entered the house just after five. I don't know what or who she was expecting; she must have been a million miles away. The news was blaring on the TV in the background, you couldn't even hear the waves it was so loud.

'Only me,' I assured her, going over to the table where she worked on her laptop and giving her a quick kiss. She breathed out in relief and smiled at me.

'I didn't hear your car come in. I was watching the early news,' she said, rising and reaching for the remote. She turned the television off. 'How was your day?' she asked.

'Same-o. A mixture of avoidable incidents and the usual number of imbeciles,' I said. 'If people stopped using their phone while they were driving, walking and crossing the road and if the 'P'-platers could remember that we can all speed, it's not a skill, I'd have had very little to do today.'

She smiled at me; it wasn't the first time I had given that speech.

I rolled my eyes. 'Yeah, I know. I'll work on it.'

'No, I hear you, and I've reported on them all,' she agreed. 'I'll pour us a drink. Why don't you get changed?'

'How does it look?' I asked, moving through the living area to the deck.

'What?' she asked.

'The yard, after the guys cleaned up?'

'Oh, of course,' she looked out to the yard through the bi-fold glass doors. 'It looks great.'

I laughed, placed my suit jacket over the chair, and went out to inspect. She didn't follow me out. I wandered around – it looked good, nice to have it clean again. The sooner they finished the better the pool, I thought, looking down on it. Then we could be done with all the tradies. I went back inside to head upstairs and see the paintwork in the attic and startled Jess again.

'You're jumpy today,' I said, as she rose and came around to join me.

She exhaled. 'Having all these guys around today... sounds silly but with the Soleil disappearance, whoever was involved still on the loose and a house full of workers,' she shrugged, 'a girl can't be too careful.'

I squeezed her shoulder, grabbed my jacket off the back of the chair and headed up the stairs to get changed. 'Don't worry,' I called back. 'If you went missing, I would look for you until the day I died.'

Chapter 29

NOW...

Coen

'Oh my God, this place is unbelievable, who couldn't live here?' Natalie said as she wandered around. 'I can't believe people live like this, with this view. But would I be bored here? What about work and could I slow down to Strand Harbour's pace?' She stood in the middle of the room wearing tight jeans, ankle boots, and a white shirt. Her hair was short and sassy, and she turned with her hands on her hip, thinking.

'Yeah, well, you don't have to worry about that now,' I reminded her. 'Besides, you haven't been into town yet, the pace may surprise you.'

She smirked at me and I laughed.

'Okay, maybe not. I'm liking the pace… in fact, I'm liking it here.'

'You could afford this place,' she declared. 'I know what you earn from your books. And you like water… me, not so.'

She continued to wander around, looking at every corner and opening a few doors. I watched; she looked great – fit, full of life, sexy.

'Where am I sleeping?' she asked, putting an end to that hope.

'This way,' I said, grabbing her suitcase from where I had dumped it in the lounge and leading the way upstairs.

'Tell me it has more than one bathroom,' she said, following. 'This huge place must have at least three!'

'It has more than one bathroom,' I parroted, as I entered her designated room and pointed out her private bathroom. She insisted on seeing mine and then made her way through my bedroom to the balcony. I went and stood beside her.

'I'm glad you came. Now remember, relax, slow down, enjoy,' I instructed.

'That sounds like the name of a new self-help book, and yes, I won't talk about work all weekend or pressure you to tell me about your project and word count.'

'I do want to talk about work with you though,' I assured her. 'I want you to see what you can glean from the locals for me.'

'Anything to get the book written,' she agreed.

We stood taking in the ocean view, then Natalie began her study of the grounds from our perch on the second floor. 'A pool as well. That's better – no sharks, no waves.'

'It's bloody cold though, plunge pools are always deep and chilly. Just like being far out in the ocean,' I said menacingly, and she grimaced at me. 'Did you bring your swimmers?'

'I brought everything,' she said. 'Clothes for a dressy gathering, hiking, casual, bike riding, running and swimming wear.'

'And all that in one large suitcase,' I said, and she laughed.

'Shut up,' she said and punched my arm. 'Yeah, I could get used to this.'

'So could I,' I agreed, on so many levels.

*****

170

That night we went down to Sandy's hotel for dinner. I'd invited Nick to join us and he missed the first round of drinks but showed up just in time to shout the second round.

'Timing is everything,' Natalie said, greeting him with a handshake, as he headed to the bar to pick up a round. I had a Holsten, then I'd get on the soft drink… I was working all the time now, at least in my head and I wanted to keep it together. I saw them studying each other with curiosity bordering on some attraction. I hadn't factored in a competitor. Sandy delivered the drinks to our table in person so she could say hello and I introduced her to Natalie.

'He's been doing nothing since he got here, you've got your work cut out for you,' she said to Natalie.

'I knew it!' she exclaimed.

Nick joined in supporting Sandy as I made my protests.

'I've been doing research, a big part of the job, big!' I insisted.

'Yeah, that's why I got him doing triathlons… he was getting fat doing his research here at Sandy's,' Nick said.

I shook my head and took the blows in good grace. You'd think we go way back for the bagging I was copping.

Nick waved to a largish girl at the bar and she came over to the table, exchanging greetings with Sandy as she left us. She had a good collection of tattoos visible on the part of her arms that weren't covered by the rolled-up sleeves of her flannelette shirt. She was what we'd call butch in my school days.

'Clare, how's it going?' Nick asked.

'Yeah, good Nick,' she said and turned straight to me. 'You're the author. Love your *Reiker* series… a seriously sick dude that killer.' She grinned.

'Thanks,' I said, offering my hand and giving her my name, I don't like to be presumptuous. 'This is Natalie, and you know Nick. Want to join us?' I didn't know who she was, but it seemed the polite thing to say since Nick had more or less called her over.

'Got to be somewhere before the hour, but I can finish my drink here, thanks,' she said and plonked herself down.

'Nice collection of art,' I said, with a nod to the dragon and fire tattoos on her arm.

'Yeah, thanks. Shame they'd struggle to show up on your skin,' she said, and Natalie choked on her mouthful of wine. Clare hadn't learned political correctness yet or maybe it hadn't arrived in the Strand. It was all good, I'd heard a lot worse than that.

'My sister's got a few,' I told her, 'she's fair, took after my father's side.'

'What's your mix?' she asked.

I liked her immediately. No bullshit, no tiptoeing around, no telling me to go back to my own country even though I was born here.

'Mum's Sri Lankan, Dad's an Aussie from the outback,' I told her.

'Clare's a journalist at the newspaper,' Nick said, as though that was a nationality. We all gave him an odd look. Then Natalie cut in.

'Were you working on the paper when Soleil disappeared? Did you report on it?'

Well done, Natalie! Worth your weight in chardonnay.

'Yeah, I worked on it,' Clare said and gulped her beer. 'Jessica – she was the other journo working it – she did the online, and I did the print content. A strange case that.'

'What's your take?' I asked.

Clare took a deep breath and then delivered her thoughts, which I suspected she'd given up a few times over the past fifteen years: 'She got the wrong ride. I reckon the guy she met was an out-of-towner cruising, giving lifts to the seasonal working girls, and he picked her. I reckon he lived nearby, and on that last day, she took her last ride with him. Then he didn't return. Ever.' She looked at Nick, who gave a nod and shrug simultaneously.

'Good a theory as any,' he agreed.

'Do you stay in touch with Jessica?' I asked, knowing that would piss off Nick because he wants to control my contact with her.

'Nuh. She was a good chick, but she wanted out and I took that to mean completely out. Besides, I'm not the write emails or social media type,' she said with a shrug. 'I miss working with her, though. She got on better with the cops than I did.' She smirked at Nick. 'Anyway, got to go. Good to meet you both and guess I'll be seeing you around,' she said and was gone as quickly as she came.

'So, Nick, about Jessica…' Natalie asked, 'do we know if she is okay?'

'She's fine,' Nick answered. 'Clare's right, she didn't want to stay in touch. After she moved back to Sydney, I got an email from her apologising for the quick exit and wishing me well. Let's face it, she was here for a minute, had a bad marriage, and left. It's not like it was a great time in her life.'

'I get it,' I said, still licking my wounds from my own recent break-up and keen to get away from the town and the relationship with all its memories. 'Let's order,' I suggested. Nick got up to visit the facilities before ordering, and I turned to Natalie.

'Getting a vibe?' I asked.

'Sure am. Soleil's still very close to the surface here, isn't she?'

'Yeah, I think she remains in the collective consciousness of most people old enough to remember,' I said.

'Clare looked about forty, so she must have been mid-twenties when Soleil disappeared, and you told me Jessica was about the same?'

'Yeah. Not that Nick gives away much on her,' I said.

'He's in love with her,' Natalie said.

My head snapped up, I glared at her. 'No? How did you get that?'

She rolled her eyes. 'So obvious. And he doesn't want a talented, handsome writer making friends with her.'

'What was that? Handsome?' I asked again.

She laughed. 'Well, given Jessica's probably in her forties now too, you'd be looking pretty good,' she teased.

I snorted. 'I'll have you know a lot of desperate and dateless women find me attractive.'

'I'm sure they do. Clare was one of them,' she said, smiling and returning to her menu.

The women in this town, even the visiting ones, were tough.

Chapter 30

THEN...

Jessica

Suspicion was an awful acquaintance – once you've met her, you can't shake her. In one day I had gone through phases where I'd say to myself 'that's enough' – resign yourself to this marriage, to town life, to live with Adam. You've made your bed. I'd tell myself how very lucky I was, and I'd agree that I knew all that I needed to know. I don't need to know anymore, those coincidences could all be dismissed.

But that itch I can't scratch, that hunger I can't feed, won't go away and I need to know everything. What if I'm pregnant now? Oh God, that just occurred to me... that's how the universe works; I bet I am, what a joke.

I don't need to know to be right; let me be wrong, please. I want to search and find nothing suspicious at all. So that after a while I'll tire of searching and then I'll know it's over, the itch will go away and everything will be okay. Won't it?

Could we divorce or does no one ever leave Adam? I wish I could tell Mum, but she'd tell me to get out now, she might even call the police – it's safest not to involve her, yet. But I need to call Mum just to hear her voice and talk about nothing. There is no one in the world I can think of to discuss this with. Nick, Clare, maybe… but no, Nick would have to take action and Clare could not hold back, she'd have to investigate. I am truly alone; trapped in my head with all of it, and trying to act normally takes so much work.

Suspicion was gathering evidence in a folder in my mind. All of my theories had holes in them.

NOW…

Coen

Natalie was enjoying being a collaborator on my next book; I'd have to give her a credit at this rate. After we got home from dinner, we had a nightcap and then she said goodnight. Bummer. But she asked if she could read the material I had on Soleil, so swearing her to secrecy and making her do the cross-your-heart and scout's honour salutes, I gave up the files. She must have read in bed half the night because by morning she had devoured the police file and was working her way through Soleil's diary – I had finished with both and felt none the wiser. I felt Detective Nick's frustration.

Then she wanted to drive past the area where Soleil regularly hitched and to see the Rest-up Backpackers' Hostel. She suggested we grab some photos while there – positionals for the book. I'm guessing the book was a done deal then! Off we headed and Natalie got me to slow down now and then while she got the vibe for the area. Once we finished the route and passed the hostel, Natalie decided she needed a double shot latte or she would die. I took her to the place Nick and I went to after the triathlon, the Pier Café.

She looped her arm through mine as we entered; I wish the walk-in was longer.

'I know you are taking me to all the best places to make Strand Harbour look good,' she said, 'and this place is fantastic. Coffee on the jetty!'

'I've only discovered good places so far,' I told her honestly. I ordered coffee and cake at the counter while Natalie selected a table. When I came back, she was still on the case.

'Did you see this one?' she asked, turning her phone towards me and flashing an old story about a Soleil doppelganger at me. Before I could answer, she began reading it out loud:

The Strand Times

Strange twist in missing backpacker search
By Jessica Steyne, crime reporter

An entry has appeared on missing backpacker, Soleil Reyer's Facebook page featuring a photo of a woman posing on the beach and resembling the 22-year-old missing backpacker.

Detective Nick Clarkson of the Strand Harbour Police said they were able to determine that Ms Reyer herself had not uploaded the photo, but a friend who had accessed her page did so.

The friend who asked not to be identified said she did not mean to cause a stir, but she had put the photo up on the page hoping Ms Reyer might come forward. The password was mutually known to the woman and Ms Reyer. The photo attracted over three hundred comments.

'We have worked through the comments but found

nothing relevant to Ms Reyer's disappearance,' Det. Clarkson said.

'While we encourage the online support and sharing, please be careful of causing any unnecessary pain or anxiety to friends and family members by posting sightings or photos without first advising the police,' he said.

*****

'So, interesting huh?' Natalie said. 'From the photos I've seen of Soleil, it looks a lot like her.'

I grimaced.

'What?' Natalie asked.

'I don't mean to offend,' I said, looking around for leggy blondes, 'but you know a leggy blonde on the beach in a social media post is as common as an author at a writers' festival. It's a red herring and the motives of that so-called friend who put it up are dubious. Why would Soleil leave her gear here? Why would she not follow through with her plans to go up north with her friends? What was she running from if she ran away? Why has she never drawn another cent from her bank account or made a call from her phone? So many questions, so few answers.'

'And over fifteen years to find the answers,' Natalie said. 'It's a bummer the phone location couldn't be more exact but I guess the technology fifteen years ago was not as good,' she said.

'True,' I agreed. 'Nick said they had some technology that wasn't available to the public – they could triangulate the cell phone's position so they knew it was still within ten kilometres of the YMCA – but that's a fair distance,' I said. 'Regardless, once that battery was dead, it was untraceable.

There's a lot to be said for big brother when it works for us.'

Natalie leaned forward. 'Aside from book sales, wouldn't it be amazing if you found her? Imagine how wonderful that would be for her friends and family, and Nick.'

'Yeah, Nick could get that monkey off his back,' I agreed. I wonder if Natalie liked Nick, I tried to read her face.

'People are looking at you,' she said, glancing around.

'They think I'm a lucky middle-aged guy with a beautiful woman and wondering how I got her out for coffee,' I said. God, I'm smooth.

She smiled and blushed just a little, not so tough after all. Just then, a young couple approached and asked for a selfie with me.

'Love the *Road Kill* series, man,' the young hippy guy said.

'Yeah? Thanks for that.' I grinned and posed with them as Natalie took the shot.

'Glad you killed off the girlfriend in the *Reiker* series too, she was going to be a liability,' he continued.

We shook hands. 'Thanks, you're the only person who has got that she was a passenger.'

He grinned and we waved them off, just as coffee and cake arrived for she-who-must-have-a-double-shot-or-she'll-die! Just as I sipped my cappuccino in a mug, the phone rang. It was Nick, was he looking for Natalie?

I excused myself and answered it.

'Hey there, Nick,' I said. We spoke for a few minutes and then, hanging up, I returned my attention to Natalie.

'So, anything important?' she asked.

I nodded. 'Could be. Jessica has agreed to speak with me.'

Natalie's eyes widened. 'This is brilliant, Coen, it will add so much—'

'But by email correspondence only,' I said, cutting her off.

'She said she's not keen to revisit the whole thing, but she's prepared to answer a few questions when I finish the first draft of my manuscript.'

'She wants to read the raw version before she corresponds with you?'

I nodded.

Natalie's eyes narrowed. 'Why? What's the point of that? So you can't quote her or include her?' She sat back and crossed her arms across her chest. I knew that belligerent Natalie look. 'Hmm. That sounds like she has something to hide or she knows something.'

'It does, I agree,' I said. 'If that is the case, and we are not reading too much into it, then it would have to be something close to home for her... something that she found out but didn't want to, or couldn't reveal. I wonder if she was in danger.'

'I wonder if she was involved,' Natalie said with a raised eyebrow. I raised mine as well and she laughed.

'Your talk with her could change the course of the book,' Natalie said.

'That's probably what she's worried about,' I agreed.

Chapter 31

THEN…

Jessica

People and the media were killing me – yeah, I know that was ironic given I fit in both camps. I looked at the *Letters to the Editor* and comments that I'm getting from my online stories, and I wondered what planet these readers were from. Such extremes of opinion – Soleil was a tramp, she's an angel, she's taken off, she was having an affair, she never existed, she embodied all that was right and all that was wrong with our society, she got herself into trouble, she should have been safe and protected here, we've all let her down, she let herself down, and on it goes.

How can everyone have such extreme views from mine? It's so black and white – she's a young woman enjoying her life, and now missing, most likely in this case by the hand of a man. A man who was duplicitous without a thought to the consequences as long as he was not caught and his needs were met.

Kissing Adam goodbye as he went to work, my lips were cold like rigour mortis had set in. I drew a sharp breath before kissing him so I didn't breathe him in. Then the impression of his lips remained on mine for a long time. He was frighteningly beautiful; would people understand that an alleged monster at worse, or cheater at best, could be so strikingly good-looking and appealing and draw you in?

My shift at the newspaper didn't start until ten today, thank goodness – it's been a big couple of weeks and the reality was that the Soleil stories were running thin… I'm depleted. At home, walking on eggshells was exhausting. Adam was worried I'm stressed by it all, frightened by the monster living in our town, living amongst us. Ha, maybe sleeping in my bed. His black car pulled out of the driveway and he raised a hand to wave to me. Was there any evidence of Soleil in his car? I'm sure Adam thought of that and wouldn't be so stupid to be caught with any. What did he do? What did Sky and Adam do? Or did he just cheat on me and nothing more?

Solid evidence; that phone that was ringing, where was it? I was alone now, no tradies, no Adam, no Sky. I waited fifteen minutes to be sure he was gone, then wandered around the house, my phone in my pocket in case he called or I needed it. I tried to put myself in his mind – if I had a phone that I didn't want to be found, where would I put it? *The car.* Well, that's just great since that's the only thing of Adam's that's not home at the moment.

Okay, where's the second place I'd be likely to put it? I stood in front of his side of the wardrobe and then reached for his gym bag and did a quick search. No surprise there was no phone there, that would be a bit obvious. But I'm thorough, no point doing something if you don't do it well. I looked in every pair of his shoes, I stepped up and looked along the shelf where he keeps his jumpers and pants – nothing. I went through the pockets of his coats hanging on his side of the wardrobe. Then, my eye was drawn to the level below, to the edge of the pool that I can see through the upstairs window.

C'mon Soleil, if you never meant to steal my husband, help me get justice for you, help me find the phone.

Gazing to the shed next to the pool, the thought occurred to me, would he store it in there? I doubt it; too hard to get at as well. Seriously, was there any point in looking for this phone? Let's face it, Adam could lie his way out of anything – he could tell me it was a spare work phone that hospital management liked him to carry. Or it could be Sky's phone that she left here like Ed the painter left his phone or Chelsey's old phone – I can think of three workable lies and I'm not even a pro at it. Maybe I'm thinking too deeply if excuses were easy to come by.

I moved to his drawers and carefully ran my hand through his underwear drawer, sock drawer, T-shirt drawer, and then I felt it before I saw it. A phone, a mobile phone.

Fuck!

My breath hitched; I had it. Is this Soleil's phone? Sky's phone? A spare for Adam? I tried to calm my racing mind and focus. Focus on the now. I pulled the slim black phone from the drawer and turned it on. It had a battery installed and it lit up so it wasn't flat, yet, probably because it had been turned off. I breathed in deeply as I waited for the screen to load and come alive. Then I swiped it open. No password, that's bizarre.

Christ, I was terrified, my body felt shaky. A glance at the door, but there was no one there, of course. I went straight to the messages and saw a list; I opened the last one which read – *C U 2night. Sx'*. Is that 'S' for Sky or Soleil? She was arriving at night, but why use this phone unless he had been communicating with her all along and hadn't told me. He kept the past and present parts of his life separate; I knew that for sure when I discovered he had a deceased wife and a sister-in-law coming to visit!

My phone vibrated with a message. I quickly slipped Adam's phone back where I found it while I checked mine.

'What are you doing?'

I reeled around in fright. Adam was standing in the bedroom doorway. I turned to face him and touched my heart. 'You nearly gave me a heart attack.'

He glared at me and didn't move. I slipped his drawer close.

'Well, you've ruined my surprise,' I said, and dramatically sighed. I showed him my phone and slid my thumb over it to unlock it again. I tried to steady my hands from shaking as I went to the notes app and opened it. I smiled as I walked toward my husband and I showed him the first entry.

Adam's details – shirt size medium or 41, shoe size 9, sports shoe 9.5, pants size 34 or 87.

He smiled. I had written the list a few weeks ago when I was birthday shopping for him. I offered a prayer – thank you, God, thank you!

'I was just getting your T-shirt size… the only one I don't have,' I said.

'I'll pretend I didn't see it then,' he said and gave a forced smile.

I smiled and rolled my eyes at him. 'Yeah, surprise! I'll think about another birthday present. What are you doing here?' I asked.

'I left my gym bag at home and I've got two hours between surgery at lunchtime. Just going to get it and head right back,' he said, giving me a charming smile.

'Okay,' I said in a singsong voice. I felt like throwing up. I headed back downstairs, my heart beating a hundred miles an hour.

Oh my God, that was close. Did he see me looking? Did he guess? I can't believe I pulled that off.

He came down after me a few moments later with his bag.

'I'm off to have a shower, I've got to leave soon,' I said, reminding him of my shift. He gave me a quick kiss goodbye, and I watched him drive off. I exhaled. My heart was thundering in my chest.

Did he believe me?

The message on my phone was an update from Clare. She had inadvertently saved me. Except I had left Adam's phone turned on! I raced back upstairs and opened the drawer. The phone was gone.

Chapter 32

THEN...

Jessica

I got to work with plenty of time to spare and on seeing me, Oliver asked for a meeting with Clare and me to go over the Soleil stories. He took us to the café on the corner and shouted the coffee. Oliver seemed pleased with our progress, but he mentioned he was thinking of cutting back the stories if there was nothing new by the end of the week. I knew that day would come, but I felt like I was letting Soleil down.

On the way back to the office, Detective Nick called. This time, he was in my 'hood' and wanted to have a coffee catch-up. How much coffee can any one person drink? Several cups, apparently. I told Oliver where I was going and left him and Clare to walk back to the office as I returned to the cafe. Nick swung his car into a parking spot and I waited for him at the front door of the café.

We got serious as soon as our coffees arrived and the waiter left. 'I have something to ask you about Soleil's phone records,' I said, 'you've got them?'

Nick nodded. 'We've got them, but they weren't much use to us. Three or four of the caller I.D.'s were blocked, but the techs could trace most of them. Two numbers went to pre-paid disposable phones and we've had no luck finding those callers yet. The text messages said next to nothing and same story, sent to unidentifiable numbers.'

'I remember you saying about the burner, but isn't identification required if you are buying a pre-paid phone?'

Nick nodded in agreement. 'In theory, but unfortunately, it's not a very well-regulated policy. You can buy untraceable two-dollar SIM cards at the self-service checkout at the supermarket… no one is asking for I.D. Some sellers accept the credit or debit card that is used for the purchase as proof of ID, so you get people with false cards or false IDs able to buy a phone easily. Phones are also gifted or sold, and the original phone owner rarely knows who they are selling their phone to, and they don't care in most instances. Plus, some places let you buy a burner for cash – you know, a phone you buy and burn after.'

'So people with a burner or pre-paid disposable are most likely up to no good?' I asked.

'Not necessarily,' Nick said. 'Some people want a separate work and private phone and think that's the easiest way to do it. I have a single, male friend who joined a matchmaking agency and got a burner because he didn't want to give out the number that he reserves for family and friends; he didn't trust the dating process. I guess people having affairs would benefit from it too.'

'People suck,' I said, summing it up so eloquently. Yeah, welcome to my life.

Nick laughed as he thought of something. 'By the way, if you're up to no good, leave your real phone at home. There was a guy who the cops picked up for murder because even though he used a prepaid disposable phone to contact the victim beforehand; he had his phone in his pocket. It was turned off, but it was still communicating with phone towers, and his location could link him to a string of crimes. Keep that in mind if you decide to turn to a life of crime.'

'Thanks for the heads-up,' I said. 'So, you've got two numbers that can't be linked to anyone and they both rang out?'

'Or were turned off,' Nick confirmed. 'Why the questions?'

I stumbled and ran off at the mouth; I didn't want to give anything away. 'I was just thinking about Soleil saying that she had a new lover. I remember her friends at the hostel said he rang there. His number will be on the hostel's phone records. Soleil told me she was keen and she was even considering not leaving if it intensified with him, so why hadn't they exchanged numbers previously?'

'Maybe if he gave her a ride a few times or expected to see her around the place, he hadn't seen the need to exchange numbers. But, yeah, if they dated a few times before the night she disappeared, then it is odd they didn't swap numbers.'

'If they did the swap and they were texting and messaging, that would still come up as an untraceable number if his phone was a burner, right?'

'Right. What do you know?' he pushed.

'Nothing, sadly,' I said, trying to sound convincing. I know my husband had sex with a blonde in my bed or Sky came and rolled around on top of our bed for some unbeknown reason. I know Adam has a burner and was messaging her or Soleil, but that's about as good as my evidence gets and I'm sure as hell not telling Nick any of that yet. I was fishing; if Adam called Soleil at the hostel or if that text message was for her, not Sky, his number should be on their phone records. But obviously, they haven't been able to track that phone back to him; there's no record of him buying it.

Did Adam buy that phone to organise meetups with Soleil or have there been other women? Had he been talking with Sky for years? Within twenty minutes Nick had to go again, which was a relief as I wasn't concentrating. Back to the job, the fading Soleil 'Sunny' Reyer campaign.

*****

Tonight, when I came in from my late shift, something happened that I don't know how to interpret, or what to think about it. We have a landline and message machine which was a little old-fashioned, but as a doctor and journalist on call, it provides a back-up in case our mobiles were out of play. Adam had gone to bed and left a light on for me, but a message was flashing on the machine. I played it and it was Sky's voice:

'Hi Adam and Jessica, I've left my phone at your place. I feel like I've lost a limb. I'm spending a week at my friend, Cam's place. Darling Adam, can you courier it to this address please?'

I stopped listening. This was bullshit. Too convenient... what the hell was going on here? If that was Sky's phone I found, why call days later to say it was missing? Who can live without their phone? If Adam called her in a panic because I found his burner, what were they up to together that she'd agree to ring and leave this pathetic message that he wanted me to hear? They were in deeper together than he admits; they must both think I am an idiot. I no more believe that was her phone any more than I believe it belonged to the painter.

Taking a deep breath, I went upstairs to prepare for bed. Adam's breathing was steady, he had to be asleep. What a relief. The house was empty, just the two of us now.

If I laid my life out on a Gantt chart, it would be clear exactly when my life changed – I had a boss once who loved a Gantt chart. It was a sort of bar chart that showed start and finish dates. On my chart, skip along the dates until you find the row that reads 'My life is shit' and you'd be in the right place.

The chart would show that it all started on that first time that I went out with my work friends, a hen's night, on the weekend that Soleil disappeared. If I hadn't gone to the hen's party, our lives would have been completely different – Adam wasn't home that night. He had to leave for the airport at around 9.30pm, but I guess he was home until then, the quickest date in history if he was having Soleil over, but it might have happened. If not, he's bedded Sky.

If I told Nick what I thought happened to Soleil, exposed Adam and if it were true, I could do an 'exclusive' – it could make my career. I could win the coveted Gold Walkley Award for courageous and extraordinary work in uncovering the murder of French backpacker Soleil Reyer, at the expense of my marriage and reputation. It could lead to a book deal and a podcast! Then, with such a high profile, I could be courted by some of the biggest programs and stations. It would be a brilliant investigative piece and expose the fear, betrayal, heartbreak, ending in doing what was right at all costs.

But at night I would be alone. I'd find love again someday, but I'd be lying in my bed and he'd be in prison. Adam would never survive in prison. I felt him move slightly behind me, his arm reaching for me and his hand resting on my hip. He slept so easily.

Do you know what's weird? When I look back on our time together – my time with Adam, I can't think of any happy times. But I'm in love with him, so there must be plenty. All I could think of were the holidays where he was moody and dark; the reduced amount of sex I was getting; Sky and Chesley sharing our marriage; and waking every day to gauge his mood as it would set the tone for the day.

We're opposites; not one thing in common. We have the security of coming home to each other and waking up together. We have this perfect, separate life together.

Eventually, I must have slept but stirred when I heard something… I didn't know if it was real… like when you dream a phone was ringing and you wake up because it was ringing. That's what it was like for me. I could hear this tapping, scratching sound. I thought it was the builders, then I realised it was night and they weren't here; the job was done. I pulled the blankets up around my ears, snuggled down further. It kept going, knocking, tapping, scratching.

What, for fuck's sake? I turned around and Soleil was at the window. Floating, staring at me through the glass pane. She was wet, her hair plastered down around her face and her eyes were huge. She mouthed the words *'help me'*. I stared in horror at her and then water poured from her mouth. She was outside, but the water was pouring into my bedroom. I sat up in bed like it was a boat on the ocean and watched the water rise. I didn't move. I just watched it rise right up to the level of the bed. I was frozen in horror; I could hear myself making these strange guttural sounds because I couldn't scream.

Moments later, I was floating next to Soleil. We were floating on our backs and I turned away, but Chelsey was on the other side of me. She smiled as if she had come for me. Soleil reached for my hand and pulled me down. It was freezing cold and got colder as we went to its depth and it was so deep – there was no bottom. I tried to call for Adam, but my mouth filled with water.

I screamed and woke with Adam shaking me. I looked around panicked; the room was dry, no Soleil, but he was real.

'You were dreaming, it's okay now,' he said and pulled me into an embrace. 'Lucky that I was home and not on the night shift.'

I looked at the window, but no one was there. No ghosts.

'Lucky,' I repeated.

Chapter 33

NOW...

Coen

My fingers couldn't move fast enough over the keyboard to keep up with the download from my mind. Getting the history down, the words flowed, introducing the readers to Soleil and her network, getting to that fateful day of the disappearance. It was methodical work, but I found it hard to stop or walk away. I had to keep putting it on hold because Natalie was staying with me and I wanted her to have a good time. If only she had come before I got stuck into this story – now I was sharing my days with two women, Natalie and Soleil.

Cross-checking and more cross-checking – the media stories, the interviews, police reports, hearsay, Soleil's diary, interviews, casual chats and imparted information. I interspersed all these influences amongst my copy. Natalie was impressed and caught up in it, so she didn't mind my distraction. I was keen to get to talk with Jessica too, so I wanted this first draft written or at least the bones laid down so I could engage with her.

As Natalie and I had spent a lot of Saturday visiting the Soleil sites and going over the evidence, I let her sleep in on Sunday morning. I went for a run, finished with a swim in the surf and then came home and plunged into the plunge pool… holy crap, that was cold. Pulling myself out of its depths, I lay on the warm tiles around its edge and dried. After a while, I could hear Natalie rattling around in the kitchen and soon the smell of coffee brewing and toast cooking wafted out poolside.

I got up, wrapped the towel around myself, and headed inside. Natalie was at the stove and turned to smile at me. This was my dream picture… back from a beach swim and Natalie living here, cooking breakfast to share. Is there any more to life?

'Hi, are you okay?' she asked, studying me.

I must have had my dream face on.

'Absolutely,' I said. 'A swim, good company, breakfast being cooked for me, what's not to love?'

'I know, right,' she said. 'This is fun; writing, researching, living here.'

'Stay then,' I blurted out, then hurried to correct myself. 'Stay a little longer and help me research this book. We could collaborate on it. You'd have heaps of holiday time owing, or you could work from here for the month. You could swing that with the boss, couldn't you?'

She narrowed her eyes, thinking about it.

'So tempting, but I don't want to distract you from your deadline.'

'You've seen how focused I am, you won't distract me. Actually, you've been opening a few doors for me.' I gathered items to set the table on the veranda for breakfast, not pushing it but encouraging the idea.

'Hmm,' she said, 'I'm not good at impromptu. Let me process it.'

'Okay.'

She was leaving soon, so I hoped she would process it quickly. She served up, and I thanked her as we ate with a full view of the ocean in front of us. Glorious. She opened her laptop that sat on the table and found the page she was after.

'Did you see this one? I found it last night; it wasn't in your files.' She turned the laptop so that I could read the online story:

The Strand Times online

Strange twist in missing backpacker case
By Jessica Steyne, crime reporter

Detectives searching for missing backpacker Soleil 'Sunny' Reyer, 22 of Lyon, France, are to question her stepfather who was previously acquitted of murder. In a bizarre twist, it has emerged that Paul-Henri Masson was charged in August 1993 with the murder of a senior citizen in his capacity as a carer at a Lyons retirement village. He was acquitted of the murder on 13 November 1993.

Email communication recovered from Ms Reyer's online account confirmed her stepfather had suggested Ms Reyer catch up with a former colleague of his while she travelled in Australia. The colleague also has a criminal record and police are following this new lead to determine if Ms Reyer met with him, although they consider it unlikely given stepfather and daughter were estranged. Mr Mason and Ms Reyer's mother were married for five years before Ms Reyer's mother's death by natural causes.

Police searching for the missing 22-year-old said they would be 'looking at' Ms Reyer's immediate family circle as part of the search, which is entering its third week.

Ms Reyer, a backpacker staying at the Rest-up Backpackers' Hostel, was last seen on Saturday 10 September leaving the hostel to meet with an unidentified person.

'In an incident like this, we always look at relatives, friends and work associates,' Detective Nick Clarkson of the Strand Harbour Police said. 'It is a normal part of the elimination process of an investigation.

'We are aware of previous histories and convictions in Ms Reyer's family and circle of friends, and eliminating these leads is a matter of course. There is nothing to suggest any family involvement or foul play at this stage,' he said.

Share: Facebook | Twitter | Email | In | g+ | Add your comment to this story

*****

Returning my attention to my scrambled eggs and toast, I said: 'I haven't seen that one, not sure what became of it.'

'I can follow it up with Nick if you like,' she said.

'Sure, that'd be great,' I agreed. She looked so enthusiastic, but I couldn't decipher if it was to be on the case or to have a chance to talk with Nick. Hmm.

THEN...

Adam

Jess was on the afternoon shift, so I had the place to myself.

The hospital management did not usually roster me on to cover Sundays, so I could do a bit of gardening, go for a swim, just chill. Then I heard my phone ringing. Not my usual phone; the phone I used to keep upstairs in the drawer but that I now kept in my gym bag. I don't think Jessica saw it when she was looking for my clothes' sizes. I can't believe I left it on, thank Christ it didn't ring.

Why do women get so hung up about affairs? It's just sex, and sometimes you just want a different flavour. God knows I love white chocolate, but I don't want to have it every day for the rest of my life. Sometimes I want dark chocolate, and just a piece or two will do; makes me appreciate my white chocolate even more.

I raced up the stairs to the wardrobe where my gym bag was just in time to hear the last few rings before it went to the message bank. I didn't make it in time; I didn't expect to. How did I forget to turn it off when I charged it yesterday? Crap, thank Christ Jessica wasn't home. I liked to keep it charged in case I needed it to make an urgent call.

Grabbing the phone, I saw the missed call and that there was a blocked caller I.D. I hate that. I put it on silent, stuck it on the charger and put it under the bed so at least if I forgot to get it off before Jess came home she won't see it charging or hear it if it rings again. What a mess. These fucking blondes were more trouble than they were worth. As I pushed it under the bed, the phone vibrated with a message. I retrieved it.

Only a handful of people know this number. I called the message bank and listened. A female voice said:

'Hello Adam, it's Soleil, come home to me. I'm waiting.'

THEN...

Jessica

Clare and the other journos on the day shift had gone home; the early evening shift was in full swing. I had filed my stories and I was writing some unrelated extra bits and pieces.

My phone rang startling me – I'm jumpy these days; it was Adam. I had just taken a bite of a kebab but I answered otherwise he calls and calls.

'Hey, missing me?' I said with a half-full mouth.

'You're eating?'

'Dinner – one of the interns just delivered my kebab, bless her,' I said. 'What's up?'

'Someone just rang here and I missed the call. It had no I.D.,' he said. 'I just thought you might have called from your work landline and it was a blocked number or you got a call too? Just checking you're okay.'

'Thanks, I'm all good. Wasn't me and no one rang my phone,' I said, glancing at it. 'They're bound to call back and it will probably be a telemarketing call that you don't want. I better get going.'

'Sure, see you soon. Love you,' he said.

'Love you.' I hung up. Adam sounded spooked. Too many ghosts?

Chapter 34

NOW...

Coen

The next day, on my way home from sharing my scarce pearls of wisdom with my delightful students, I swung by the post office. I've had my mail redirected to there, rather than my personal address, it was just safer. Sometimes you get an overzealous fan but most of the time it was a budding author who has hunted you down and was sure that he or she will make it with your support if they can drop in and we work together. Scary, especially since I'm barely meeting a deadline myself these days.

The post office lady was cool and not interested in me. I wasn't special, she didn't appear to be interested in anyone. Perhaps she had grander ambitions than caring for her community and their postal needs. I felt sorry for the poor old fellow in the queue behind me who was charming and up for a chat. She gave me three envelopes. One was from Natalie's assistant forwarding on some fan mail that had come to the publisher's premises. Not much traditional mail arrived for me these days – emails, on the other hand, were prolific. The second was a contract for a Writers' Festival that I was invited to talk at later this year and the third was a small padded post-pack with no address. Hopefully, it wasn't filled with a white powder and death threat from someone unhappy with one of my book endings. It happens.

When I got home, I got distracted by several emails and Natalie, and I forgot about the small package until later in the day when I spotted it again on my desk. Natalie was on a call so taking advantage of my momentary solitude now was a good time to open it safely and privately. I cautiously slit it open and found a USB stick. It wasn't a secret that I was working on the Soleil case, so I suspected this was related… yep, I'm becoming a top-notch sleuth. Carrying on that thought, I removed the USB from the envelope with a paper towel so I didn't put my fingerprints on it – genius stuff – logged in and stuck the USB into my laptop. I dropped into my office chair, waiting and hoping it wasn't virus ridden. A watched computer never boils, or something like that… it eventually opened and on it were three very short audio files and nothing more.

I hit one after the other and played them. I froze, confused as a soft female voice with what sounded like a French accent said to me:

'Hello Adam, this is Soleil; I miss you my darling.

'Hello Adam, it's Soleil, come home to me. I'm waiting.

'I have a surprise for you, Adam.'

What the hell was this? I grabbed the envelope again but there were no markings. Why did someone send me these? Did Soleil send them? Did Soleil send Adam sexy messages? Were they having an affair? How old were these? What did they mean? Was she still alive or was this a motive for murder, Adam murdering Soleil? Or Jessica murdered a cheating woman who she thought was a friend? Or even the sister-in-law, would she have a part? Who sent these and does Detective Nick know about them?

I stood up and paced, so what am I supposed to do now? Reveal them to Natalie and then to Nick? Why weren't they sent to him originally? Natalie would say no, make it unique to my investigation and the book, but my gut instinct told me to tell him or it would cause a massive rift between us down the track. But then again, it was my clue meant for me. This was too big a decision to make on the spur of the moment. I decided not to tell either of them just yet; I'd sleep on it and run on it in the morning, then act on it.

Was this really Soleil's voice? And if it was, who owns these recordings and who has held onto them all this time?

I'm glad I'm a water guy because I sure as hell felt like I was treading water now, trying to bring all the pieces together so I could feel the ocean bed beneath my feet again.

*****

By the next morning, I had decided to tell Detective Nick about the voice recordings but not Natalie just yet. It might be significant evidence and I thought it was best to follow the protocol – cops before the publisher. When I rang, his young constable sidekick told me that Nick was in Sydney at a compulsory training and catch-up session. I messaged Nick that I had something and we agreed to meet for a drink. I was becoming weighed down by secrets.

Fortunately, Natalie had an online book launch, so she couldn't join Nick and me, which would leave me free to talk. I headed to Sandy's Hotel about half an hour before

I was due to meet him that night. As I entered, I saw Sandy talking with a guy who was setting up an amplifier, microphone and his guitar in the corner; I gave her a wave; she must live and work at her hotel because she was always there. I liked the atmosphere of Sandy's place; I felt very at home. Tonight, half a dozen of my students were there and they invited me to have a drink with them. They were all too young to remember Soleil. Those who were born in Strand Harbour were three or four years old when Soleil went missing. Their parents would remember the whole sordid affair. I happily accepted their invitation and diverted the subject away from me so I could sit back, relax, listen to them talk (research for my younger fictional characters) and have a drink.

I had just about finished my Coke when Nick arrived and I excused myself to join him, reminding them jokingly that they had assignments to do. Seeing Nick, my students started to organise a collection to bail me out. They were a good lot.

We picked a table and Nick settled into the chair opposite me with a sigh. It must have been a casual conference, he was in jeans, a black polo shirt and a jacket.

'Has Natalie gone?' he asked.

'No, she's got a work thing online tonight. You look like you've had a bad day,' I said, observing his demeanour.

Nick sighed. 'The training and catch-up was the usual boring shit but I finished the day with a dickhead drunk driver who wrote himself off on a street pole and I got to break it to his wife,' he said, and then he ordered a bottle of red wine to share. I'd get a glass if I was lucky, I was pretty confident Nick would polish the rest off.

'So we'll both walk home,' I added. He gave a small chuckle

and what looked like a relieved smile when the wine arrived post haste and he took his first large sip of the red.

'Going to eat eventually?' he asked me.

'Happy to if you are.'

We indicated to our young waiter that we'd look at the menus. After we made some small talk about life, work and our next triathlon event, we got to the main subject. Must have been a bad day if it took him that long to get to what I had found. He clearly didn't expect me to unearth anything revolutionary. I pulled the small padded post envelope out of my jacket pocket and handed it to him. I'd made a copy of the recordings on my laptop.

'What's this?' He peered inside. I filled him in and then he sat silently. I could hear his brain whirring.

'Did you touch it?' he asked.

'Just the envelope. Got any recordings of Soleil's voice that it could be compared to?'

He thought for a moment. 'Can't say we have. We never found her phone and it's pretty unlikely that friends kept messages from her fifteen years on, but maybe the sentimental did.'

'What are you thinking?' I pushed him.

'A thousand things.'

'Good. You're going to work this with me, aren't you?' I reminded him. He looked at me like he had forgotten I was there.

'Yeah, sure. In fact, let's agree absolutely no media on this. Only you and I know about it and whoever sent it, right?'

'Agreed,' I nodded, 'although I'd like to tell Natalie.'

Nick's lips thinned as he considered this. 'Risky. You know what will happen if it hits the media. The attention and pressure on both of us will overwhelm anything we are trying to do.'

Yeah, no Natalie. 'Let's keep it between us then and whoever you need to give it to for analysis for now, and let's thrash it around.' I wanted him thinking out loud, this was goldmine stuff for my book.

We threw around possibilities. And then I had to wait until prints could be checked and audio authenticity confirmed if it could be tested, but it's fair to say it opened a can of worms.

Chapter 35

NOW…

Coen

For a person who can't do impromptu, when Natalie made her mind up, all action broke loose. She insisted I spent the morning writing, as she placed a call to Nick and organised to meet him for coffee to talk about the case. He accepted, naturally. Hmm. She decided before she left to meet Nick that she would stay another week. So Natalie called her boss, emailed the office assistant to get some files she needed to be couriered to her overnight, advised her flatmate, and organised to meet me for lunch and to go shopping for a whiteboard. I was wrapped, exhausted and in awe. I'd organised to get changed out of my swimwear into shorts and a T-shirt.

What a pisser if I've invited Natalie to town, hoping to spark a romance with her and Nick gets the girl. Life sucks sometimes. Anyway, not much I can do about it now… a shame I wasn't psychic. Which got me thinking – was a psychic ever consulted, Lord knows they usually came out of the woodwork. I did a quick search online to see if I could find someone who stepped up to predict Soleil's outcome and bingo, I found it. Wouldn't you know it? Jessica covered the story, she must have been getting desperate.

The Strand Times online

Psychic blasted after predicting the death of missing backpacker

By Jessica Steyne, crime reporter

Psychic Deirdre Barnes is under fire from viewers of *The Day's Begun* breakfast program for claiming that missing French backpacker, Soleil 'Sunny' Reyer was dead.

Ms Reyer, 22, of Lyon, France, was last seen on Saturday 10 September leaving the Rest-up Backpackers' Hostel to meet with an unidentified person.

Ms Barnes spoke of her past work with the police in assisting to find missing persons and said she knew Ms Reyer was dead.

'If she had any relatives here, of course I would have prepared them for my announcement before going to air, but she doesn't, and I'm sorry to say the young lady is no longer alive,' Ms Barnes confirmed to *The Strand Times* after her breakfast appearance.

Breakfast host Anne Miller asked Ms Barnes directly on air, 'can you tell us where her body is?'

Ms Barnes responded she was working with the police but she believed Ms Reyer's body was underwater.

The Day's Begun's switchboard received over one thousand calls of complaint about Ms Barnes' revelation claiming it was inappropriate and could harm the investigation.

The Police are asking the public to call Crime Stoppers with any useful information.

Share: Facebook | Twitter | Email | In | g+ | Add your comment to this story

*****

Underwater. Yep, she's good this psychic. Strand Harbour was a beach town – that narrowed it down, phew, Soleil was underwater, thanks Deidre Barnes for nothing.

I printed out the first half a dozen chapters I had drafted for Natalie to peruse and mark up if she found anything that didn't make sense. I don't work that way and I don't like it, but I agreed with her that if Jessica met with me, and anything got unveiled, we wanted to strike while the iron was hot. I'm feeling the pressure. At least the first half of the book would be largely about Soleil and the investigation, so I'm presenting history and facts. Not much can go wrong there. It made me remember the good old days – my last book; it was so much easier writing fiction; who would have thought I'd be missing my serial killer character!

THEN…

Jessica

After hours in my head and days of analysis, I had one clear thought – get out of this marriage and this town. I was dying here. I couldn't pretend I know nothing or that I am not sleeping with a cheater and maybe, just maybe, Soleil's killer or co-killer. I didn't like Adam with Sky, the looks they shared, the history they had, something was not right there.

I knew I was risking my marriage for what could just be a roll in the hay, but now I'm not even sure this relationship was going to go the distance. I want to go back to the city, I want to feel safe, and I have come up with several plans.

Okay… *Plan One*: give the blonde hairs to Nick for analysis. He's got Soleil's DNA, see if they match. If they do, she'd been in my house; if they don't, they were Sky's hairs in my bedroom. Ask him to do it completely on the quiet – in fact, I won't tell him where I got the hairs from until his team analysed them. Journalists' sources were privileged. The upside, at least he'd have grounds to investigate Adam and I hadn't thrown Adam under the bus for what could just be an affair. I can then tell Nick about the phone, and where I think Soleil might be buried – a grave in my garden, the plunge pool for her headstone. Nick would arrest Adam; I'd break the story if I was up to it and disappear myself for a while. That was *Plan One*. The scary part was if Adam somehow got off the charges – would he come looking for me?

'If you went missing, I would look for you until the day I died.'

Would I be safe or, like Chelsey, have an accident? I'd always be seeing him in a crowd, looking over my shoulder or sleeping with one eye open. I'd be scared to answer the phone, check emails; scared to love again.

Plan Two: here goes… I disappeared. It's easy to disappear; people disappear all the time. Close to forty thousand people disappear every year nationally. I know, I'm writing the stories, doing the research. This could work. I disappeared and then suddenly the newspaper where I worked asked questions. Two young women were now missing. Clare would crusade this one, make it her own and take on the lead reporter role; it would be as if she knew me forever and could write from the heart.

The police had to investigate Adam then, even just to eliminate him. Everyone knew that the husband, lover, boyfriend, whatever, was usually the first person to have the spotlight put on them. Almost two-thirds of victims knew their offender – more stats I've uncovered. They would find my blood spatters where I left them; Soleil's hair too. Before I disappeared, I would slip into the conversation with Clare that I thought Adam was having an affair and about seeing the burner phone. I'd mention something about the plunge pool – how weird he was about it, asking me to stay home while it was being concreted. She'd get that and run with it, she's a bloody good journo. Soon, the police would uncover it all and arrest my beloved husband. They might re-open the Chelsey case in the light of one dead backpacker and a missing wife whose body was never found.

But what do I do then? Do I resurface and say he hit me and I ran? Then he's charged with Soleil's murder only. Who do I become? He might only get fifteen years for Soleil's murder or get out early on good behaviour and then when I'm middle-aged, I'll be on the run from a very revengeful ex-husband hunting me down. *Plan Two* had some flaws.

This led me to *Plan Three* – do nothing. Stay with my husband, turn a blind eye to his affair. Or tell Adam I know about his affair and I'm going to have one with Nick to balance it out. That would get a reaction. Maybe a very telling reaction.

Or *Plan Four* – call out his affair and ask for a divorce and head back to the city. If he has harmed Soleil, he'll get away with it. Surely he won't hunt me down because I want a divorce – he can save face and tell everyone I wanted to go back to the city, he didn't. If he and Sky have hurt her, they'll eventually come unstuck… they were leaving a trail. But I'd be safe. Selfishly safe. Sorry, Soleil.

Chapter 36

NOW...

Coen

Nick had no analysis back yet on the USB or the voice on the tapes. It was fair to say it was killing me. Fortunately, Natalie got 'home' just after midday and plonked herself down beside me, handing me my car keys. She saw the printed chapters.

'Oh, fantastic, I'll get to work.'

'No way,' I exclaimed, sitting back in my chair and refusing to type another word. Her face fell. 'I know you're excited about this book, thank goodness, but you've been out all morning sipping coffee while I've been slaving away here over the keyboard. You promised me lunch.'

She sighed and rolled her eyes. 'Artists, they are so temperamental.' Then she grinned. 'Goodo, let's go and I'll tell you what Nick said. I feel like seafood.'

'Is that what Nick said?' I teased, and she groaned. Yeah, lame joke.

'I know just the place,' I said, and we got organised. I made myself presentable to go out in public – clean shirt and ran a comb through my hair, then we locked up and headed out.

The *Pearl and Oyster* was a lovely little restaurant, and even though it was a little expensive, it had a Strand Harbour casual dress code. Perfect. We scored a table on the deck overlooking the beach; Natalie ordered a Chablis, I also got us both a glass of sparkling water with lime, and we got some oysters to start with. I could get used to this. I saw a few heads turn our way… just about everyone should have seen me in town by now, so the novelty was wearing off. I just hoped when and if this book came out that I'd still be welcomed in town and I would not expose anyone's favourite Strand Harbour resident.

Our drinks arrived pronto. We clinked glasses and toasted our health.

'Glad you came for a visit?' I asked, fishing.

'Hell yeah. But I don't think I could relax and do nothing, so it's been good having this project, your book. It's intriguing, I'm enjoying it.'

'So, what did Nick have to say?' I prodded.

'Poor Nick,' she sighed. 'You know, it must be tough being a cop with an unsolved case that just haunts you. He's had offers of promotion if he leaves Strand Harbour, but he said he just can't leave. Unfinished business.'

I nodded. 'Yeah, but it might do him good to get away and not be the cop with the cold case that never moves on.

'Maybe,' Natalie agreed. 'Anyway, I was right. He is keen on Jessica, but from what he said, I don't think that's mutual. I also found out he doesn't have her phone number. She had a work mobile phone when she was here and changed the number when she left.'

I swallowed a mouthful of my sparkling water. 'Bummer!'

'I know. I told Nick that you had as much to lose as Jessica, so you were hardly likely to risk doing anything crazy, neither would my publishing house. But he stuck with his story that he didn't have her number. I'm inclined to believe him.'

'You are worth your weight in ink,' I told her.

Our oysters arrived. They were delicious. There was nothing like sitting by the sea, smelling the salt air and eating fresh seafood. I could feel the sea and salt on my skin, so good.

'As for the stepfather and local criminal friend lead,' Natalie continued, 'forget it. Nick said it was a waste of time and the so-called criminal friend was in New Zealand and had been there for the past year. His passport was unused.'

'Well at least he's out of the running,' I said. 'Got another couple of leads for you to chase up in between proofing pages.'

'Great,' she enthused, 'shoot.'

'Okay, but we need to be very subtle, we don't want locals or the media getting wind that we are looking at any one person or event in particular, so if you could just say that we are checking back over every statement taken.'

'I understand,' she said.

With a sip of my sparkling water, I started. 'First one… Dr Adam Steyne, Jessica's husband, went up to Sydney to pick up a friend at the airport. Jessica was at a hen's party and came home later to find him asleep in bed on the night Soleil went missing.'

She nodded. 'I read it. He'd texted her earlier too and people saw her there at that party.'

'That's right. But he didn't leave until 9.30pm. Can you confirm who he picked up and that the flight came in that night and his guest was on it? Getting CCTV footage of him at the airport fifteen years ago will be impossible, but let's be sure he had a reason to be there,' I said.

'Sure,' she said, scribbling down some notes. 'I'll start with Nick and then the airlines.' She sat back and looked at me. 'So you think he could have picked up Soleil, had his way, knocked her off, dumped her, got to the airport and been in bed when Jessica came home?' Natalie summed it up.

I nodded. 'Highly unlikely, but let's pursue it. I'm going to suss out the witnesses who gave Jessica an alibi and make sure she was at that Hen's Party all night.'

'Ooh, a female suspect, that'd be great for the book,' Natalie said.

I narrowed my eyes at her. 'Remember it's not fiction.'

'Oh yeah,' she said, sheepishly, and lowered her voice. 'Still, it would be good for marketing.'

Yeah, I smiled at her – always working. I continued: 'I've had to rule our Julian from the hostel because his alibi is watertight. Everyone in the group he was with that night at the hotel could vouch for him the whole night.' I shook my head. 'Who'd be a detective?'

Natalie sighed. 'Much easier to write stories about them. Besides, we're asking a lot of people to remember stuff that far back.'

'I know, but worth a try.'

'Do you remember how long your talk was at the Byron Writers' Festival ten years ago or who was on the panel with you at the Sydney Writers' Festival five years ago?'

She had me there. I was desperately trying to recall so I could be a smart ass and surprise her.

I sighed. 'Fine you win.'

She grinned and polished off her last oyster.

'Don't worry, I'll happily ask the questions, but I just wanted to make sure you were living on Reality Lane,' she teased. 'What else? Give me a couple of things to follow up on. I work better with pressure.'

'Okay, do you believe in clairvoyants?'

'If I have to,' she grinned, and she held my eye for a little longer than usual. I didn't want to read too much into it, but it was a romantic setting, even if we were talking about a cold case, a missing girl, and a possible murder.

Delegating, I gave her the clairvoyant to follow up as well. Let's hope the clairvoyant tells her that love was right in front of her!

Chapter 37

THEN...

Jessica

Plan Four – I convinced myself that was the plan to go with. I could barely stand to be near Adam anymore; I had gone full circle. The things he said to me about not wanting Sky to visit and then he probably had her in our bedroom, on our bed. How they must have been laughing at me. I hated this house. I'm sick of this small-town, trapped day in and day out in this life. It's scary how you get stronger and grow from adversity, and I was getting angrier. Adam took me for some fool that he could cheat on and I'd just hang happily on his arm like a trophy wife. It's not even the seven-year itch, a long way from it.

Sky, Soleil and Chelsey were beautiful, nothing like me. But was Sky, even Soleil, so irresistible that it was worth losing a marriage over? Did they flirt with him and seduce him, or was it the other way around? I kept trying to remember what Soleil said about her *Matt*. She was keen; she liked him enough to consider staying longer, that much I remember. I guess now she's staying forever – three or more in this marriage.

Poor Soleil, I'm judging her unfairly. She may never have met Adam and if she did she may have honestly believed he was Matt.

Then I had a very scary thought. What if Adam won't let me leave? What if suspicion fell on him? Would he and Sky plot to make me look guilty for Soleil's disappearance? The jealous wife. Were they in this together? That phone call about the missing phone seemed orchestrated. I needed help. I was getting in way above my head and I needed someone to have my back.

A glance at my watch told me Clare was knocking off in thirty minutes but I was on the late shift; I had to see her before she left. I sent her an email and she looked over at me like I was an alien – our desks were only about ten metres apart. She fired one back asking if my legs were broken, and yes, she'd slip out of the office to meet me for a coffee. She hated to miss out on anything, and she suspected I had a scoop going on.

I told Oliver I was having a quick handover with Clare and picking up an afternoon coffee, offering to get him one which was a sweetener. My phone rang on my way out of the office to meet her; it was Adam – he usually rang before he headed home. I used to love the way he called me so possessively. I took a deep breath to calm myself before answering.

'Hey, how're things?' I answered as casually as I could. I was becoming the queen of casual. It scared me how I could sleep with the devil and put on this front like everything in our world was great. Meanwhile, on the inside, I'm boiling with questions, anxiety, rage, fear, uncertainty… a hundred feelings, some I didn't know what to do with.

'Where are you?' he asked.

'Heading out with Clare for a coffee. She's not happy unless she gets a double shot in the afternoon.'

'Thought you'd see enough of each other at work all day without going out for social coffee,' he said.

'It's work, a handover,' I told him. 'What's happening with you?' I diverted the conversation.

'Nothing. Just letting you know at this stage I'm on track to be home by six. Quiet day.'

'You've jinxed it now,' I said to him, and he laughed.

'You sure you don't want me to save you some dinner?' he asked.

I thanked him but told him I wouldn't be in until about nine. 'Go ahead and don't save me anything,' I said. 'I usually get a kebab on my late shifts.' I wonder if he was checking that I would not be home before nine because he had company. Sigh, let it go.

'Okay. Love you,' he said.

'Love you too,' I said, automatically and hung up.

I kept expecting to turn and find him right behind me, then feel his hands around my neck, or feel a pillow over my face, or be pushed underwater in the bath or pool when it was filled. I can't sleep, can't eat, can't function. I looked like rubbish. My work was suffering… all I've done today is drink coffee and plan my escape. That's not a day's work, it's a life sentence.

The time to act was now; every time I looked at his perfect face, I kept waiting for it to split open and this evil mask to appear.

*****

Clare had gone straight to the nearby coffee shop and had ordered for me; I'm so predictable. She looked like she had just pulled herself away from tinkering under the bonnet of a car. You'd never pick her for a journalist.

'Thanks for ordering, I've got to be back in twenty minutes or Oliver will have a fit,' I said, sliding into the booth seat opposite her. We knew our editor well, and yeah, he does freak out if everyone was not on hand as the deadline approached.

'Sure,' she sighed. 'So what's happening? Why did you want to catch up?'

'I have a hunch on the Soleil case and a plan,' I started.

Clare held up her hand to stop, and we said nothing while the waiter placed the coffees in front of us and we thanked him.

'Okay,' Clare said, 'tell me your hunch.'

'I'm onto something and I'm not sharing.'

'Well, thanks. Anything else you want to talk about?' She looked unimpressed, her lips thinned in a straight line.

I smiled. 'I mean I want to tell you, but I'm not going to involve you in case it backfires and we get in trouble. But I want to tell you what I've got so if anything happens to me, even if it appears natural, it's not.'

Clare rubbed her arms. 'You're giving me goosebumps, and I don't goosebump easily. I don't like the sound of this.'

'I know, but I need someone to know, please.'

She straightened, looking more serious.

'Sure Jess, shoot.'

'Can I trust you will keep it to yourself – completely to yourself?' I leaned forward to emphasise the gravity of what I was going to tell her.

She nodded. 'I don't like it, but I appreciate you using me as your backup.'

'Okay, in strictest confidence...' I looked around and

continued. 'I've got something that could incriminate Soleil's boyfriend or killer, they might not be the same, but I think they are,' I clarified. I had her attention now.

'You're assuming Soleil is dead even though you didn't say her "murderer",' Clare said.

'I don't know.' I left it at that. 'I think I've found Matt... the guy Soleil was talking about.' I took a deep breath. 'Clare, in a handbag in my closet, is some evidence that you won't need to access unless something happens to me. You promised me you would keep this to yourself, don't forget? I'm only telling you in case something happens to me.'

She nodded. 'I'll keep my word.'

I smiled and patted her hand. 'Thanks, Clare. In one of my old handbags, you will find a plastic bag with two blonde hairs inside—'

'Are you fucking kidding me?' she snapped.

I sat back and narrowed my eyes.

She cleared her throat. 'Okay, sorry, my lips are sealed, but you are asking a fucking lot.'

'I know. The handbag is a small silver bag at the bottom of my closet. They might not be Soleil's hair, but they might be.'

'What the fuck? Where did you find them?'

'I can't tell you that just yet, but you'll find a note in with the hairs telling you where I found them, and a few other things that I think are relevant. If anything happens to me, even if it is accidental, find that Clare.'

'Fuck,' she muttered again. 'When are you going to bring this stuff out?'

'When I know the truth.'

'Why not now?' she pushed. 'You should tell your husband, he's a doctor, he'll know what's an accident and what's not if anything happens to you.'

'No, no-one,' I said. 'I don't want him at risk,' I added. Ha, imagine! I wanted to say especially not him, but that would have let the cat out of the bag. 'I don't have any actual evidence and I want to give Nick enough to do the job right. Just trust me. Think of the scoop you'll have if anything happens.'

'I don't want a scoop because you know what that means?' she said, running a finger theatrically across her throat.

I nodded, feeling my throat swell. Then I smiled. 'Could be all melodramatics, too,' I said and forced myself to laugh.

She smiled. 'I'll be pissed off if anything happens to you.'

'Me too,' I agreed.

Chapter 38

THEN…

Jessica

All I was doing was waiting to get out of the house every day. I should have gone into acting; my performance around the house was truly impressive. Great life.

As we had breakfast together, I studied him discreetly – it was Chelsey's birthday today. He didn't know I knew, but I remembered the date from a press story. He was fine this morning, the same as usual. Maybe he wasn't mourning her or the pain had eased a little. Maybe he forgot the date and would remember it later in the day. She would be thirty-seven today if she was alive, eleven years older than me. I bet days like today still caused him pain, maybe they always will. He'd probably think about her all day, what they would have been doing if she was still walking the earth and how they would have celebrated her birthday, and how they did in the past. And then he'd look at me. I wonder if he thought I was his new saviour or a poor substitute.

Next week's shift was back on normal hours – what a bummer. I wanted those late shifts because I had time without him in the morning and less time with him in the evening. But, one step at a time; I was working mainly on not being jumpy because that was going to give me away, it was exhausting. But I feared him, hated him and sometimes loved him – those emotions were so entwined I wasn't sure which one was the stronger at the moment.

Oh, the irony… I asked for the dream bathroom but now I'm too scared to get into the spa bath and I never, ever, want to swim in that pool; all of which Adam seemed not to be too worried about. If only I could get away with not being in the same bed.

THEN…

Adam

I heard the phone ringing this time and got to it before it went to the message bank. Luckily, I'd just got out of surgery and was at my locker.

'Hello,' I panted.

There was a pause.

'Soleil?' I whispered, and then it was the French woman's voice again. I spun around. I don't know why… I expected someone to be watching me.

Hello Adam, this is Soleil; I miss you my darling.

'Who are you? What kind of sick joke is this?' I spat the words out, and then the caller was gone. 'I'll get you, you fucker.' I looked around. No one had heard me and I got myself back under control.

Who was doing this? What was this? What the fuck was this? Christ, calm down, calm down. Is this Sky's idea of funny? Could be a trap from the cops? Are they sending these messages randomly to people with dark cars, people who gave Soleil a lift, or the town's males to flush them out?

Stop, breathe, get a grip.

I went to the nearest window and looked out; everything looked normal. The ambulances were bringing people in, a couple was walking in with flowers, all as it should be. Calm down, it's just someone's idea of a prank.

What's next? Does someone think they'll bribe every guy in town and get money? That one of us will pay?

Jessica? Did she find the phone, see my messages? Is this her idea of playing detective? No, I doubt that. She's a shocking poker player, she wouldn't be able to pull it off, her face would tell me everything. Besides, when she found the phone, she would have gone into panic mode and a meltdown. Or did Jess receive the same call? Was someone trying to convince her I did this? Would Sky do that? God knows she's desperate enough... she'd think if Jess left, she could move in and stay.

Throw the damn phone away, I told myself. Then another thought came to me – could it be someone connected with the past... someone who has joined the dots – Chesley's death and now Soleil missing? They know about me; they think it could be me? A journalist, amateur sleuth, private detective, someone who hated me? No, that's too much of a stretch and they'd have a hard time finding the Chelsey stuff online unless they were watching me. Unless they were family or in-laws. Sky knows.

I rang Jessica; she was on the day shift and would probably break for lunch soon.

'Hey,' she answered, 'how's your day?'

'Okay. Just wondering if you got a blocked call or missed call just then? I'm worried it might be someone from home trying to reach me?' I asked, bullshitting to minimise my urgency for asking. I held my breath.

'Yes, but I had Oliver here talking to me so I didn't answer it, but let me check….'

Dying here.

'No, there's nothing in my message bank and the phone's ID is blocked. I hate it when people don't leave a message,' she said.

'No drama, it's just I've had a few now, so I thought it might be something pressing. So you'll be home about four?' I checked.

'Yes, and you're still on late shift?'

'Afraid so,' I said. 'Don't wait up.'

'Okay, see you in bed.'

'Love you,' I reminded her.

'Love you,' she said and hung up.

Was that caller intending to tell Jessica something? Imagine if they put that thought in her head, that I knew Soleil. Fuck, she'd be looking at me like I was a monster.

Chapter 39

NOW...

Coen

Monday was the day of the week where I put a plan in place – the work I wanted to achieve. I needed to do this coming out of a weekend, then the rest of the week flowed for me with my lecturing and writing. After writing my book for a while, I wrote the email that I had drafted in my head and sent it.

To: jessicawrites@outlook.com
From: Coen Watson
Subject: Soleil

Hi Jessica,

My apologies for the subject line that will no doubt bring back sad memories. Thanks very much for agreeing to talk with me via Nick. He's a good guy, and I'm enjoying my stay in this pretty town... a change of pace which no doubt you found as well.

I'll cut to the chase, Jessica, so I don't waste your time. My last book release burnt me out with its punishing publicity schedule; I needed to get back to basics and to get back to where I felt at home – by the water. A friend suggested Strand Harbour to me and the real estate agent found me a house by the beach to rent for six months; I now know it was your former house. Incidentally, several townsfolk mentioned they liked you and were saddened you left, and that they were sorry to see the good doctor depart as well.

I stumbled across Soleil's missing posters and the story unfolded. I started investigating and met Nick. Now, having read everything you wrote at the time, along with the police files and Soleil's diary, I desperately want to find Soleil, as I imagine you do to this day. I know you were probably thinking I want a bestseller, and that would be nice too, but I've got bestsellers. I want to tell this story. I would love to give Soleil a resting place if she has passed away – and that is the most likely scenario – and I'd love to give Nick some peace of mind and closure. I suspect you could use it as well.

So, I'm not out to write a sensational novel, that doesn't interest me. I'm writing a book covering what happened, who Soleil was, the frustration, the despair of the town, and the desperation of those who worked the case (and reported on it) to find Soleil. I am happy for you to read my work, but I'd prefer to talk to you before I finish it… your insights may change the way I structure the story.

Would you consider working with me or at least speaking with me now and regularly through this process? I have completed the early chapters, which were just establishment chapters to introduce the reader to Soleil and Strand

Harbour as it was fifteen years ago. I am happy to forward them to you but I would much prefer to meet. I can come to you, or of course, you know where I am.

My very best wishes.
Coen.

After I pressed send, I sat back and wondered how long Jessica would take to respond if she responded at all. Then, I saw my car turning into the driveway with Natalie behind the wheel, back from her hunting day, as she called it. She came in wearing an enthusiastic grin and bearing takeaway coffee, bless her.

'Can you break for an update?' she asked.

'Hell yeah, I'll just save my work.' I saved the file, put the laptop in sleep mode and joined Natalie on the verandah, accepting the coffee. Great view of the beach, magnificent view next to me, all was well.

'How's it going?' she asked.

'Powering,' I told her in all honesty. This book was writing itself; sometimes that happened. 'What did you find?'

'Nick didn't have the flight information in his file for Dr Steyne's guest – it was his deceased wife's sister, Skylar Kotze.'

'I wonder how they got on – Skylar and Jessica,' I mused.

'I can't imagine they were bosom buddies. Regardless of the flight information, Skylar definitely came to town and stayed for a short while. There were plenty of witnesses, including Nick. But she didn't arrive until after Soleil disappeared as far as the statements in the file were concerned.'

'Hmm, nice work,' I said, pondering that.

'Plus,' Natalie added, 'there was a guy who ran a servo

that told Detective Nick he didn't remember every car or driver that came in on his shift, but he remembered Dr Steyne came in that night for an energy drink. Adam Steyne was definitely on the road to the airport at the right time.'

'Why would he know Dr Steyne?' I asked.

'The servo is only about thirty minutes out of town and supposedly the good doctor had treated the servo's son for a broken arm.'

'Right. Handy. So, Dr Steyne was definitely on the road to the airport that night, but he still had about three hours beforehand, and he could have picked someone up on the way to the airport, someone hitchhiking. He had a dark car, not blue, but near enough.' I took a deep breath. 'In my mind, he's still in the running. So is Jessica. So is every transient person who passed through in a blue car.'

Natalie smiled. 'Stay on it, Sherlock.'

Truthfully, I had nothing.

THEN...

Jessica

Another day, another night – I'm losing weight, I can't sleep, can't eat, can't breathe. I volunteered for every extra hour I could get at work to stay at work. When I was with Adam, I'm willing myself to relax and to keep the hysterical tone from my voice. Every time he touched me, I was so angry I wanted to smack him. Even angrier when I thought about the night I was ovulating and he preferred to drink with Skylar. No wonder he didn't want sex, he probably had it that day! How many call-outs to the hospital were genuine and how many were bed-hopping? See suspicion, it took over.

Last night I awoke and Adam wasn't in bed next to me. Holy crap, where was he? Fear coursed through me; he wasn't in the bathroom either, I could see through the open door of the ensuite. What now? Where was he? I opened my eyes, slipped out of bed, and I moved to the door. There were no lights on downstairs, not even the glow of his lamp from the study. I moved back into the bedroom and to the window; I moved the curtain aside just a little and I saw him. He was standing looking down into the plunge pool, just staring into the earth pit. Soon it would be concreted, then filled with water. A watery grave.

I watched him, riveted; his face was unreadable – a blank mask – no anger, no fear, he was just staring into the bottom of the pool at the earth. Then he turned and went to the shed. What was in the shed? Had he put his second phone in there or was he getting something to bring back upstairs… rope, tape… I had to control my breathing so I didn't panic and start hyperventilating; I'm not a woman who can live on the edge. Chelsey, Soleil, what if he killed them? What if he's planning on adding my name to the list?

A glance at the clock – 4am. I was on the day shift but I couldn't justify heading to work at this hour. I didn't want to get into the shower in case – well, no one wants to re-enact the *Psycho* scene. I was so screwed; my heart was racing. He came back out of the shed carrying nothing. Thank God. I slid back into bed, closed my eyes and prayed. Ten minutes later I heard him come back into the room; I kept my eyes closed and tried to control my breathing. Impossible, I couldn't do it. I opened my eyes and saw him undressing.

Making a stirring noise so he knew I was waking, I whispered: 'Are you okay?'

He turned to me, surprised to see me awake.

'Sorry, I didn't mean to wake you, I just couldn't sleep and wanted to call in and check on a patient.'

'Are they doing alright?' I asked, knowing he was lying.

'Yes, stable.' He slid in next to me and reached for me. I turned so he could spoon me and I lay in his arms that I once thought were so protective.

Chapter 40

NOW...

Coen

The '*Week of Natalie*', as I was calling it, went past in a blur. Our days were busy... I wrote after breakfast each morning – we ventured out for breakfast twice – but then I got straight to work afterwards. Natalie researched and did her own out-of-office work; in the afternoon she would edit my pages and we'd talk about them when we had our dusk beach walk followed by cocktail hour, not that we ever had a cocktail, but you get the gist. If I was happy with her thoughts or changes, she would go into our shared folder and make those changes the next morning, otherwise, I'd add her suggestions to my list of reworks and think on them for a while.

Nick came by twice; I suspect he wouldn't have done that if I was working at home alone, but he wandered around the house fascinated with it. Clearly, Jessica never invited him over. On one occasion, we stopped for a coffee break and the three of us sat on the front veranda enjoying the view. I felt happy, really happy, with the company, my work and the house I had rented – I didn't expect that so soon as a new kid in town.

How does Nick do this job? Waiting for results – especially as a small-town cop – was arduous. I wouldn't have the patience. When Natalie went to take a call, he told me he had no news about the recordings, and I had no further contact with whoever sent them despite haunting the post office. Nevertheless, when Natalie returned, I put Nick on the spot about other areas of the case; he might offer more information with Natalie there, should he wish to impress her.

'What happened between them, Nick?' I asked, 'between Jessica and her husband?' He was elusive last time I asked, but I know him a little better now.

Natalie gave him a warm smile. 'Go on, spill it,' she said.

He couldn't help but smile and then took a deep breath before answering. 'I hate to add to the rumour mongering, and trust me, you get a lot of that in a small town, but it was big news at the time.'

I leaned forward, keen to hear this.

'The doctor was married before and was widowed,' he said and held up his hands. 'Don't jump to any conclusions, his first wife died in a fall that the coroner ruled was an accident. But his sister-in-law came to stay. She was a looker, and she was seen around town a lot with Dr Steyne during her stay.'

I nodded. 'Oh, the affair, how cliché.'

'From a writer's point of view?' Nick asked. 'Maybe. Anyway, I'm not saying they had a fling, but the rest of the town said that. Jessica packed up and left not long after the sister-in-law did. The doctor, who was respected and liked at the hospital, allegedly didn't want to be here without Jessica, so he left too. But...'

'Yes?' I said, probably too keenly.

'There was also a rumour and not one that I can substantiate, that he resigned with a push – the good doctor had been dabbling into the pharmacy supply.' Nick added.

I sighed: 'You can't blame the poor bastard. His first wife dies, his second wife clears out and he'd have seen a fair amount of trauma in his job.'

'Did the sister-in-law leave with him?' Natalie fired at him.

'Skylar? Let me think, it has been a while… no, she left before Adam and Jessica departed.'

Hmm, I gave that some thought. 'So, all of those departures had no connection to Soleil?'

'Not that I found,' Nick said.

I was just about to ask another question when he continued.

'I always wondered about Skylar; the picture that Jessica painted of her was interesting.'

'I haven't seen her name come up in anything yet,' I said, a bit confused about Skylar's intrusion in my story.

'That's because you won't find her in my file. Technically, she arrived after Soleil went missing, but if she broke up that marriage, why did she leave without Adam? I'm not buying her role in the split,' Nick said, more candid than usual – Natalie was relaxing him, I imagine. 'Something happened for all of them to clear out. I never learnt what it was, but it has crossed my mind over the years.'

'You think…?'

He shook his head. 'Nope, not thinking a thing,' he said.

I sighed and rolled my eyes. 'Anyone would think you're a writer providing red herrings.'

He laughed. 'Yeah? Anyone would think you're an investigator!'

We gave each other a sly grin. I left Natalie to see him off as I returned to my work and he returned to the cop shop.

Message check number 101 for the day... I was hoping Jessica might respond, but the week passed with no contact. On Sunday afternoon, Natalie departed. She promised to return in a few weeks for another three-day weekend if not longer... I lived in hope. She would have stayed longer, but she had two authors on deadline and she wasn't ready to hand them over to her assistant.

I waved her off and then the house felt so empty that I went for a run, and then showered, changed and went to Sandy's hotel for dinner – someone inevitably adopted me, which they did and fortunately, the older couple who sat with me was happy to talk about their Winnebago adventures and football. I had the night off from talking about writing and books.

I got home just before nine and took the rest of the night off, especially since the slave driver was gone. Besides, the cricket was on and the boys needed my support to beat the Poms. I made myself a mug of tea and sat in front of the TV when my phone rang. I answered, but the caller waited and then hung up.

Only a few people had this number. Did Jessica decide to call me and then change her mind?

THEN...

Jessica

Tonight I was going to look for more clues at home – I was wearing my investigator reporter hat. My shift finished at 5pm and Adam wouldn't be home until later; I can breathe for a while.

I logged out, said my goodbyes to the team that was still in the office, and headed home. It was still light when I pulled my car into the garage and headed inside. Normally I would go for a beach walk but I saw something in his drawers when looking for the phone – a small pile of papers and cards right at the back secured by an elastic band. I wanted to go back and look at them when I knew for sure that he wasn't coming home anytime soon, and that time had arrived. Placing my handbag in our room, I made my way to Adam's side of the wardrobe.

This was the act of a paranoid person, but I checked to make sure he hadn't placed a thread or something near the drawer which would indicate someone opened it. I know, I know, too many crime shows. I leaned down to the bottom drawer, pulled it out, and moved some of his socks out of the way. The small pile of papers was still there; I guess he didn't think I was snooping or he would have hidden them. After removing the bundle, I had a quick look in his T-shirt drawer where I had found the spare phone; it hadn't been returned. I suspected that might happen.

I took the pile of papers and went to my desk, which gave me a good view of the driveway; I'd see his car if he came home early. I took the rubber band off and read the first card – an anniversary card from Chelsey. She had written inside:

On this our first anniversary, Bear, know that I love you more deeply than ever. You are my life, your wife. Cx

Great, that's just what I needed to read. Nothing better for the heart than a good stab of jealousy even if the rival was dead; maybe it's worse if the rival was dead. Bear, huh? I wonder if that was because he's so grouchy, it suited him.

The next was a birthday card with the same message.

Love you forever, blah, blah, blah, *want to share this and every birthday with you until the day we die.* That could be arranged. There was a time when I wanted that same thing, once upon a time in another fairy tale. I glanced up to the door, then the driveway – all clear, all good. I saw a folded sheet of paper with her image on the front – she was so beautiful – it was the memorial service brochure from her funeral. No matter whether she was a threat, dead or alive, this was so sad. My God, she looked like Soleil. I folded it and returned it to the back of the pile.

There were several receipts: the settlement from Chelsey's life insurance, another for a car service, don't know why he bothered keeping that and then, holy fuck, I couldn't believe it… no!

I stood up and then bent over, getting some air into my lungs, panting as if I had just done a race. I reached for the receipt and read it again. It was a receipt for a vasectomy.

Stop. I looked away and looked back again. It was definitely confirmation that a doctor had performed a vasectomy on Adam Steyne. My husband. It was dated eight years ago when he was married to Chelsey then. Did they not want kids… did she know he had done this?

We had been trying to get pregnant and all this time he didn't want kids and thought he would just conveniently forget to tell me he'd had a vasectomy. I rifled through the rest of the papers; there was no receipt for a reversal. How could he do this to me?

Snap.

I heard it loud and clear – the straw that broke the camel's back.

Chapter 41

THEN...

Adam

There had been no calls from 'Soleil' for a few days. The tension was easing in my body or so I thought until today. I nearly ran off the road. What the hell was going on? Every day on my drive home from work, I glance at the pole and the MISSING sign to see Soleil the poster girl. Today, it's new and bigger. Is this some kind of joke? There's her picture with the large red word above it reading 'FOUND'.

Seriously! What the hell did it mean? Who had found her? Was she found? Who put that up?

Was it just for me? Was someone taunting me, knowing that I drove by here regularly, or was it a hoax meant for everyone to see? Had that poster been up all day? I haven't seen the news today. Was there a breakthrough?

I was almost home when my phone rang, the other phone. It's not linked to my car's Bluetooth hands-free; I scrambled into my gym bag to get it. I answered it just in time and it was that French voice again:

I have a surprise for you, Adam.

'I will hunt you down,' I hissed, but she, the caller, was gone. Was this poster the surprise?

Jessica and I had to get out of this shit town.

THEN…

Jessica

Angry doesn't come close to describing how I am feeling. This man I wasted time supporting, loving, marrying – and I didn't take that lightly – cheated, lied and allowed me to blame myself for months of failed pregnancy tests. This beautiful man of mine just lined me up like the perfect faux wife in his life. Tick that box, wife done, next…

Well, I wanted more – to be happy and have good times and be loved and romanced. To have damn good sex and to have truths spoken to me. To laugh. Ha, laugh, imagine that. To sleep safely and I wanted Soleil to be buried with dignity with her kin and with a headstone. You went too far, Adam; you threw back in my face all the love I gave you and now it was all going to come down around you. For the first time, I felt an allegiance with Chelsey and Soleil. I was now fighting for them – we were three women on a mission. The worm had turned. I wanted out. Actually, I wanted more than that. I wanted revenge, cold and unpalatable.

*****

Today Oliver called Clare and me into his office. He instructed us to cut back on the Soleil stories from next week; we had taken it as far as we could with no new leads and he was putting us back on general news. I would miss her; I felt like I had failed her, but I would not give up on Soleil even if I couldn't file a daily story.

But clearly, someone else wasn't giving up either. Just after 3pm, reception put through a call to me from a member of the public saying a strange poster was on a pole en route to the hostel, near to the café. I slipped out, told the boss I had to check it out, and taking the camera, I headed to the area. I drove up the road, counting off poles, and there it was. There was once a missing poster on this pole and now someone had replaced it with the same image of Soleil but the word FOUND. What the hell? People suck, who would do this? Is this supposed to be a joke?

I pulled over where I could see the length of the road and any cars coming and looked around for a moment, but no one was in sight. I raced out of the car, took a photo, and then grabbed the poster and I was back in the car heading away in a matter of minutes. Phew, done.

I rang Detective Nick to tell him about the hoax poster and said I'd send him the photo. After arriving back at work, I folded it up, stuck it in my car glove box, and headed inside. This was my secret now, until I investigated it a little more. I didn't want to give the prankster a platform just yet in case it encouraged him or her and took the focus off finding Soleil. People suck.

✶✶✶✶✶

The work day was done and on arriving home, I saw Adam's car in the garage. Sigh, reality kicked in and I entered the house of my cheating and snipped husband and called out, 'I'm home.'

239

He appeared a few minutes later; he didn't look happy; he had the furrowed brow thing going on. I kissed him hello.

'I'm going up to change, then let's have a walk or cocktail hour,' I said, keeping everything as normal as possible.

'A drink, good idea,' he said, heading to the kitchen. 'We need to talk.'

'Oh, okay,' I said casually, while my blood roared through me. I ran upstairs and got changed, constantly looking at the door to see if he had followed me.

We need to talk. I kept looking over my shoulder. *We need to talk.*

What if this was it and he finished me off? I glanced at my phone. Maybe I should call Detective Nick before I go back downstairs. My stomach was whirling. But what if he just tells me he's cheated?

Just go, just face whatever was coming.

I returned downstairs casually dressed and he was already on the veranda with our wines poured. That's a relief; at least he's sitting down and not hanging around the kitchen knife drawer or hiding somewhere – overactive imagination, not me. I joined him.

'Thanks,' I said, sliding into the chair next to him. 'Good health.' I clinked my glass with his. He was in his workout gear but hadn't worked up a sweat and he didn't smell like he had done anything.

'I've been thinking,' he started, 'maybe you are right. Maybe we should return to the city.'

I brightened – it wasn't fake, this could be a good out for me.

'Really? What has brought this on?' I narrowed my eyes and studied him.

He took a sip of wine before answering. 'I think both

of our careers may need a city boost. I need some new challenges; I'm sure you do too.'

'But we've just finished renovating,' I said, using his old excuse.

He slammed his hand on the table and I jumped. 'You've been nagging me to return to the city since the day we married. Now you want to stay?'

I swallowed. 'No, I want to go,' I said, in a calm voice. 'Lose the attitude.'

Tick, tick, the time bomb...

'Sorry,' he said and breathed out. It's what he would have expected me to say, I wasn't a total doormat just yet, and I was trying to be as normal as possible in an impossible situation. I cleared my throat.

'I just don't understand why you want to go now when you've almost got it all – the house finished and the secure job. You know I would go in a heartbeat,' I said.

'Maybe what I want has changed,' he muttered. 'We'll sell this and get ourselves a townhouse in the city, a bit of a yard for the kids or a dog if you like.'

'Then let's go,' I said, and I watched as he visibly relaxed.

Over my dead body, I thought. I hoped that wasn't an omen.

THEN...

Adam

I slept fitfully, stressing all night long about those fucking phone calls – who was playing with me? And Jessica was acting differently; I had put it down to her being freaked out about Soleil missing, but something had shifted; an undercurrent – confidence, no that's not it, indifference – I can't put my finger on it. Is she having an affair? Fuck, that's why she's not in a rush to leave anymore. I've got to get a look at her phone and if she was cheating, the bastard she's sleeping with better be sick of living.

Later that night, she took ages to fall asleep. I fell asleep and woke up twice while she still stirred – her breathing gave her away. About 2am she was finally out to it. Thank Christ. I rose, trying not to make a sound, ventured towards her study and saw her phone on the charger. I thumbed the screen open and went straight to the messages she had sent – a few to me about her work leaving times, a couple to Clare, some guy called Simon – I opened these, my blood boiling and read them. No, false alarm, he's the newspaper's photographer by the look of it. The text messages included addresses, the subject of the photo and times to meet her there. I moved down the list, nothing. I breathed a sigh of relief.

I put the phone down and took a leaf out of my book – I'm no stranger to hiding stuff – so I checked for her hiding places. I'd start with the usual places – her car and drawers. Has she got a second phone or any love letters? The drawers would have to wait since she was sleeping nearby. Next, the garage, Jess's car was unlocked. I always locked mine in the garage, but Jessica never did. Clearly, she didn't grow up in South Africa.

I opened her car door as quietly as I could, flicked off the interior light, and looked in the door pockets, and console and found nothing. Flipping open the glove box, I pulled out a large wad of folded paper. A quick scan told me there were no other phones in there. I unfolded the paper; what the hell? The poster I saw on the pole – *FOUND, Soleil Reyer* – did she put this up to get me and then pulled it down when I passed? Was she watching for me to drive by?

Maybe she's getting the Soleil messages too, and she doesn't want to tell me. Perhaps someone is bribing her or feeding her lies. If she thinks I am the killer, she's probably terrified of me, which explains the change in her demeanour. If Sky hadn't left, I wouldn't put this poster past her, but I saw her on the plane. She's gone.

I left the poster unfolded on the passenger seat; let's see Jessica's reaction when she knows I have found her out.

Chapter 42

THEN…

Jessica

The walking dead – that's me, so exhausted, but I managed to fall asleep. I don't know what jolted me awake, but Adam wasn't beside me; he was downstairs again. This time, as I looked out from our upstairs bedroom window, I could see the dim light through the garage window, then it went out. What was he doing? This could be the night – the night he took my last breath too. Lack of sleep was depriving me of thinking rationally. This had to stop now. I had to decide and whatever I decided, just do it and live with it. I loved him once, but I don't know him at all. I could almost see myself appearing in one of those documentaries – *When Partners Turn Bad*, or *I Married a Stranger*.

I moved away from the window for fear he would see me and I returned to our bed, listening for his footfall on the stairs. About twenty minutes later, he came back upstairs and I faked sleep this time. He didn't touch me and I waited, frozen and trying to emulate sleep. I was sure for a minute or more he was leaning over me, watching me. I was too scared to open my eyes, but I could feel his breath on my face. And then he moved away. My heart was beating like a drum.

*****

My eyes shot open like I was expecting drama; there was none – Adam was asleep beside me. As he stirred, I whispered I was going for a run and kissed him on the cheek. I couldn't sleep, so I may as well do something useful. I ran for about twenty minutes one way down the beach and then walked back watching the sunrise. The sea was oddly calm this morning, as if it was trying to calm me. Despite my yearning to return to the city, this was beautiful, breathtakingly beautiful. Soleil and Chelsey would never see beauty like this again and it reminded me to stop and smell the roses. It reminded me of how dangerous my life was at the moment. I realised I was thinking of Soleil in the past tense, accepting she was dead.

When I came back, Adam had gone. I took the spare key from our key hide and let myself in. He'd left me a note – they had called him in for an emergency and I breathed a sigh of relief; I could get ready without putting on an act that everything was alright, it was so exhausting. On a whim, I checked the garage and yes, his car was gone. I was being paranoid, but I thought for one crazy moment he could lurk in the house. Enough already!

An hour later, when I was ready to go to work, I opened the front door of my car, slid in and gasped. The FOUND poster was sitting on the front seat. I locked my car doors, locked myself in. I don't know why I did that, I just thought it might be a trap. He might hide in the garage. Why did he leave it on the seat? I haven't harmed Soleil, surely he can't think that I created this poster as some sort of stunt.

I unlocked the car door, raced back into the house and grabbed the evidence that I had stashed in my small silver handbag – I planned to keep everything close to my chest now, I'd bury it at the back of my desk drawers in the office. I was back in my car moments later, doors locked and driving away. I was so terrified that I'm sure I hyperventilated all the way to work. Now that Adam had found the poster, I didn't know what he was thinking. I had to tell him where I found it, why it was in my car. But why was he in my car?

Nick – I had to get away or go to the police station and tell Nick all my suspicions about the hair, the phone, the message signed 'Sx', Adam's pool obsession and hope I was right. But what becomes of me then? If the police arrested Adam, his lawyer could have him out on bail in five minutes because there was no evidence unless they dug up the pool and found Soleil. If she was really there. He was, after all, a respected doctor.

'How did this happen; how did this happen to me?' I mused aloud, as if saying it might provide an answer. You hear about women being in frightening relationships, but you never believe for a moment that you would let yourself be that woman. Yep, the girl most likely married a killer. See kids, it can happen to the best of us. I wish Soleil could just surface and then all I'd have to worry about was a cheating husband.

It was a relief to be at work and I entered the office and offered the usual round of greetings to anyone around. I placed my bag on the ground under my desk and put my silver handbag with the evidence enclosed in the back of my office drawer, then logged in. Oliver wasn't at his desk;

I looked around for him but couldn't see him. While my computer went through the motions, I grabbed my mug to make tea, and then my phone rang. Adam, and so it begins. I let it ring out; I wanted to hear his tone of voice before I called him back, but he didn't leave a message. I went and made my mug of tea and returned just in time to hear the phone ring again, Adam again. If I didn't answer he'd be suspicious. He might even come here. I let it go to message bank, then I messaged him straight back.

In an editorial meeting, can't talk. Call you when I escape. Love you, Jx

I'm an idiot to think I'd outsmarted a guy who could close down parts of his life so clinically and continue as if nothing happened. We were on completely different planets. I rose and headed to the I.T. department and stopped at Dev's desk.

'Jess, computer dramas?' he asked.

'No, just need to pick your brain if that's okay?'

He sat back, looking pleased that he was needed. 'Sure, shoot.'

I began. 'Dev, is it possible to file an online story as a draft and ensure no one internal or external sees it until I choose to make it live?' I asked. 'It's a police matter requiring complete confidentiality.'

'Yes, you can put a private tag on it so you can choose who sees it or only you until you want it to go live,' Dev said, fiddling around on his screen. 'Just here,' he said, putting to the private elective.

'Perfect, thank you. And to make it go live, I simply take private off and press the publish option? And absolutely no one in-house or outside the building can see that story until I do that?'

Dev nodded. 'Absolutely safe.'

'And can I do that if I log in externally as well?'

'You can. You'll get the same mirror screen,' he said.

'Thank you,' I breathed a sigh of relief.

'Anytime, Jess.'

I returned to my desk, gave Clare a pathetic smile as she headed out with a photographer. I hoped my smile conveyed '*hey nice day*' but it was probably more like '*I'm drowning*'. I placed my tea on the desk, sat, and wrote the story of my suspicions. It was a back-up if anything happened to me and if I was not around. Dev would remember that I asked him that question and could search and retrieve it for the cops, maybe. I'm covering all of my bases.

Oliver was back at his desk but he had his weekly conference call with the Sydney editorial management team this morning, so I knew I had an hour free. I finished the first draft. It would have to do, and I put it in private mode. *Done.* I was sick to the stomach; it made me wonder if I would ever eat or sleep normally again. My body felt cold and hot with flushes of anxiety; my breathing was like small panicked gasps for air, my mind raced continuously. Get a grip.

It was time to tell Clare more.

Chapter 43

THEN...

Jessica

About thirty minutes after I finished my declaration, Clare walked back in with the photographer – she wandered over.

'Coffee?' she asked, with a nod outside, and started walking towards the door like I had no choice. I grabbed my purse and followed. I caught her up outside the door and we strode to the coffee shop on the corner without sharing a word. We ordered and then we sat at our regular table.

'So, any leads on this Matt guy?' she probed.

'Nothing yet,' I said and sighed dramatically.

She nodded and accepted my lies. At least someone knew I was playing a dangerous game.

'Guess that's that. Love to know what happened to that chick,' she said.

'Me too,' I agreed. 'Drives me nuts. Must keep Nick awake at night.'

'Yeah, cops, who'd be one?' she asked.

We sat in silence for a moment, but there was still something I had to discuss with her.

'Clare…'

She said nothing, waiting for me, patient with me.

'You know how I said I was trusting you with some information but not to react or do anything?'

'Hard to forget,' she said and frowned.

'Does your promise still hold?'

'I'm good for my word.'

I nodded. I told her where the silver handbag was in my desk drawer and slipped her a piece of paper with the password on it for the story I had just written.

'Please don't look at either unless I disappear off the face of the earth.'

She nodded. 'Agreed. But the curiosity is killing me… I'm a journalist after all.'

'I know. But I promise it's not a story if nothing happens. There's more.'

She groaned. 'You are putting yourself in so much danger.'

'Maybe,' I said. Then, I mentioned the recordings, and the day that Soleil and I recorded them, and my part in using them to flush out who I thought was the guilty party – I didn't mention Adam's name but if she broke her word and listened to them, she'd hear his name. I told Clare she could find them in the same file as the one with the password.

'Tell me more about them, about Soleil,' she said, 'we have time.' She took a sip of her coffee.

I nodded and took a breath before starting.

'Soleil and I had fun, even in the short time we were together. One afternoon when I gave her a lift, I remember trying to greet her in her native tongue, but my French needed a lot of work; at least it amused Soleil,' I told Clare.

'On that day, she taught me a couple of French sayings that I could use with a lover.'

'Uh, huh,' Clare said, sounding suspicious of where this was going.

'She recorded them for me. One of them was "*I miss you my darling*" which is something like: "*Tu me manque ma chérie*" or near enough.'

Clare nodded.

'The other two were "Come home to me, I'm waiting – *Allé à la maison à moi, J'attends*" and "I have a surprise for you? *J'ai une surprise pour vous.*" So I cut those up, and sent them via phone to the person I thought was Soleil's killer to get a reaction.'

'Holy crap, are you for real?' Clare asked.

I gave a small nod, not sure what she would say next.

She grinned and said, 'that's brilliant.'

I exhaled with relief. 'Well, it won't win an award for best editing in a horror film category, but I did a pretty good job of it. It was weird hearing Soleil's voice, scary... I kept looking over my shoulder like I expected her to appear.'

'You are quite a brilliant investigative journalist,' she said, looking at me with admiration.

'Thanks. We'll see if it works.'

She gave a small shudder. 'Scares the shit out of me.'

'Me too,' I agreed. I straightened, cleared my throat, and felt better. 'So, what's Oliver got you working on now then?' I asked, diverting the conversation. The game was over for me. Adam wanted to move back to the city, but we sure as hell weren't moving back there together.

No, today was the day I was going to bring it all to a head.

THEN...

Adam

Lucky she sent me that message because I was going to get in the car and drive straight to her office. What the hell was going on with her? So she might not be having an affair, but what's with the 'FOUND' poster? I'm worried someone's filling her head with ideas; the same person who was playing the sick joke on me with the phone messages. Jessica might not tell me so that it didn't upset me. She's like that.

I needed to speak with her and tell her everything was okay; she can believe in me. I drove to work on automatic pilot this morning; can't remember getting here. I needed to find out who was doing this, fuck them!

When I got a break mid-morning, the first thing I did was make a call. Might not have been the smartest move, but I can't sit around powerless, waiting for someone to reveal their hand. I took my spare phone, went outside the building, and moved away from the entrance. I checked the caller I.D. was blocked and then I rang the hostel. The kid at reception answered.

'Rest-up Backpackers' Hostel, Lacey speaking,' she said in her high-pitched voice.

I took a deep breath.

'Hello?' she said again.

'Is Soleil there?' I asked. I heard her breath hitch.

'No. Who is this?' she stumbled.

'Are you Soleil?' I asked, keeping my voice low. 'Have you been calling me?'

'Who is this? You're sick, you know she's not here.' She hung up.

I turned the phone off. It wasn't her. She was too freaked out. If she had been making calls pretending to be Soleil, surely she wouldn't be so shocked, she would have sounded cagey, maybe defensive.

Who else? It could be Sky, but she wouldn't leave town if she thought she could get into my bed. I tried her number anyway, but it went to message bank, I didn't leave a message. That left Jessica and she'd never, ever do that. Would she? Maybe I've underestimated Jessica. She changed when Sky came to stay… did Sky tell her about my past, about me and Chelsey, about how Chelsey died? Sky would say anything for her own gain.

With a performance as good as some of my hypochondriac patients, I told the hospital administrator I wasn't well and couldn't be around the patients, and headed home. I would wait there for Jessica as long as it took. Driving into the garage, I could feel myself buzzing with… I don't know what it was – dread, adrenaline, nervous energy – I was wired. I headed inside, removed my coat and tie. And then I returned to the pool… the empty pool. One more week until the pool construction guys filled it with concrete and not long after, water.

I walked down the ladder onto the dry and hard dirt. I imagined what it would be like when it was full of water – cold and deep; it made me homesick. I lowered myself down and sat on the ground, waiting. I didn't care if it was dirty. This was the end of my road.

I turned at the sound of a noise behind me… that was quick. But it wasn't Jess. I was imagining things, shadows. I could have sworn I just saw Chelsey.

Chapter 44

THEN…

Jessica

Adam responded to my meeting message, firing back a note asking me to come home ASAP. I stopped, closed my eyes, drew a breath and opening my eyes messaged him back so that he wouldn't be suspicious.

Are you sick? I'll get home as soon as the meeting is over, about twenty minutes. Jx

He's sick alright. Game time. I was going to confront him and stall him, and I was going to use Nick to help me, but without telling Nick the entire story, in case I got it wrong. I hope it all worked.

I rang Nick and he answered on the first ring.

'Jessica, hey, what's up?' he answered like that more often these days, as though he expected me to have some big breakthrough every time I called.

A white lie: 'A guy from the hostel wants to talk with me privately. I asked could you be present and he said yes. Are you free to meet me at home in thirty minutes?'

'You organised to meet him there?' he asked incredulously. 'What if he's Soleil's killer?'

'Well, if you can't come, I'll change the venue, but he didn't want to meet in a public place,' I said.

'I can see you rolling your eyes, by the way,' he said.

I laughed. How bizarre that felt to laugh.

Nick continued. 'I'll be there, and by the way… not for publication yet, but the receptionist chick, Lacey, from the Rest-up Backpackers' Hostel just rang. Someone called and asked for Soleil and then they asked her if she was Soleil.'

What the hell? I got over my surprise and said in the best normal voice I could muster: 'Well, that's weird. What does that mean? Do you think it is related to the FOUND poster prank? You know about that, don't you? Did I tell you?' I couldn't remember who or what I told anything or anyone these days – my head was spinning.

'Yeah, I heard, and it might be related. Lacey said the voice was similar to the guy who rang Soleil for a date. She said he had a sort of haughty, upper-class accent. Not much of a lead, but an interesting twist.'

'Can you trace the call?' I asked.

'We're trying.'

'Hey, thanks for letting me know,' I said. 'See you at my place.'

'Thirty minutes,' he confirmed and hung up.

I returned some emails, stalled for about ten minutes and then grabbed my bag, told Clare that Nick wanted to see me about a story and bolted before Oliver saw me or she could ask questions. I got in my car and drove automatically, heading home on the route I had done so many times by myself, with Soleil, when I had trusted my husband. I'd have about ten minutes with Adam and then Nick would arrive. If I was wrong, I'd say the guy from the hostel didn't show and Adam was home from work early; if Adam was going to attack me, Nick's entry might be timely. God almighty, what a bloody circus.

I pulled into the driveway and saw Adam's car in the garage; the door was up, but I didn't drive in. Parking it on the driveway allowed me quick access to my car if I needed to get away. Once I used to be so excited to come home and find Adam's car in the garage and know he was inside waiting for me – this beautiful man and I were living our life here, until death do us part. I got out of the car and made my way to the front door. It was locked. I used my key and entered the house; I was shaking.

'I'm home. Where are you?' I called. The house was silent and he didn't answer. I felt sick. Please don't be dead… maybe it was best if he was… I prayed he hadn't killed himself. The thought made me stop momentarily in my tracks; I couldn't bear the thought of finding him and facing that.

I started again, slowly moving through the living room and made my way to the entertainment area, to our garden, to the pool, to where I thought Soleil might lay.

I couldn't find Adam, and then I moved closer to the edge of the dirt hole and he looked up and smiled at me.

Chapter 45

THEN…

Adam

Her eyes were enormous when she saw me in the empty dirt pool. I smiled up at her. I didn't say a thing; I wanted to hear what she was going to come out with.

'What are you doing sitting in there?' she asked. 'You'll get your suit filthy.'

It was such a practical thing to say that I laughed aloud. 'I was waiting for you. I thought you arrived before,' I said and pulled myself up from my sitting position. 'My mistake, hearing things, you know?'

She nodded.

I leaned against the earthy side of the pool. Jessica stayed silent. This should be when she asked again, why. Or looked confused; thought I'd gone mad; asked me what was wrong; what had happened; why I was in the pool in the first place; was everything okay; did something happen at work? I'm no expert, but I thought all those reactions would be normal if you came home and found your partner who was supposed to be at work, sitting in an empty pool.

But her reaction was what I would expect from someone who knew more. She said nothing, she just stared at me.

I breathed out. She thinks I killed Soleil. She read the messages on my phone from 'S' and thinks I did it. The FOUND poster was her idea to get me to react.

'Come and join me, Jess,' I said with a smile. She froze, standing above me on the opposite side of the pool. And then she said the strangest thing, it threw me.

'I found the receipt; you had a vasectomy.'

My mouth fell open. Of all the things she could have said, with everything else that was wrong, where did that come from?

'You deceived me, Adam.'

That's it? I thought. Not murder, not cheating, but the bloody vasectomy. That's what she's been so cold about… holy fuck. I've got this so wrong. Okay, this was salvageable, I can get out of this. We can still save all this. Fuck, I can get around this.

She started talking. 'You let me go through all those months of hoping and monitoring my ovulation, wanting a baby, wanting your child. Every month I went through the heartbreak of getting my period, having to start again, wait another month, live in hope, and yet you knew all the time that we couldn't.'

Tears welled in her eyes, my poor Jess.

'That's the cruellest thing anyone has ever done to me, Adam.'

I was staring at her, and I pulled myself together.

'Jess…' I cleared my throat, preparing to say something, trying to come up with some words. My mind was working overtime, I hadn't planned for this outcome. I held up my hands, trying to placate the situation. She just stared at me, looking down from the edge of the pool.

258

'It was wrong of me, the worst thing to do to you, Jess, I'm so, so sorry... but after Chelsey died, I didn't want to love again, ever. I didn't want to marry, have kids, have anyone I could lose,' I said and stopped to see how I was going. No comment. Okay, keep going.

'Then I met you, and I didn't want to have a relationship or love you, but I couldn't help it,' I said, with a small shrug. I gave her a helpless look, which I hoped would get me across the line.

She nodded. More needed; I kept going.

'I'm scared to have kids. I see children come into the hospital all the time; so much can go wrong and not just to them, to you in childbirth. So many complications. I just... I can't lose you and I can't face the risk of losing a child. I won't survive it.'

I let that sink in. That was pretty damn good, I nearly brought myself to tears – a few would have been handy, but I was as dry as a desert.

THEN...

Jessica

Adam. God, he was good. The lies rolled off his tongue so effortlessly. The Jessica of yesterday probably would have lapped all that up, bought it all – his need for me, his fear of losing me and how it would kill him, the vulnerability, the broken man – boohoo. I gave him a small smile, which he took as encouraging because I saw him breathe out. Then I came in with the killer blow. Let's start with my biggest suspicion and hit hard... Nick will be here shortly; he might even hear how this plays out.

'How's Soleil today? Still dead? You visit her often?' I asked with a glance to the corner where he was standing and maybe had buried her.

His whole demeanour changed in front of my eyes. He went from vulnerable to arrogant. His body straightened, his eyes narrowed, and he smirked.

'Just for the cheating manual, if you are going to deny knowing someone, then it is probably best to clean the blonde hair out of the spa bath,' I said.

Adam scoffed. 'Storing your evidence, were you, Jess? So you asked me did I know her, knowing I did just so you could catch me in a lie? Was that fun? Enjoy that?'

Shaking, I didn't expect him to tell me. In my heart of hearts, I didn't think he killed Soleil or Chelsey.

'No. I wanted to be wrong, Adam,' I said with sincerity, my voice hitched. 'Couldn't you just screw her and let her go up north as she planned?' I asked. 'I can't be hurt by what I don't know about. Ignorance is bliss and all that.'

His voice rose. 'That was the plan; she was supposed to hit the road, the stupid bitch,' he said, hissing the word 'bitch' through his clenched teeth.

'But she fell in love with you.'

He shrugged. 'There are worse things in life than dying, Jess. Soleil… Chelsey… at least they'll never know half of life's dramas.'

I scoffed. 'Good of you to save them then.'

We both stood in silence, staring at each other, tap dancing around the issue.

'I love you, Adam, I loved you enough for life,' I said, my voice trembling. I stood frozen. I should have turned and run.

'Oh Jess, that's why she had to go,' he said with exasperation.

'She was going to tell you and I wasn't going to give you up for anything. You're my world. That stupid bitch was just passing through.'

I was so busy hanging onto his words like they were a life raft that I didn't notice him moving closer, slowly, and then he lunged forward, grabbed me behind my knees and pulled me into the pool.

Screaming, my fear of this man taking over; Adam caught me hard against his body. He straightened me and held me tight against his chest.

Through gritted teeth, he muttered. 'I love you, Jessica. So what the fuck are we going to do about all this?' His hand moved up to my throat. 'Were you pretending to be Soleil? Did you call me with those messages?'

'What do you mean? She's messaging you?' I tried to raise my voice to sound a little freaked out. Acting freaked out wasn't beyond me at the moment. 'Are you sure Soleil's dead then?' I said and glanced at the edge of the pool. 'What if you didn't kill her? What if she's still alive?'

'Oh, she's dead, she's very dead.' He narrowed his eyes. 'C'mon, Jess, you sent those messages, didn't you? Why?'

Where the hell was Nick. And then my phone buzzed with a message. I pushed back from Adam and he released me. I grabbed my phone and read the screen. If I was a real actress, I would have faked it, but my face fell. It was from Nick. He'd been delayed and asked me to move the meeting to a public place.

I was alone with Adam.

Chapter 46

THEN…

Adam

I pried the phone from Jessica and read the message; Nick wasn't coming, no one was coming.

'Looks like it's just you and me, babe,' I said.

Then she surprised me. I've been around dying people for years and they fought and struggled for life, but as calmly as though she had nothing to live for, Jess looked at me and said: 'Can you take my life, Adam? Knowing I truly loved you for you.'

That threw me I've got to admit. I swallowed.

'I don't want to, Jess. I'd like to own this secret together and continue as we were. But I don't think you could do that.' I studied her.

She said nothing. She didn't start making promises, and I knew she could never stay in this house with me like nothing ever happened.

'How about a bargain?' I offered.

Her head snapped up to look at me.

'Okay,' she said. 'What?'

'You'll leave today. You'll tell your editor that you've got a family emergency – you know, someone is sick or dying – and you've got to go to them urgently. Then I'll call your boss in a week to say you're not coming back, you've decided you want to stay in the city. That we're separating, that you never liked the smaller town life, you're too ambitious. I'll put on the drama, the despair. I'll resign, say that I can't stay here without you… too many memories.' I confess my voice caught for a moment, and I swallowed. There was truth in this.

I waited to gauge her reaction, and she nodded.

'Those lies would fit,' she agreed. 'What will you do?'

'I'll work somewhere else in Australia. We'll keep our secret, our little pact forever,' I said.

'How can you be sure I'll keep the secret?' she asked.

I laughed. 'This is the part where you're supposed to be promising to keep it. You know how my mind works too well, Jess. You will keep this secret because if I go down, you'll go down.'

She nodded. I continued. 'They'll never find Soleil,' I said, 'but if they do, I have evidence of the phone messages you sent me. I'll tell the police it was a game for you. You caught me having an affair, you tried to blackmail me. You fought with Soleil and she fell, hit her head, it was an accident. But you said if I didn't help you bury her, that you would tell the police I had a history of this. I'll tell them I felt like I had no choice. Who wouldn't believe that feasible lie?' I waited.

'Yes,' she said.

Standing straighter, I rammed the message home. She needed to know I wasn't being generous, she was up to her neck in this with me. 'Make no mistake, darling, I will bury you in this,' I told her.

That was it. We looked at each other for a moment, our lives to date streaming by us.

'We're bound forever, Jess,' I said.

She nodded and then she pulled away and took the ladder out of the pool, her legs were wobbly. I offered her my hand, but she didn't take it.

She was leaving me.

It took all my willpower not to grab her back – to kiss her or kill her.

Chapter 47

NOW...

Coen

T he phone rang; I suspected it would be my sister, Carmel – she was the family member who took it upon herself to call everyone regularly. I didn't recognise the number, probably a time-waster, as Natalie calls them. But it turns out it wasn't.

'Coen, it's Jessica, I believe you are in my house?' she said and gave a soft laugh. 'Is now a good time?'

I think I froze with the shock. Jessica Steyne? Jessica was calling me.

She sounded older than I thought; I must have been thinking about her being in her mid-twenties the whole time I was writing, but now she would be in her early forties.

'Jessica!' I gathered myself, 'of course, now is good. Thank you for calling me.'

She laughed a breathy, sexy laugh… she'd be in the alto section of a choir.

'You didn't expect I would.'

'No. Well, maybe eventually, if and when you read the manuscript.'

She asked me how I was enjoying Strand Harbour and told me she read my *Reiker* serial killer series.

'I felt so sorry for Eloise. I wish you didn't have to kill her,' she said. 'I knew she wouldn't be able to redeem him, but I thought maybe she'd see the light and get away.'

'Does that ever happen?' I asked and chuckled. Then I realised that might be her story – *good work, Coen!*

'Yes,' she said, 'sometimes it does.'

I wanted to keep Jessica on the line for as long as I could, so I couldn't believe I had already potentially put my foot in it about women and serial killers, but she just laughed and blew it off. She sounded relaxed.

'So, what have you got?' she asked. 'I promise I won't reveal anything you tell me.'

'You're not working in the media anymore?' I asked.

'No,' she said and didn't elaborate. I thought I could detect a small accent, even a plummy sound. Maybe she was doing podcasts or voice-overs these days, her elocution was good.

'So, what have I got...' I said and told her about the people who had shared their thoughts and how much of my writing to date had been just getting down what happened, not so much the theories. I didn't tell her I was checking out her and her ex-husband; it needed to be handled sensitively and I didn't know how she'd react.

'Would you consider coming back here and giving me a hand?' I asked, a bit tongue in cheek. 'I've got a few days' commitment lecturing at the university, otherwise, I'm completely dedicated to this book.'

'It doesn't sound like you need any help. Besides, I don't think I could come back.'

'It's a beautiful house,' I said.

'Yes, I know. I have to go now but I could call again if you had a few questions, or you can email me anytime.'

'I'd love to talk again,' I said hurriedly, so uncool.

'Tomorrow at about 7pm, if that works for you?'

We locked it in. I was going to suggest a video call but I figured the face-to-face might be too much, too soon. I'd focus on the interview. I had more than a few questions, but I got her emphasis on the word 'few' and didn't want to push my luck.

*****

I spent the next day making a list of questions for Jessica and then narrowing that down to four that I needed and wanted to know immediately. She rang right at 7pm.

'Hello again,' she said. 'Do look just like your book jacket photo?'

'I do, believe it not,' I told her. 'I won't let the publisher touch me up in Photoshop. Fans get too disappointed when they are expecting Chris Hemsworth and they get Quasimodo in person.'

She laughed again. 'Hardly that,' she said, flattering me.

I knew what she looked like in her twenties – she was stunning – sophisticated, attractive, and natural. Now, she sounded like a confident woman in her forties.

We talked for a while about our day and it was a warm and comfortable conversation, and then she suggested I fired away with a few questions. Again with the 'few', and so I did, starting with the obvious.

'You worked the case; Nick says he has a gut instinct for who did it, but he can't prove it. Do you?' I asked.

I heard her draw a breath. 'Yes, I do.'

And that was all she said. I laughed; I couldn't help myself.

'You're going to be a tough subject to interview,' I said.

She laughed. 'I have a very strong hunch who did it, but I'm not ready to share that with you yet. That's not saying I won't down the track. Next question.'

'Righto. Did your leaving have something to do with Soleil?'

'In more ways than one,' she said honestly. 'It took a toll on all of us involved in the case.'

'I'm getting the feeling you are holding back on that answer too,' I said.

'Yes, but a lot of it is based around my relationship with Adam, stuff I don't want to share yet and maybe it is not relevant to your book.'

'Fair enough. Then you won't like the next question. I can't rule out Adam as one of our suspects—'

'Why?' she cut me off.

'He had a dark car, he had a few hours before going to the airport – unaccounted hours.'

There was silence on the line, and then Jessica spoke.

'Off the record?' she asked.

'Absolutely,' I agreed.

'I think you would be wise not to rule him out.' Then she added quickly as if she should not be too obvious, 'or anyone else for that matter.'

Message received.

Chapter 48

NOW...

Coen

The following morning when I came back from my run, I left a message for Nick. He rang back while I was having tea and toast on a stool at the kitchen bench, admiring the view. I will never tire of watching the ocean.

'Got something?' he asked, hope in his voice.

'Maybe,' I said. 'I spoke with Jessica by phone last night.' I had his attention now.

'Oh yeah? How is she?' he asked, sounding anything but casual.

'She seemed well. An intriguing lady.'

'Yeah.'

'She asked after you.'

'Yeah?'

'Yeah.' Good talk, bonding here. I continued. 'I had some questions about her husband and I wanted to know who she thought was ripe for the murder.'

'Did she tell you her thoughts?' I could hear the ice in his voice that she might have thought her husband capable all along and didn't talk with him about it.

'No... we barely scratched the surface, she doesn't trust me yet.'

'Right, yeah, of course,' he said, relaxing.

'I didn't mention the four-voice grabs,' I said.

'Bloody hope not, but it would be good to hear her reaction to those,' Nick said.

'My gut reaction... she's going to give us nothing.'

'Just like it was all those years ago,' Nick agreed.

****

I spoke to Jessica again that evening by phone – she rang me and did not offer me her number. I didn't tell Nick that she was planning to call again because I didn't want him involved as yet. Jessica might clam up and I need her to talk, journalist to a writer. I felt in my bones that she was holding out on me – she was formal, not unfriendly, but not forthcoming. After some chitchat for the sake of politeness – the weather, the beach, my students, where she was up to reading my book series – we got down to business, or rather Jessica did.

'I will not say anything today unless we agree on a few things,' she said, the journalist coming out in her.

'Go on,' I encouraged her.

'This discussion is important, but how it is recorded in history is even more important. Do you understand what I'm saying?' she asked.

'Yes. What do you need from me?' I cut to the chase.

'I don't want my conversation recorded and I want us both to agree on how we present my findings. If you don't agree to that, then let's just enjoy having met via phone, and I'll be on my way.'

I absorbed her words. 'Understood and I agree.' I said, 'However, in return, I request exclusivity for anything you are prepared to share concerning this case and exclusivity to publish anything that comes out of what you tell us that doesn't incriminate you.'

She thought about that for a moment and then said, 'Agreed.'

'Did you want to start rather than me asking you questions?' I asked.

'Yes,' she said. 'This is all off the record. It didn't come from me, but it's an exclusive and you can run with it.'

I felt my adrenaline rushing, the words were music to my ears.

'I think I know where Soleil's body is.' Then she told me her story – how Adam kept looking at the dug-out pool, how she learnt he didn't go to the airport that night, and how he had an affair. Afterwards, I sat in stunned silence for a few moments.

'So, I had no choice but to leave and keep my mouth shut or I would have been under the concrete eventually too,' she concluded.

'And you never told Nick this?'

'No.'

'Was Adam's sister-in-law involved in any way, do you think?' I asked.

'No, I don't know why she would be.'

'Wow. I can't believe Soleil could be in that pool shell.'

She agreed. 'Perhaps it's time the pool was dug up.'

Chapter 49

TODAY...

Adam

It's funny how some memories remained with you in great detail, like that night. Yes, I planned to do the airport run, but I didn't have to leave until 9.30pm. Three hours with nothing to do, plenty of time for a quick fuck and I knew just the girl for that. Soleil was thrilled to hear from me, too easy. I'd set up my phone to send a message to my pager at 9pm. I'd tell Soleil a client had been arrested – I was Matt, his lawyer – I'd have to drop her home and go. Then I'd head off to the airport. Bloody genius. Except that stupid blonde wrecked it.

I gave Jess a ten-minute head start before I got my car out of the garage. I hoped Soleil would not keep me waiting because I'll be driving off if that's the case. I drove down the street and there she was, standing on the footpath. She looked sexy in a short, red summer dress and flat sandals – fresh, tanned and glowing. She saw me and smiled a smile that would melt most red-blooded guys. I didn't have to get out of the car; she was at the car door and slipping in onto the leather passenger seat within seconds. I gave her a quick kiss hello, ordered her to put her seatbelt on and I pulled the car back onto the road.

'I'm pleased you were free,' I said.

She threw a sexy smile in my direction. 'You were at the top of my best offers list. Besides, my destiny is my own.' I think that was a hint that her plans could be changed if I, that is, if Matt wanted her to stay on.

Placing my hand over my heart, I smiled. 'Touched, I am, touched.'

She laughed. 'So, what have you got planned?' She twisted in her seat to look at me.

'Champagne, a spa bath, great sex,' I said.

She pushed her blonde hair behind her ear and shook her head. 'I wouldn't be upset if you changed the order a little,' she teased and turned to face the front again as we came along the beach road. It was dark now, but the moon lit the white horses on the waves. She clarified: 'I would be inclined to change it to great sex, champagne and a spa bath,' she suggested.

'Duly noted,' I nodded. 'I'm sure we can accommodate that.'

She gave me a look like she was seeing her future with me, so I brought our date back to reality.

'I'll miss house sitting at my friend's place,' I said, reinforcing that lie I told her. I threw in a sigh as I admired the dark view of the ocean as we drove along. 'One day I would love to live beachside like this.'

She glanced at me and I couldn't read her expression.

'What is it?' I asked her.

She looked away and then looked back at me. 'I just had a funny feeling during the week that you were married.'

'Married?' I laughed like that was such a crazy idea.

She gave a little shrug. 'You made a mistake.'

Fuck! Should I turn around now and drop her straight back where I found her?

'What do you mean?' I played along.

'You called me the wrong name after we last met in your car… you called me Chelsey.'

My eyes widened. 'Chelsey?' I made a scoffing sound as I pulled into the driveway and cut the ignition. 'That's a nice name, but I don't even know anyone called Chelsey. I should be better at remembering names, especially with my work, and especially with beautiful ladies, but I struggle. Forgive me?'

She smiled. 'No apology necessary.'

We exited the car. *Fuck!* I can't even remember saying that, but she looks like Chelsey. I swear Chelsey never leaves me alone. I held the house door open for her and turned off the alarms. I would have made more small talk, wined her a bit before sex, but she'd been upfront about wanting it straight away. Let's not kid ourselves, there's not a guy on the planet who will give up the extra foreplay in a heartbeat to get to the main event. I indicated the stairs and followed her towards the bedroom.

She moaned as we came upon the main bedroom with the beautiful view, even at night; the moon was suspended above the sea like a painting for our pleasure. I didn't put the lights on, we didn't need to and the moonlit room meant we could keep the blinds open.

She had a great body and her dress was off in moments, along with the rest of her lace underwear. She was fit and soft, glowing and exciting. We spent no time on niceties; we fucked, hard and fast and needy. After, we laid on the bed next to each other, staring at the ceiling, until she rolled over and put her head on my chest and sighed – a contented sigh. She ran her nails lightly down my chest.

'Good for you?' I asked.

'Very good for me,' she said with a smile.

'Happy now Miss Impatient?' I teased.

She smiled and pinched me. 'I wanted you.'

'Not complaining here,' I said. God, I was sick of dominant women. I stroked her hair.

I pulled myself upright, pulling Soleil up with me. 'Why don't you run the spa bath and I'll get us some champagne.'

'Yes please,' she said, and I watched her walk naked into the bathroom; she was something else. I stretched like a contented cat, then I leapt off the bed, and didn't bother covering myself. I was comfortable in my skin and walking around the house with nothing on felt very natural. I headed downstairs to get the champagne and glasses; I could hear water running upstairs in the bath Soleil was preparing.

I glanced at the clock, then checked my phone while I was in the kitchen and sent a quick text message to Jessica telling her I loved her. Minutes later, I headed back up to the bathroom with the champagne and two glasses. Soleil was standing at the bathroom window, looking between the timber blind slats down to the garden below. Established trees blocked the nearest neighbour, but the glow from the lights downstairs and the moonlight gave Soleil a view of the yard.

'It would be easy to get used to this life,' she said.

'Yes indeed,' I agreed. I went to close the blinds beside her and looked down below in the yard as I did so; it was a bloody mess with that pool undone. I snapped the timber blinds closed, turned back and as I poured two glasses of champagne, she slipped into the bath. The water had just covered the spa jets, so she turned off the taps and accepted a glass of champagne. I slid in beside her and we clinked glasses and sipped.

'This is so nice,' she said, sighing. 'Thank you for finding and inviting me.'

'My pleasure,' I said. We made some small talk, usually a requirement before or after sex unless you're paying for it.

'So, are your friends – the homeowners – building something in the garden? I saw some materials by the side of the house.'

'Building... um...' she caught me by surprise. 'Yes, Jeff the owner is putting in a pool. I'm overseeing it in his absence, part of the deal with me staying here. It's a mud bath.'

I drank a mouthful of champagne; I'd have to pace myself since I was driving. I changed the subject but she talked on.

'A small pool,' she said. 'Guess you won't be doing laps in it then.'

I laughed at the thought. 'No, not this type of pool, it's a plunge pool, small and deep. It's dug out; the concrete is being laid soon. They've had to cancel twice because of the weather and some other hold-up. Jeff had the right idea to get out while the work went on.' I added a sigh for dramatic effect. 'I'll do a bit of gardening for him, clean it up. Like to garden?'

She didn't answer, but looked at me strangely.

My brain was working overtime, like a Tetris game where little pieces were falling into place – what have I told her? It was Jeff, wasn't it, the name I told her for my friend?

'Are you okay?' I asked her.

She cleared her throat.

'What is your friend's wife's name?' she asked.

276

My mind froze. *Keep your lies close to the truth, they are easier to remember.*

'Jess,' I blurted out. 'Jeff and Jess.'

'Jeff and Jess,' she repeated. 'They are so lucky to live here.' She smiled. 'I have a friend, Jess… Jessica. She's at a hen's party tonight.'

Fuck, fuck, fuck. I didn't make the connection before – was this the hitchhiker Jess had given a few lifts to? What had Jess told her? That the pool was late being concreted, that she'd get time off to oversee it, who knows. Fuck!

My heart stopped. I'm not sure what I looked like, but I tried to keep a neutral look and not increase my breathing. Thank God the spa was going and it wasn't dead quiet in here.

Soleil continued. 'She was telling me about her husband, a doctor, and how they were renovating a house along the beach, putting in a plunge pool.'

I laughed. 'Bit of that going on,' I assured her. 'You only need to drive up and down this street to see the work in action. Nearly every beach house has a pool, odd I suppose.'

She took a large gulp of champagne. 'I'm sure,' she said and smiled. It was a weak smile. 'Well, we shouldn't stay too long in here in case we shrivel up.'

I rose and she said, 'Adam?'

'Yes?' I answered.

Then I realised what I had said and so did Soleil.

'You're Adam, not Matt. You're Jessica's Adam,' she said.

Then there was silence except for the buzz of the spa jets.

Chapter 50

THEN…

Adam

Soleil was staring at me as I removed the glass of champagne from her hand. She stayed seated in the spa; it was surreal as the water continued to froth around us like the charade hadn't stopped the date. She said the words again, slowly and deliberately processing every word: 'You're Adam, not Matt. You're Jessica's Adam.' Her eyes were huge and she glanced at the door and then at me, calculating her next move.

'Who are Adam and Jessica?' I scoffed. 'I have no idea what you are talking about,' I said.

I can't believe this was the hitchhiking chick and that Jessica told her about the pool, our house, and renovations.

I could hear the sound of my marriage tearing in two – Jessica would leave me if she found out about Soleil and I would not lose her, not for anything, not for anyone, not for a fling with a bloody transient backpacker.

Calm the fuck down, slow down, breathe.

I put our champagne flutes on the ledge under the window and turning back around, I sat on the edge of the spa, my feet in the water and looked into her eyes. I took a deep breath and I leaned forward and put my hands on her knees. I grabbed underneath them and pulled her legs straight up. She went down into the water, thrashing, trying to grip the side of the bath. I pushed her legs against her chest, keeping her head underwater. She was strong, but I had the advantage of surprise on my side. Soleil thrashed. She flayed, her hands beating the sides, her head trying to push up through the water. I couldn't see her features through the whipped-up water, but she struggled against me with all she had.

Fucking hard work. Die for fuck's sake!

I could hear a low growl and realised it was coming from my chest as I fought her and then she was still. I held her there waiting, making sure and releasing her legs, I reached for the spa button and turned it off. Her face came to the surface; everything was quiet now.

'You stupid, stupid bitch,' I hissed at her and thumped the water. If she had just played along, she would have had a great time, been driven back to the Y in a few hours and been on her way to Cairns sometime really soon. Now my night was ruined, and I had a shitload of work ahead of me when I had to leave in two hours. I thumped the water in anger.

Flipping her, I turned her over, face down, and left her floating in the water as I pushed myself out of the tub. I dried and put on a black T-shirt and black boxer briefs – the fewer clothes I needed to wash, the better. First things first – I raced down the stairs and out to the backyard. It was a cool night; I'd need that for the next hour. From the shed, I grabbed the shovel and slipped on my gumboots. I went over to the freshly dug out plunge pool. I jumped

279

down on the shallow mound where the stairs would go and dropped into the level depths of the pool. It was small and deep all over and the soil was only recently turned, so it wasn't too compact. I shovelled dirt like a crazy man; it was a blessing in disguise the concrete hadn't been laid; to think I was complaining about it all week. I dug a grave... not too deep – I didn't have time – just deep enough to ensure she'd be nicely covered until the concrete sealed the deal.

I dug with fury, swearing and cursing the stupid bitch who put me in this situation. When it was deep enough, I threw the shovel aside, climbed out on the dirt step mound and, stopping at the back door, pulled off the boots. I wiped my arm over my face, gathering sweat and dirt. Thank God the house was tiled, even so, I left a small dirt trail as I took the stairs up to the bathroom. A glance at the clock. It had taken me close to an hour; it was nearing nine. I had to leave soon. Fuck!

Sheet, I needed a sheet and grabbed one out of the linen closet on the way through – a black satin sheet from my bachelor days. At least it wouldn't stand out like a beacon if any dirt got moved.

I entered the bathroom, half expecting her to be there drinking champagne. Her head floated in the water, her knees and legs folded up. I lay the sheet down on the floor, put an arm under her knees and head, and lifted her out of the spa bath and onto the sheet. Fucking hard lifting a dead weight. I stood, got my breath back and then leant down and wrapped the sheet around her. I bent at the knees and hurled her over my shoulder. Christ almighty, the weight. As I carried Soleil down the stairs, I thanked God Jessica was staying the night at Clare's place and that Sky would get here late, go to bed and sleep in due to jet-lag.

At the backdoor, I tried to keep my balance holding Soleil and slipping on the gumboots again. I walked to the edge of the pool nearest the newly dug grave and threw her into it. It was then that headlights came up the street and turned into my property.

I froze.

I'm a goner.

This is the end. After all I had lived through, it was going to be over for me.

The car didn't move into the garage but pulled up out the front of my house. It was black. I couldn't see who was behind the wheel and then the door opened and I saw the driver in the light. It wasn't Jessica. It was Skylar!

Fuck, fuck! I panicked and looked down into the pool where Soleil lay wrapped in a sheet. I was filthy and sweaty and Skylar was coming up the driveway. She saw me and grinned, opening her arms wide for a hug. Stunned, I moved towards her, away from the pool, and returned her embrace.

'My flight got in hours ago, so I thought I'd hire a car, get here myself and surprise you! Why are you filthy?' She glanced over my shoulder and looked down into the pool. In the moonlight, she could make out the figure on the earth at the bottom of the plunge pool. It was obviously a body wrapped up.

'Adam, what have you done?'

Chapter 51

TODAY...

Coen

I rang Nick and he came straight over. I told him everything. He wanted to call Jessica immediately, but I could truthfully say I didn't have her phone number. I understood now why Adam didn't want to sell the house, the last thing you'd want was a new owner doing renovations, especially around the pool.

Nick secured a search warrant for the property and I stayed around for the dig... professional curiosity and a front-row seat to the pool being ripped up. The reason for the dig was leaked and the media went crazy – the population of Strand Harbour doubled. It was no surprise that Jessica didn't call me again when she saw that unfolding.

I stayed in the house... I suspect many people found that morbid, but I also had quite a few people who offered to come and stay with me. People, we're a funny lot.

For the day of the dig, there was a large gathering of people outside the fence boundaries, waiting for news and a huge media scrum. Some people brought flowers in case we found Soleil. I gave up trying to go anywhere and resigned myself to writing inside, often with Nick for company, but truth be known, I didn't want to leave the premises. This was my reward and the setting created the ambience for my book. Natalie couldn't believe it. I think she wanted to come back to stay with me while it all unfolded, but we both agreed that having a publisher there might be in poor taste as if we were hoping for the news that would make the book a bestseller.

After the concrete was broken, Nick and I were on-site, right beside the pool, or as close as I could get. I took photos and video. I prayed Jessica wasn't wrong… not only because everyone, including me and especially Nick, wanted to find Soleil, but I'd have serious egg on my face if her bones weren't there.

Soleil's clothes, bag and phone were found first in a shallow grave. The dig kept going, and then there was a cry to stop and bones were revealed. Nick turned to me.

'We've found her,' he exhaled. 'You've found her,' he added.

I shook my head, looking down into the pool grave with dismay. 'It was Jessica. I'm just the agitator. If she had told you her suspicions twenty years ago, all those years of pain would have been avoided.' I looked at him. 'For Soleil's friends and family, and you.'

'Even if she had just hinted at it,' he agreed, 'sent me an anonymous tip, anything.'

I swear, right in front of my eyes, those twenty years of stress fell off Nick's shoulders. He looked like a man freed.

It took several days before we received the coroner's news. The bones weren't Soleil's.

Chapter 52

NOW...

Coen

I was at my desk writing what had unfolded when Nick pulled into the driveway in his cop car. I saved my work, ran downstairs to unlock the front door – which I had to do these days with all the 'tourists' checking out the death house – and I invited him in, following him back upstairs. Something wasn't right. He looked like a man with bad news.

'What's going on?' I asked, now worried and thinking about my elderly folks and family. Had someone died and he was sent to tell me? Cops are usually given the death knock duty.

He spun around when we got into the living room.

'It's not Soleil.'

My mouth dropped open and I glared at him, stunned.

He repeated himself. 'The woman lying in the pool grave was not Soleil.'

I sat down on the couch behind me; it was well placed for a man in shock.

'Who is it then?' I asked, my voice laced with dread.

Nick sat opposite and cleared his throat. 'It's Jessica. Adam Steyne's wife, Jessica.'

Jessica Steyne was dead.

Beautiful, talented Jessica was buried below the pool.

I rose and put my hands behind my head. How is this possible? I didn't know what to do initially. I think I paced around for a few hours after Nick left. He was shattered. And then, I wrote an email to the person I had been corresponding with by phone and email.

'*Who are you?*'

And again later that day… '*Who are you?*'

And again, and again.

'*Who are you?*'

'*Who are you?*'

'*Who are you?*'

But no answer came, ever.

THEN…

Adam

In the early hours of the morning, I woke with a start; Jessica was getting into bed beside me. Jesus Christ, I thought it was Soleil for a moment. My heart was racing.

'You're home,' I said, realising what was happening. Holy fuck, thank God I thought I had to go to the airport and get Sky, or Soleil might have stayed the night with me… technically she did, but not in my bed. Fair to say that's one of Soleil's dates that didn't go well.

'I missed you, I wanted to come home,' Jessica said, sleepily.

I glanced at the clock; 2am. I pulled Jess into my arms and cocooned her. I felt her body relax.

'I missed you too,' I whispered.

'I love you,' she said.

Eventually, I slept. Until the phone started ringing. I can't believe that Jessica bought the painter's phone story when Soleil's phone rang… must have been one of Soleil's Y friends looking for her! I played casual, closed my eyes and pretended to sleep, all the time raging and waiting until Jessica's breathing became steady and I knew she was asleep again. I wasn't expecting Sky up for hours. I snuck out of bed and did my checks again in the morning light – the bedroom and ensuite, the living areas and around the pool deck; everything looked clean and unmarked. I made my way up to the new bedroom, grabbed Soleil's gear, turned the phone off and I checked the hallway was clear.

I raced downstairs with Soleil's bag, grabbed the broom by the back door and headed out to the shed, hiding Soleil's pack behind the toolbox. Jessica won't look there. I'll bury it in the pool dirt when Jessica leaves for work – for the love of God, I just want a simple life. I returned the broom to where I found it. I took a deep breath, everything was okay.

I left the shed and casually walked over to the pool in case Jessica got up and saw me from the bathroom window. I looked around it and the yard, pretending to be inspecting everything. There was a dirt trail but nothing that would raise suspicion. The night frost had levelled out the colour of the dirt on the base of the pool nicely.

Nothing protruding because nothing was there, thanks to Skylar. It was a good night's work. I thought it was over, my life, my freedom, but just like she did with her sister, Sky gave me a grin like it was another great chance to conspire.

Once I told her the story, hurriedly, briefly, with enough spin so that she thought I was some poor sad bastard having a flashback to my days with her and Chelsey, she had a better plan.

'If anyone associates you with that girl, the first place they're going to look is the pool,' she said. 'She drowned, right?'

I nodded.

'Get her out of there and in my hire car. Where can we take her where her body won't wash up?'

'I've got just the place, near a blowhole, there are always rips. She'll be washed out to sea and be fish bait in no time,' I said and jumped down the ladder into the pool again.

'Bring something to weigh her down,' Skylar suggested.

Christ, I can't believe we were having this discussion so practically, like it was something we did together every day. I was running on adrenaline, Sky was running on power – she had something over me, again.

I hadn't filled in the grave yet, I'd do that when we got back. I grabbed Soleil's body; she hadn't got any lighter. I heaved her up and out of the pool, climbed up and threw her over my shoulder, steadying myself. Skylar brought her car into the garage, and no one saw the movement of the "parcel" from the pool to the car. Let's just hope we don't get pulled over by the police. I asked Skylar to wait while I went back into the house and cleaned up. She followed me in.

I raced upstairs. The bed was okay; I had worn a condom so there was no wet patch or telling signs. I quickly scanned for telltale blonde hair and re-made it. I grabbed Soleil's handbag, shoes, dress and underwear and stuffed them all in a plastic bag and tied it, taking the package up the steps to the recent additions – the second and third bedrooms. I entered the second room and threw the bag on the top shelf of the built-in wardrobe, pushing it to the back out of sight. I'd get rid of it tomorrow, bury it in the pool when I'm home alone. Hopefully, the sea creatures will dispose of Soleil's body, and no one will ever find her package of clothes once concreted into my pool. Job done.

I retraced all my steps ending up downstairs and again wiped any marks I had left on the stairs and through the living areas. Skylar had already cleaned up some of my dirty footprints. I grabbed my car keys, wallet and phone and followed her to the hire car.

I checked my phone and Jess had returned my message. *Love U darling. Miss U heaps, C U 2morrow, Jxx.* The whole thing was surreal. Sky and I drove as normally as we could. I was spent in more ways than one. I felt like I was on speed; I knew soon I would hit a wall and be exhausted, but I was still operating on an adrenalin high. What a disaster of a night. Soleil left me with no choice. She would have told Jess or ruined my reputation, and a man with a dead wife doesn't need more attention focused on him – I've worked too long and hard to have some bloody transient chick pull my life to pieces.

Soleil was a lot like Chelsey – not just because they had that tall, blonde, tanned thing going on and they waxed everything off and I mean everything – but they were both so self-assured. An attractive quality in a woman; it makes you want to own them and control them.

I couldn't believe Skylar needed petrol, but she stayed out of sight while I filled it and grabbed a drink. I only bought one given I was the only one that could be seen; we can share. I didn't realise later how well that would serve me as my alibi, driving to the airport to pick up Skylar.

'I'll call you, don't answer,' she said as we drove away from the servo.

I wasn't sure what she was doing, but then it became clearer.

'Hi Adam, darling, it's Sky. I'm arriving earlier, I hope I haven't missed you. I'll see you at your place.'

'You're a born criminal,' I told her and she laughed.

'Takes one to know one. Now if anyone asks, you got the message on the way and turned around. But can we fool your wife?'

I scoffed. 'Jessica is the most trusting soul you'll ever meet. You'll see.'

So kind, so trusting, so loving. I couldn't let her leave me.

Chapter 53

NOW...

Coen

The police on the other side of the country had issued a warrant for Dr Adam Steyne. In the interim, Nick traced the source of my 'Jessica' email correspondent, and the truth blew us away. Another unlikely source also helped blow the case wide open. Clare. The journalist who had worked with Jessica all those years ago.

The day after Jessica's body was identified, we met at the police station, the three of us – Nick, Clare and me – in a meeting room. Clare had a small silver handbag with her and a USB stick. We were a motley crew – Nick was in a dishevelled suit and looked like he hadn't shaved for a month, I was in jeans and a black T-shirt and my eyes were as dark as my shirt from lack of sleep, and Clare looked like a farmer, in jeans and a checkered cotton shirt.

'I sent the audio tape to you,' she started.

My jaw dropped in surprise. 'Why? How did you have it?' I asked.

Nick held up his hand. 'Can we start at the beginning?' He turned to Clare. 'The very beginning.'

She nodded and took a deep breath.

'Just before Jessica left town, she made a discovery. She gave me some items to mind in case she ever went missing.'

'Jesus, and you never thought to share?' Nick said.

'She never went missing,' Clare said. 'You told me you corresponded with her.'

Nick held up his hands in apology. 'Sorry, please continue.'

Clare gave a nod. 'Jessica said she thought she had found out who murdered Soleil, but she was short on evidence. She was going to meet you when she confronted the killer and if that person came clean, you'd be there.'

Nick groaned and ran a hand over his mouth. 'That was the day, it was a misunderstanding… never mind.'

'When she left town suddenly, I assumed she'd got it wrong,' Clare continued her story. 'I waited for her to contact me but she didn't. So, I grabbed the handbag she had in her bottom drawer and emailed the password-protected document she wrote to myself at home. That's it on the USB,' Clare said and pushed it to Nick. 'Here's a hard copy for you.' She gave it to me.

'It outlines her suspicions of her husband. She thinks he was having an affair with Soleil but he swore black and blue he'd never met her.' She opened the silver handbag and slipped a small plastic envelope to Nick that looked empty.

'Hair that she found in her bed and bathroom that she thought belonged to Soleil.'

'Christ,' Nick swore.

'We still haven't found Soleil,' I said, pointing out the obvious.

'And she's definitely not buried under that pool,' Nick said.

That was the truth. The pool was demolished and dug down to a depth way past what a man with a shovel could achieve.

Nick continued. 'But with Soleil's clothes and phone bundle buried there, and with Jessica's body now identified, Adam Steyne's as good as going away forever.'

Clare asked what we both wanted to know.

'Who were you emailing all those years?' she asked Nick.

His breath hitched as if he was mortified or embarrassed. 'The email address I was using was created after Jessica "left town". She contacted me to say sorry that she had run out without saying goodbye. We didn't correspond much, maybe twice a year to just say hi. It's the same one Coen was just using to correspond with "Jessica".'

'Or the person pretending to be her,' I added.

'Who owns it?' Clare asked again.

'Skylar Kotze.'

I had to stand. I pushed my chair back and walked away from them for a few moments. I felt revulsion... that's the best way I can explain it.

'Why?' Clare asked. She wanted the story as much as I wanted it.

'We're about to find out, but I'd say she's an accomplice,' Nick said. 'From what I remember Jessica said she was crazy for Adam. Chances are she'd do anything for him, even lie and give him an alibi on the night of Soleil's death.'

'Do you think they are a couple now?' I asked.

Nick gave a small shrug. 'It's possible, very possible. The *whois* search we used to track down the email's IP address location listed it as Perth.'

We all took that in. The years of life that two talented, beautiful young women had missed, was most likely because of Adam Steyne and his lover, who were happily living together on the other side of the country.

'You know about his first wife falling, don't you?' Clare asked.

'Yeah,' Nick said. 'He might be responsible for three deaths.'

'Dangerous to love,' I said, sitting down again. 'I thought her voice sounded plummy, but it still had an Australian twang to it.'

Clare shook her head. 'Jessica's voice was not plummy. It wasn't really Australian either, but it was what the radio folk call well moderated. I have the uncut version of those recorded lines she did with Soleil, you can hear her. I'll send it to you.'

'Thanks,' I said. 'I really would like to hear that.'

'I suspect Skylar Kotze has been putting that voice on for years,' Nick said. 'The emails listed go back a long time. Lots of bullshit to Jessica's mother about not being able to come home because she's working. She even had Jessica's mother believing she was working in London and emailing from there.'

'Probably said it was a terrible line when she rang home to disguise any voice differentiation,' I suggested.

'Jessica's mother died about 15 years ago, and Jessica had no siblings. Not that hard for Skylar to get away with it,' Nick said. 'Any friends, like me, have probably long dropped off.'

'But why correspond with me?' I asked. 'Why risk it?'

'There'd be two reasons I can suggest,' Clare said, and we looked at her to elaborate. 'Skylar either wanted to know what you had found so they could cover themselves, or Adam Steyne's done the dirty on her and she wants revenge.'

I thought back on what "Jessica" aka Skylar had said to me and told Nick and Clare: 'She told me three things, and it makes sense now because it is three things that she would have known from her time visiting, or if she were involved.'

'Tell me,' Nick said, desperate for anything that would help put her away.

'First, how Adam kept looking at the dug-out pool; second, how she learnt he didn't go to the airport that night—'

'Because he was picking her up!' Clare threw in.

I nodded. 'And finally, that she knew Adam had an affair.'

'With her or Soleil,' Nick finished, 'or both.'

'All of those involved her first-hand and she could pretend Jessica discovered them,' Clare agreed.

I sat back and gave a small smile.

'What is it?' Nick said, reading my expression.

'Skylar suggested to me to try the pool. I think the honeymoon is over.'

Chapter 54

THEN…

Adam

I couldn't let Jessica leave. I loved her. I raced out of the pool, up the ladder, and to her. She whirled around in fright as she heard my footsteps and then felt my breath right behind her. I grabbed her and kissed her hard, and then I took her last breath from her.

I walked around to the dirt steps and lowered myself back to the pool floor. Reaching up to the shallow edge, I gently lifted Jessica's body in and kissed her forehead. She looked beautiful. Grabbing the shovel, I got to work. It was daylight, so I dug at a speed I didn't think I was capable of digging, but it wasn't hard. I'd only recently shovelled that dirt out for Soleil's grave, so it was loose.

While Soleil vanished before my eyes into the depth of the blowhole, I felt it was fitting that Jessica would rest here forever, in the home that we created together. That would bring me some comfort. I rolled her in, said my goodbyes and covered her. Now I was crying. I truly loved her, the only one of them I loved. Standing back, I acknowledged I did a good job digging that grave – soon it was level and I spread a layer of the new dirt wide so you couldn't tell that any dirt had been upturned.

Next, to cover my boot marks on the way up and out of the pool. I walked to the shed and returned the spade and my boots. I grabbed the straw broom from the shed before closing it and swept the loose dirt back into the pool dirt cavern. Entering the house, I locked the door behind me and headed to the bathroom to shower. I was hot now, and flicking the tap on, I started with a cold blast, letting the water wash the sweat and dirt off me. Can't believe my good luck not having that pool concrete laid.

I turned up the heat and scrubbed down with Jessica's shower sponge. After, I cleaned the bathroom and threw the towels into the laundry; the cleaning lady was due Tuesday and she'd do a load of washing then.

Back into jeans, a black t-shirt and runners, and then a quick look around. I'd have to let Jessica's boss know she'd left me, gone back to Sydney. I knew just the person who'd be happy about that news and would help me. Skylar.

Chapter 55

NOW...

Coen

My book – *The Girl on the MISSING Poster* – went straight to number one... there is nothing like true crime to capture the imagination of readers. It put me, Natalie, and the publishing house in a very nice position. I didn't have a book launch. Natalie didn't think it was necessary, and I wasn't keen to 'celebrate' someone's death or resurrection. So, she just lined me up for a thousand interviews – okay, maybe it was only two hundred, but it felt like a thousand.

The good thing about the media interviews was that no one asked me when the next *Reiker* book was coming out and why I killed his girlfriend, Eloise. Although one reporter asked me was it easier to write real death than fictional death. No. I'm not sure I can write non-fiction death anymore... I have a new and profound sadness in me for the victims and their families. Perhaps that might ease a little in time.

I left the week after Jessica's body was found. Soleil's body never was found, but we learnt from the court circus that followed that Adam Steyne weighted down her body and buried her at sea.

I didn't have to pay out the lease… a tenant with a body on his premises had good grounds to get out of any lease. The university was kind enough to release me as well on the basis I appeared at their annual open day next year to give the welcoming lecture. Done.

Strand Harbour was great. It would always have a place in my heart, but I felt like I was brought in for a reason and that job was done. Anyway, the house was Adam's problem; it might sell to a ghoul and horror collector, or in time to someone who didn't care what happened there. But it would need a new garden, the plunge pool was broken and gone.

The highlight of the book's release was not that we could celebrate Adam and his accomplice Skylar being arrested, or that Jessica and Soleil's family and friends would have justice. The highlight for me was about two months after it was all over, Natalie, Nick, Clare and I had a very, very long lunch. It was a release for all of us and we felt proud of what we had achieved. Nick looked different… his face was relaxed; he didn't look like he was carrying a burden. Natalie looked like a publisher with a bestseller on her hands and a crush on a cop. Clare looked more confident – a nomination for a Walkley Award for her reporting of the story will do that to you.

As for me, I was proud to author that book. I felt like I had given my three friends – two of them new friends – something they needed. I had extended myself beyond my skills and somehow gotten justice for the two young ladies. It was also truly satisfying to know that at last, Soleil would not be forever missing, alone, in a foreign country, even though her body was never recovered.

Sometimes while sitting at my desk, I played the audio file Clare sent to me with the messages Soleil recorded for Jessica. I play the uncut version, where I can hear Soleil and Jessica talking and laughing. Skylar, when she was talking to me pretending to be Jessica, sounded nothing like her. I didn't know that at the time, I only heard Soleil's voice on the edited version I first received. How clever Jessica was when she cut those up to flush out her murderous husband. Too clever, sadly.

I liked to hear their voices – Soleil's soft French accent – and the one sentence she recorded just for Jessica. I listened to it now and then. It was my way of giving Soleil the last word: *Être libre et heureuse, Jessica* – be free and happy, Jessica.

On the day I left town, I drove that very road that Soleil hitchhiked on. In my mind, I metaphorically opened the door and offered her a lift. A lift out of this town.

Thanks for inviting me to visit, Soleil. We can both go home now.

THE END

Also by Jack Adams:

Two childhood friends find themselves working together as a Private Investigator and Psychologist in the *Delaney and Murphy* series:

Asylum

Ten-year-old best friends, Nathan and Adam, really liked Joe. He was their friend, an artist, the man they spoke to through the wire fence of the lunatic asylum.

But something happened behind those walls, in those rooms, on the grounds, at the river.

The inmate sketched it all – fine lines, truth in the negative space, truth in the pencil strokes.

Then one day Joe was gone.

Twenty years later Nathan and Adam receive a letter.

Stalker

Adam couldn't wait… his Uncle Allan was coming to watch his cricket game this afternoon; Adam's father was always too busy to get there. Uncle Allan believed Adam and his best friend, Nate, would one day be chosen for the State side if they kept practicing… Adam's bowling was really improving.

Adam didn't have an Uncle Allan.

Coming next in the *Delaney and Murphy* series: *Cult*

From the author

This has been a book that has been ten years in the writing. Every time I read it and re-read it, I was dissatisfied. I received endless feedback from agents and publishers and made the changes they suggested, but feared the book would end up not being my book. It sat in my bottom drawer so I could visit it again with a fresh perspective.

My thanks to fellow authors over the years who helped me along this journey – Simona Moroni, Dr Amanda Apthorpe, Sally Odgers, Kris Sheather and sincere thanks to proofreader, Brenda Telford.

I believe I am happy with it now and thus, this is Coen, Soleil, Jessica, and Nick's story. The town is fictitious but it is not dissimilar to a lot of lovely little coastal villages in Australia. I hope you enjoy *Poster Girl* and I invite you to explore my other series featuring childhood friends, Nate Delaney and Adam Murphy – a work in progress – *Asylum, Stalker* and *Cult*.

Contact Jack:

I am not much for social media but can be found at:

Facebook: https://www.facebook.com/jackadamswrites
Email: jackadamswrites@gmail.com

www.ingramcontent.com/pod-product-compliance
Lightning Source LLC
Chambersburg PA
CBHW020336120726
47904CB00002B/428